The Devil's Reaper
(Matt Drake #34)

By
David Leadbeater

Copyright © 2023 by David Leadbeater
ISBN: 9798867878603

All rights reserved.
No part of this publication may be reproduced, distributed, or transmitted in any form or by any means, including photocopying, recording, or other electronic or mechanical methods, without the prior written permission of the publisher/author except in the case of brief quotations embodied in critical reviews and certain other non-commercial uses permitted by copyright law.

All characters in this book are fictitious, and any resemblance to actual persons living or dead is purely coincidental.

Classification: Thriller, adventure, action, mystery, suspense, archaeological, military, historical, assassination, terrorism, assassin, spy

Other Books by David Leadbeater:

The Matt Drake Series

A constantly evolving, action-packed romp based in the escapist action-adventure genre:

The Bones of Odin (Matt Drake #1)
The Blood King Conspiracy (Matt Drake #2)
The Gates of Hell (Matt Drake 3)
The Tomb of the Gods (Matt Drake #4)
Brothers in Arms (Matt Drake #5)
The Swords of Babylon (Matt Drake #6)
Blood Vengeance (Matt Drake #7)
Last Man Standing (Matt Drake #8)
The Plagues of Pandora (Matt Drake #9)
The Lost Kingdom (Matt Drake #10)
The Ghost Ships of Arizona (Matt Drake #11)
The Last Bazaar (Matt Drake #12)
The Edge of Armageddon (Matt Drake #13)
The Treasures of Saint Germain (Matt Drake #14)
Inca Kings (Matt Drake #15)
The Four Corners of the Earth (Matt Drake #16)
The Seven Seals of Egypt (Matt Drake #17)
Weapons of the Gods (Matt Drake #18)
The Blood King Legacy (Matt Drake #19)
Devil's Island (Matt Drake #20)
The Fabergé Heist (Matt Drake #21)
Four Sacred Treasures (Matt Drake #22)
The Sea Rats (Matt Drake #23)
Blood King Takedown (Matt Drake #24)

Devil's Junction (Matt Drake #25)
Voodoo soldiers (Matt Drake #26)
The Carnival of Curiosities (Matt Drake #27)
Theatre of War (Matt Drake #28)
Shattered Spear (Matt Drake #29)
Ghost Squadron (Matt Drake #30)
A Cold Day in Hell (Matt Drake #31)
The Winged Dagger (Matt Drake #32)
Two Minutes to Midnight (Matt Drake #33)

The Alicia Myles Series

Aztec Gold (Alicia Myles #1)
Crusader's Gold (Alicia Myles #2)
Caribbean Gold (Alicia Myles #3)
Chasing Gold (Alicia Myles #4)
Galleon's Gold (Alicia Myles #5)
Hawaiian Gold (Alicia Myles #6)

The Torsten Dahl Thriller Series

Stand Your Ground (Dahl Thriller #1)

The Relic Hunters Series

The Relic Hunters (Relic Hunters #1)
The Atlantis Cipher (Relic Hunters #2)
The Amber Secret (Relic Hunters #3)
The Hostage Diamond (Relic Hunters #4)
The Rocks of Albion (Relic Hunters #5)
The Illuminati Sanctum (Relic Hunters #6)

The Illuminati Endgame (Relic Hunters #7)
The Atlantis Heist (Relic Hunters #8)
The City of a Thousand Ghosts (Relic Hunters #9)
Hierarchy of Madness (Relic Hunters #10)

The Joe Mason Series

The Vatican Secret (Joe Mason #1)
The Demon Code (Joe Mason #2)
The Midnight Conspiracy (Joe Mason #3)
The Babylon Plot (Joe Mason #4)

The Rogue Series

Rogue (Book One)

The Disavowed Series:

The Razor's Edge (Disavowed #1)
In Harm's Way (Disavowed #2)
Threat Level: Red (Disavowed #3)

The Chosen Few Series

Chosen (The Chosen Trilogy #1)
Guardians (The Chosen Trilogy #2)
Heroes (The Chosen Trilogy #3)

Short Stories

Walking with Ghosts (A short story)
A Whispering of Ghosts (A short story)

All genuine comments are very welcome at:

davidleadbeater2011@hotmail.co.uk

Twitter: @dleadbeater2011

Visit David's website for the latest news and information:
davidleadbeater.com

The Devil's Reaper

CHAPTER ONE

Bushida paced the tiny, squalid room with his fists clenched, trying to focus on anything but the damn television. He wore dirty jeans, a sweat-stained t-shirt and shoes that had seen far better days. His knuckles were scarred from years of fighting, his face the same. He walked with a slight limp, but could overcome it if he needed to teach someone a lesson. And, Bushida found, that was often the case in his line of work.

Bushida was the leader of what was left of the Tsugarai.

He was a proud man, proud of everything the name Tsugarai once represented. They had been a fearsome fighting force, a force of nature to be sure. They had numbered in the hundreds, had their own township, and had trained and indoctrinated many new members. Yes, most of those members had been coerced into their ranks, but they soon settled in.

Take Mai Kitano, for example, he thought. She'd been coerced into the ranks of the Tsugarai, purchased from her destitute parents who were forced to choose between siblings. They trained Mai in the art of fighting and stealth. The Tsugarai taught her how to be a Ninja; she was one of them, part of the primary team that went out into the world and completed missions, earned money, grew a solid reputation for doing the best job. Mai had never been happy with the Tsugarai, but she had performed well for them, worked at the top of her game alongside several others who had also been coerced for countless years. It had been assumed that she had become a part of the clan, at peace with them.

How wrong they had been. Mai Kitano tore the Tsugarai apart.

That had been years ago. The Tsugarai were reduced from a world power, a wealthy, renowned, admired and much-sought after gang to a threadbare outfit that could barely rub two cents together. They were evicted from their home, chased down like animals by the police, forced to turn to the streets and the hovels and the open spaces in the countryside. The Tsugarai were branded criminals, shoot-on-sight antagonists, lepers in their own country, *their own province*.

All from a direct impact on their infrastructure, an impact caused by Mai Kitano and her bunch of friends.

Ever since that happened, what remained of the Tsugarai had been struggling to make ends meet. Most of the clan were killed, captured, and imprisoned. Those who remained, who escaped that terrible day and night, stayed apart for a while, and then came together gradually, living now as different people under different guises. Now, they had been forced to form a small, largely impotent gang to survive. They existed by carving out a small territory of Tokyo for themselves, strong-arming businesses and people, doing a little contraband, and trying hard not to step on the bigger gangs' toes. It was a hard living, and not what they were used to. The Tsugarai were still good at what they did; they just couldn't show their true identities anymore.

So they were left with this, Bushida thought. A sordid collection of seedy structures in downtown Tokyo that were marked for demolition. Unsafe. Unsound. They were uncertain, living day to day, running on empty, just crawling through the wreckage of their lives. What little money they earned from local businesses and a bit of dealing was soon eaten up. Bushida, in charge, felt keen humiliation.

It had been like this for years; he knew. They made a little more each year, but never more than a little. They kept the real estate developers off with a few threats here and there. Barely kept their heads above water. It was a meagre, fruitless, soul-destroying existence, not worthy of the great clan once known as the mighty Tsugarai.

Bushida had tried for years to rise above the squalor, to make things just a tad better. In his heart, he knew it wasn't working, knew that, as a leader, he was failing. But what could he do? How could he help the clan any more than he was doing?

Finally, his attention turned back to the damn television. *Was* there something he could do? The images on the screen turned his stomach, made his blood boil. There was no way *she* should get such good publicity.

He made himself watch. Standing there, body sweating, eyes ablaze, he saw that a nuclear explosion had just been prevented in London, and he saw who was getting the praise. There was no mistaking her powerful frame, and no mistaking the figures of her friends. No forgetting that appealing, hated face, those deep black eyes that knew betrayal as well as they knew the back of their hand. She was right there... the despised one... Mai Kitano.

The television was showing a London department store where the explosion had almost taken place. The heroes were all standing around – uniformed cops and plainclothes agents as well as what he knew was now named the Ghost Squadron. They were smiling, some with relief, others with pure happiness, still others with nervous tension. Mai Kitano was standing quietly trying not to get sucked into the chaos, but Bushida could see her as plain as day, in what he envisioned as the 'winner's circle.'

Mai Kitano.

Such a reviled name among the Tsugarai. Bushida hadn't know what she was up to these days; his organisation was now too weak to keep track. Seeing her like this was a stroke of good fortune.

If he could rid the world of the loathsome creature and her team, his standing would grow. Maybe he would even become a legend, an iconic figure. The man who destroyed Mai Kitano. Maybe the Tsugarai would start growing again, attract more members. Right now, they were festering, depleted.

But just maybe...

He watched the television, grating his teeth together. The camera kept flicking across Mai and that annoying, pleased smile that was plastered on her face. It showed the other members of her team too, Matt Drake and Alicia Myles and all the others. Bushida knew exactly where they were right now.

But what could he do about it?

What resources did he have left? Bushida thought about it. There was precious little. They made their living day to day. Contacts? Well, the old Tsugarai had mountains of them. The new Tsugarai? They had been pretty much forgotten.

Bushida forced himself to watch the television until the coverage ended. It fed the darkness inside. He felt like throwing something at the screen when it had finished, but knew the clan couldn't afford to buy a new one. It was an odd and embarrassing situation to be in.

Bushida sat down behind a small, messy desk, faced with papers and documents and several stained glasses half full of alcohol. He downed one quickly, then another. He picked up his mobile phone, hit the speed dial.

'Han,' he said shortly. 'Come in here.'

The door opened less than a minute later. Han looked in. He was a short, weasel faced man and was Bushida's second-in-command. Bushida could never get used to his constant squint, imagining the guy was always staring strangely at him.

'You rang?'

'What do we have that is still of value?'

Han blinked, caught by surprise. This was a question Bushida had never asked before. He thought for a moment and then shook his head.

'What do we have...' he repeated. 'In storage, you mean?'

Bushido shrugged. 'Anywhere. What did we filch from the old ranch? The houses? What have we gained from the locals? What have our subjects given us in lieu of yen? Anything at all that may be of value.'

Han thought about it for a while, his head cocked to the side. His perpetually squinting eyes narrowed some more. 'We have the documents.'

Bushida licked his lips. That was interesting. The

documents were old scrolls covered in Ninja legends, legends of the Tsugarai and other clans that had long since died out. They were plentiful, and genuine, and worth something to someone. A collection of ancient, authentic stories that covered many yellowed scrolls and dog-eared leather-bound books.

'To the right person,' he said. 'They could be immensely valuable.'

Han nodded. 'We have tried to find the right person, to no avail.'

'But have we tried *her?*'

Han screwed his face up and shook his head. 'Her?'

'The Devil's Reaper.'

Those words, that sentence, caused Han's face to go slack. His eyes shone with terror. The man's mouth fell open.

Bushida had known this would happen. He held up both hands. 'I know. You don't need to say anything. But it is necessary.'

Han struggled to pull himself together. 'Surely nothing is *that* necessary.'

'You struggle with death and murder now? After everything we've done?'

'I don't... struggle... with it. I know it's necessary for survival. It is our world. But... the Devil's Reaper? She's on a whole different level. We're talking the worst of the worst.'

'She is a necessary evil.'

'But the things she does. Her *modus operandi*. I can honestly say there is nobody worse in this world.'

Bushida nodded with satisfaction. 'Then it is only right that we visit her on Mai Kitano and her team.'

'Kitano? I had forgotten about her.'

Bushida bristled. 'Forgotten? Be careful. That

disgusting woman was the architect of our destruction. The reason we eek out a living with the gutter rats. Nothing is too bad for her. And I will have vengeance for the Tsugarai.'

Han nodded. 'That is admirable, and probably expected. We number so few now and are so downtrodden. Do you think reaping vengeance will help our position?'

Bushida shrugged. 'I think many people, once they hear how we took care of her and her team, will embrace the Tsugarai once more. Perhaps we will become a world power again.'

'It's daring,' Han admitted. 'Bold. Undetermined,' he sighed. 'And reckless.'

Bushida held up his hands. 'We're dying, Han. The Tsugarai are *dying*. What you see is all that we have left. We were once a great clan with governments in our pocket, world leaders depending on us. We had influence, wealth, power, and we were feared. Oh, how we were feared. Now... they spit at us in the street. They laugh. They mock our name. The great wrong has to be righted. Seeing *her* bathed in the limelight like this,' he gestured at the television. 'Has convinced me.'

Han stared at him and suddenly there was no more fear in his eyes. There was a splash of determination, a glint. Bushida's words had had a powerful effect on him. He straightened and took a deep breath.

'The Devil's Reaper, you say?'

Bushida allowed himself a small smile. 'I can't think of anyone I'd rather introduce Kitano too.'

'It's a bold choice.'

Bushida accepted that. 'When you engage with her, there is no going back.'

'She could ruin us.'

'We cannot fall much further into the cesspit.'

'Do you think she will accept the documents as payment?'

'I think it is worth a try. By all accounts, she is cultured, sophisticated, polished. She would appreciate the age and beauty of the documents. She is a collector of fine art, of antiques. I believe she would enjoy the documents.'

Han couldn't help but bite his bottom lip. 'Then, perhaps we should start the process of contacting her.'

'I think,' Bushida said. 'That that is a good idea.'

CHAPTER TWO

Rhona King was a six-foot-two brunette with long, straight hair, midnight black eyes and full red lips. She stood ramrod straight on her feet, had broad, muscled shoulders and spent a good part of her day working out. Today, she wore designer-branded black leggings and a baggy jumper and training shoes. Her face was stern, hard, often harsh. She painted her nails blood red and kept them trimmed.

Rhona King was a dark, evil legend. She went by the name of the Devil's Reaper.

It had been a hard few years since her mentor, the Devil, was murdered. She remembered that day well, the sheer hell of knowing the man she looked up to, the man who taught her everything he knew, was dead. And not just dead. The Devil had been a legend of criminal enterprise, a creative, bloody mastermind. Some jobs he'd done... Rhona marvelled. Even now, in her mind at least, she hadn't come close to eclipsing his expertise.

But she was the next best thing. She had clients far and wide, people who came to her to... take care of things. Rhona was at the top of her game and much in demand. If an accident needed to happen, a man needed to die and his death not be suspicious, a woman killed in a certain way and not arouse the attention of the authorities – that was Rhonda's speciality.

And she loved her job.

Take now, for instance. She sat before a bank of monitors, surveying each screen in turn. She was watching news coverage of a large protest in New York City. The screens showed different angles from separate TV stations, all focused on singular parts of the protest. One screen showed a body of men and women waving placards. Another showed the slow stream of traffic trying to cruise past. Still another showed the police watching on, the ambulances waiting just in case; the people shouting into their megaphones. There were long shots of surrounding establishments and drone shots of the street layout.

The Devil's Reaper monitored it all. Crunch time was fast approaching. The monitors flickered and flashed and kept her attention. Her desk was otherwise tidy, a black slab of carbon fibre that weighed little to nothing yet was as strong and sturdy as iron. The room itself was spacious, with a drinks cabinet in one corner, a bar, and a mini kitchen. Rhona was self sufficient in here to a point. She could stay here all day, working.

These days, years into her solo job, she still got nervous, still got excited. It was very rare when a job didn't go according to plan. Yes, it happened, but Rhona soon made it right. She always had a contingency, and then another.

She sat watching the screens, moved, scooped her hair out of her eyes, tied it back. She picked up a mug of coffee, sipped at it. Rhona's lair was in the basement of a large house that sat on the outskirts of a small town, somewhere in America's south. The house

Devil's Reaper

was unremarkable. She kept herself to herself, didn't draw attention. At the moment, she employed no guards, no helpers, and had no prodigy of her own alongside her, although one existed. At the moment... she was a one-woman band.

But she had access to others at a moment's notice. They knew she paid well, and they knew the horrors she could wreak if they crossed her. She also knew the calibre of men and women she should hire. She knew not to employ the dumb ones.

Right now, on the screens, the furore of the protest rose a notch. That was good. Rhona saw the crowd swell, saw the placards wave furiously, countless people start to yell. Some of them were pushed out into the road, close to passing cars, a good sign. She let a wicked smile play around her full lips.

The time was almost here.

She had several people placed among the crowd, all ready to act. Rhona saw one of them... accidentally... push a woman into the road. Gently. It was a kind of foreshadowing. She saw another do the same. The cops hadn't noticed the danger yet, and wouldn't until it was too late. Now, the moment approached. Rhona had planned everything. She'd incited this very protest, used social media to fan the flames. She'd made sure her prey was going to be a part of it, made sure the woman... named Rita... would show up on the day and stand in the right place. It had taken careful planning, precise organisation, utmost concentration. It would be beyond most people, but this was what she did. Granted, her attacks were usually large and messy and attention grabbing, but she could do low-key too.

Was it low-key, though?

Rhona let her eyes wander over the sizeable crowd,

all the unknowing players. Not one of them knew they had all been gathered to facilitate the murder of a single person. Her client, the woman's husband, was safely at work, surrounded by people, and would be sufficiently shocked and upset on hearing about his wife's death at the protest.

Rhona leaned forward. The time was nigh.

She watched, able to pick out the woman who was about to die because she had a tracker on the person who had been assigned to kill her. The woman in question was a curly-haired blonde wearing a long white coat and oodles of jewellery. She actually stood out from the throng. Most of the other people involved in the protest were dressed more conservatively. Rhona watched the last few seconds of the woman's life tick by.

Then it happened. A truck came rumbling up the street, trying to ignore the protesters. It approached steadily, air horns blowing. Rhona saw the killer get into place, the perfect position. The woman in the white coat opened her mouth to shout out her protest.

It never came. At that moment, she received a shove to the back, a hard shove that sent her sprawling out into the path of the big truck. She stumbled, staggered, and the front grille hit her hard, smashing her off her feet. In her isolation, Rhona couldn't help but grin. The woman's head bounced off the truck and then the sidewalk, and then there was blood all around.

Her people melted away. The woman who'd done the deed retreated into the crowd. They wouldn't wait around to ensure the victim was actually dead. They'd done their bit.

The truck ground to a halt, its grille covering half

the woman's body. Her white coat was soaked in blood, her blonde hair streaked with it. The red substance pooled into the road, ran into the gutters. Rhona saw it all as a job well done. She saw people running towards the woman, raising the alarm, the trucker climbing out of his cab. She saw the assembled cops move into gear, an ambulance start moving. From here, right now, she couldn't be certain the woman was dead, but she would keep watching.

There was no doubt the cameras would stay focused on the dead or potentially dying woman. This was what they lived for.

Rhona kept watching. The cameras didn't move. Paramedics arrived, pushing everyone out of the way. More cameramen pushed their way through. Several of Rhona's screens were now focused on the downed woman.

And the downed woman wasn't going anywhere.

Rhona drank her coffee. Keeping an eye on the screens, she walked across to the bar and poured herself a celebratory merlot. She sipped it, unable to stop the grin from curling her lips. A job well done, well executed. The target was surely dead.

But she wouldn't stop watching until she had clarity. That clarity came as Rhona took her fourth sip of wine. The medics stepped away from the body and covered it up.

Rhona let out a little laugh.

She wouldn't contact the husband. He had already paid her and would find out soon enough. She hoped his act of misery on hearing about his wife's death would be suitably convincing and that he could hide his own private smiles.

Rhone sat back. A job well done. She crossed her

legs, contemplated leaving the basement, heading up to the shower and taking a long, hot, celebratory soak. She had the time. There was only one other job on her books, and she had three weeks to complete that.

A red light started blinking. She stared at it for a moment, surprised. The red light signified an incoming call.

Someone had taken the time to fight their way through all her protocols, through the passwords, the procedures, using the correct etiquette. Someone who had been vetted down to the last pubic hair really wanted her attention.

A new job?

Rhona felt a shiver of exhilaration. She loved the "new job" feeling. Loved the thought of coming up with some new idea, a new ruse, a special kill. There was nothing like delving into a new set of opportunities. And the beauty of her job... every kill was different.

She picked up her mobile phone, connected to the incoming call, which was at a top level of encryption. 'What can I do for you?'

'Am I speaking to the person known as the Devil's Reaper?'

She was confident enough in the encryption and the raft of protocols to answer: 'You certainly are.'

'Good. My name is Bushida. I have a job for you.'

'Can you afford me, Bushida?' she enjoyed a bit of playful banter with her potential employers. It helped her gauge what kind of person they were.

'That's one thing I couldn't find out,' he said. 'Your rates.'

'I differ,' she said in a breathy tone. 'Depending on the job requirements. If I love the job, I can be had quite cheaply.'

'I guarantee you will love this job.'

Rhona found her interest piqued. 'I'm all ears.'

There was a deep intake of breath from the other end of the line. Bushida was nervous. Rhona often found that people were nervous when they spoke to her. It made her feel tingly and comforted.

'First,' he said. 'I represent the remains of the Tsugarai. Have you heard of us?'

'Old Ninja clan,' she said, frowning in memory. 'Consummate killers yourselves.'

'Our clan was all but wiped out,' Bushida told her. 'But that's a long and an old story. The reason I mention it at this moment is because of the issue of payment.'

Rhona listened as the Tsugarai leader explained he had in his possession a collection of ancient documents that related to several Ninja clans, all genuine. Stories of their exploits through the years. From the earliest centuries to the present day. He was willing to give them to her if she would do his bidding.

'That depends on the job.' Her interest was still on a high level. She didn't need money, and the documents did sound as if they might keep her occupied. 'What exactly am I going to be asked to do for you? Is it bloody? Is it hard? Is it sleazy? Is it wild and batshit crazy? Does it involve the decimation of thousands, or just hundreds? Is there a celebrity involved, a politician, a news reporter of the highest order? Oh, Bushida, give it to me. I can't wait.'

Another gulp of apprehension and maybe it was her way of speaking. She enjoyed keeping them off guard.

'I believe you know the name: Mai Kitano.'

Rhona froze. She said nothing.

'Not just Kitano, but her entire fucking team. You

know them. Now, as the Tsugarai dwell in squalor, *they* are out lording it up. You know that recent nuclear attack in London that was thwarted? They did that. And they're fucking celebrities now, getting all the praise. Well, it isn't right. I want them taken out, and I want it to hurt. I want them to suffer. And nothing obscure. Each death will hit the headlines, if you know what I mean.'

Rhona had been listening to him, growing increasingly excited. The death of her mentor, the Devil, had rocked her world, and she knew it had come at the hands of Drake's team. She had considered instant retaliation, but the Devil had trained her differently. Part of the reason they stayed in the shadows, on the peripheries of evil deeds, was that they remained impartial. Giving no one a reason to suspect them, nor to believe in their existence. It was said that Satan's biggest coup was in making people believe he didn't exist. Well, *her* devil had been the same, except for those he wanted to. They didn't accept anything where they might produce a clear motive.

So Rhona had stayed clear of Drake and Kitano and the others all this time. But it had always concerned her, always rankled in the back of her mind. Since her mentor died, they'd already drawn thousands of breaths that they weren't entitled to.

'Do with me as you will, Bushida,' she said.

He hesitated. 'Does that mean you will work for me?'

'In any way you wish.'

'I want Mai Kitano to suffer. And Drake, and Alicia, and all the others. I want them to feel what it is like to have your world ripped out from under you, as mine was. To lose everything you have ever known. To feel your heart ripped out.'

'Stop it. You're making me horny.'

Bushida cleared his throat. 'Can you handle that?'

At those words, Rhona sat up ramrod straight. 'You are insolent,' she said. 'Asking the Devil's Reaper if she can handle such a job. Is that really your question?'

'Sorry. It just slipped out.'

'I'm sure it did. But do listen when I tell you to never let it slip out again. That would be bad for you.'

Bushida remained silent.

'That's better. Now, consider me hired. I will look into Kitano's team and I will inform you of my plans so that you can watch in relative real-time. I will lead you on every step of the journey. This will be my masterpiece. Are you ready?'

'Show me the way,' Bushida said.

CHAPTER THREE

Clive Ingham woke with the sun on his face, glad to be alive. He lay in bed for a while, basking in the warmth. It was going to be a good day.

He rose, took a shower, dressed and went to make himself a fresh breakfast of croissants and coffee. He was a tall, gangly man with awkward arms and legs and a way of walking at a stooped angle that made him appear shorter. He was bald, clean shaven and liked to dress in smart shirts and trousers even on his days off.

And today was a day off.

It was Wednesday, and he'd called in a lieu day. Ingham lived alone. He sat at his breakfast counter, ate the croissants and downed three cups of coffee before sitting back and reflecting on his life. He worked in the centre of Los Angeles, at an accounting firm that looked after highly paid stars – celebrities, footballers, market traders, that kind of thing. Ingham knew his job and worked it well, reaped the rewards.

But it hadn't always been that way.

His formative school years had been brutal. Somehow, he'd fallen victim to a terrible bully, a boy who made his life a living hell. Ingham had never known how it happened, it just did. One day, the bully was taunting someone else, the next day it was him.

And the bully took a shine to him. Maybe because of Ingham's reaction, maybe because he fancied him... who knew? Ingham certainly didn't.

Those days had been all about survival. He clashed with the bully five times a day, sought help from the teachers, but that just made everything worse. Ingham would never have survived if it wasn't for Drake.

Ingham blinked. Yes, that was his name. *Drake*. Ingham tried to remember the kid's first name, but couldn't. Jack? Dave? Matt? He wasn't sure. It didn't matter. The Drake kid had stood up to the bully, driven him off, and the two had become fast friends. In fact, Ingham believed Drake was once his best school friend.

He wondered what had happened to him.

Many people often pondered over what had happened to old school friends, Ingham mused. It was one of those facts of life. Ten, twenty years down the road, you wondered what had happened to Drake, or Sharon, or John. Of course, you rarely found out, but with social media these days, it was far easier to try.

Ingham tried to shrug the old memories off. He didn't enjoy remembering weaker times. He'd put those days behind him, moved on. And now the memories had turned a promising day into a melancholy one.

He got to his feet, thinking maybe he should go for a walk. It was one of those balmy, bright LA days outside, and that was sure to invigorate him. Ingham had got used to the Californian heat a long time ago. These days, he embraced it.

But once more he found himself dwelling on the old school days and his best friends. They had been quite a team and made sure everyone knew. There was strength in numbers, in comradeship.

Ingham poured himself another coffee. This one wasn't as fresh, so he set about brewing another. It was gone nine a.m. and, yes, a day off should start with a better mindset than this. Ingham drank another cup and then got ready to go out for a walk.

Outside, it was hot and humid and sweaty. Ingham lived in the city, away from the coast, so didn't benefit too much from the sea breezes unless they were really strong. Today wasn't one of those days. He bent down to tighten the laces of his trainers, then set off, heading west away from the house. The road was tree-lined and quite wide, and he thought he'd cover ten blocks or so before heading back. If he managed the ten blocks, there was a row of shops there where he could grab something nice to eat for lunch.

Ingham walked for a while, letting his mind wander from work to women to shopping. He contemplated the state of his life, decided he liked it. When he'd moved to the US, he'd been more nervous about going forward than at any other time of his life. His entire existence uprooted. But it had turned out to be a brilliant move, helped, of course, by finding the right job that suited him.

He waited for traffic, skirted young adults on electric scooters and even a skateboard, smiled at young women pushing prams, chatted with a guy he knew vaguely who was out trimming his hedges, felt sorry for a guy who was having to change a tyre in the middle of the road. It was a long, refreshing walk, something to drive the cobwebs away and make him sweat a little, get the blood pumping. It was just what he needed before an indulgent, lazy lunch on a relaxed day off.

Up ahead, he saw the telltale signs of the row of

shops he'd made his destination. There was a grocery store, an electrical repair shop, a convenience store and a couple of older establishments that changed hands too often for him to keep track of. One week they were Chinese takeaways, and then Thai, and the next month they were Italian. Still, the food was always good.

But this was lunch. He would pick something nice up from the deli in the grocery store.

Ingham went in, heard the bell sound as he pushed through the door. There were a few people inside, browsing, and a guy at the counter who looked to be buying an entire week's shop.

Ingham headed straight for the sandwiches. He took his time, eventually choosing something in the meal deal section and then took his selection to the counter. He waited in line. A few minutes later, he was back outside.

It was darker. Clouds had scudded in, or had they? When he looked up at the skies, they seemed just as bright as before. Maybe it was his own outlook... maybe he was looking at it all differently.

But why?

For no reason, Ingham felt a sense of foreboding. He blinked, looked around. There were two shady alleys to the left and, at the head of one of them, a dark figure leaned against the wall, its arms crossed.

The figure watched him closely.

Ingham frowned, trying to shrug the strange feeling off. Had he felt the guy's eyes on him as he exited the shop? Was that what it was? Ingham shrugged internally. Strange guys didn't really bother him. He started walking back to his house, now passing the alley.

And that was when the guy stepped out.

Ingham sent him a strained smile. This was broad daylight, almost lunchtime. Nothing was going to happen. Ingham noticed the guy had others with him. There were a few of them crammed down the alley. He put his head down and tried to walk by.

The guy got in his face.

'Excuse me,' Ingham said and tried to walk around.

'Sorry, dude,' the guy said. 'This isn't personal.'

Ingham stared at him. 'What?'

The guy reached out, grabbed Ingham's sandwich bag, and snatched it off him. For a moment, Ingham glared with righteous indignity, wondering if this was all a joke, but then he felt a powerful blow to the abdomen.

He doubled over, felt his pockets rifled. All this was happening in the street. From the blurred corners of his vision, he saw the others emerge from the alley, and saw their legs surround him. There were at least eight of them. Someone had his wallet. Another, his keys. The objects were then thrown to the floor.

Someone punched him in a kidney. Another person smashed a fist into his arm. For now, they stayed away from his face, but they beat him, firing in blow after blow until Ingham fell to his knees.

From behind, he heard the shop's bell ring, someone either going in or out. Would they help or call the police? Or would it just speed up whatever was happening to him?

Ingham groaned in pain. His arms were on fire, his body throbbing. Why was this happening? It suddenly reminded him of the old days, the bully in school, dishing out harsh treatment. This was like that, but far worse.

Ingham cried out as a punch smashed into his left ear. Someone brought a fist down onto the top of his head. There was a kick to his thigh. Ingham saw the lone sandwich now on the ground and wished he was still on his way home, looking forward to eating it.

Ingham saw the flash of a blade. His stomach lurched. Was this not just a beating, then? They were all carrying blades. His heart almost stopped. He looked up, asked them why they were doing this. He knelt in the darkness of the circle they had made around him and saw only a field of knives above his head. Ingham shivered. This couldn't be happening.

The first blade snicked out, sliced across his forehead. Ingham felt a gush of blood flow from the wound and then saw red before his eyes. He still couldn't believe it. A second knife struck him, this one flashing across his right bicep.

And then a third.

Ingham screamed. A knife flicked across his face, opening up his cheek. Another took a chunk out of his nose. The pain was so bad he could hardly breathe. He tried to look up, beseeching his attackers.

'Why?' he asked.

There were grunts in reply, nothing more. None of the faces staring down at him betrayed any sign of pleasure. Their expressions were business as usual.

'Please,' he said.

More knives flashed. They cut his shoulders, his thighs, his chest, none of the blows designed to kill. Blood was everywhere, dripping off him. Ingham couldn't believe that he'd woken up, just a few hours ago, in the best of health, happy, content. They were cutting him to ribbons.

More knives flashed. Ingham knelt in agony. His

strength was ebbing away as fast as his blood was flowing. He panted heavily, stared at the ground. What would they do next?

He found out soon enough. The knives disappeared to be replaced with a few guns. They aimed the small weapons at him. Ingham was already too far gone to be surprised.

The guns went off. Bullets slammed into his legs, his arms. Ingham wailed in agony. He collapsed onto the floor. They fired four shots into him, none of them lethal, all of them excruciating. Ingham was seeing double, blacking out. He couldn't take much more of this. He was heading down a long, black tunnel from which he knew there would be no return.

It was only when the liquid hit him and then the powerful stench of petrol brought him back to consciousness, at least for a little while, that he realised their final, terrible act would be to set him on fire.

CHAPTER FOUR

Matt Drake looked up as Torsten Dahl sat down at the table. The others were already here, and the big Swede was the last.

'Finally graced us with your presence, did you?' The Yorkshireman asked.

'Well, I am a superstar,' Dahl made himself comfortable. 'You should think yourselves lucky.'

At that, Drake made a face. 'We're all superstars,' he said. 'Unfortunately.'

The team were seated around a large table in a small restaurant. Alicia sat to Drake's right, reading a menu. Mai was to his left. Hayden and Kinimaka were opposite, near Dahl. Cam and Shaw were to the far right. Almost everyone was engrossed in their menus. Drake didn't know why. They came here once a week and knew them off by heart.

'I'm not seeing what I want on the menu,' Alicia muttered from the corner of her mouth.

Drake glanced across. 'Really? What do you want?'

'You. Naked. Your big–'

'Hey, hey,' Drake looked around uncomfortably.

'I was going to say something about your big, hairy chest.'

'Tone it down,' he smiled. 'We're in public.'

'Don't tell me what to do. And there's nothing wrong with doing it in public.'

Drake coughed. 'Well, there *is*.'

Alicia shrugged and went back to her menu, still searching.

Drake caught Hayden's eye. 'Have the phone calls stopped?'

She wobbled her right hand. 'Kind of. They're not coming through as regular.'

Drake nodded. That was good. Recently, the team had completed a major mission in London where they had prevented a nuclear explosion and, rather than melting away at the end as they usually did, had been caught up by all the publicity. They had found the cameras turned on them. With nowhere to go, the Ghost Squadron had taken all the plaudits, and was forced to even do a few interviews. Unable to escape, they had been the subject of the spotlight and, even days and weeks later, the publicity hounds were still chasing them. Hayden had been fielding their calls.

'So there is light at the end of the tunnel,' Mai said with relief in her voice.

'I thought you looked good on camera,' Drake said without thinking, and then winced as Alicia elbowed him wickedly.

'Thanks. But it didn't suit me at all.'

'It suits none of us,' Kinimaka said. 'Not in our type of business. Publicity is the last thing we need.'

'As we know from before...' Drake said, a bit ominously.

Dahl bit his lip. 'Well, I, for one, enjoyed it,' he said, stroking his blonde hair. 'I look good on TV.'

Drake laughed. 'So does a gorilla, mate. Actually, I can see the resemblance.'

'Piss off.'

The waiter arrived and took their drinks order. They didn't hold back since they were all able to walk, or stagger, home. They hadn't met up for a week and, truth be told, Drake missed his team when they weren't on a job.

'You think the London exposure will ever die down?' Kenzie asked.

'Did you get any?' Alicia asked archly. 'Were you there?'

Kenzie gave her the finger.

'Sure,' Hayden said. 'We just need something else big to happen. Nothing dangerous, obviously.'

'Some big celeb scandal would be nice,' Kenzie said.

'But hopefully nothing concerning our old friend, Haley Rose,' Hayden said. 'That was a pretty high-profile case, too.'

Drake remembered the Hawaiian escapade well. 'From which we escaped unscathed,' he said. 'From the press, I mean.'

They all nodded. Their drinks arrived, and they got stuck in. Drake was starting on bottled beer, but was already looking forward to the shots later. He took a sip of the cold beverage, savouring the taste. The waiter hung around to take their food order and, as expected, they all ordered the same thing as usual. No need for all the menu searching. Drake shrugged. He wouldn't labour the point.

'Any news from Bryant?' Shaw asked.

Drake liked the question. Bryant was their boss, the owner of the private security firm *Glacier,* and was the man they relied on for new jobs.

Both Mai and Hayden looked up, about to speak. Hayden was their team leader and liable to hear about any new jobs first. Mai was Bryant's girlfriend.

'You go,' Hayden said.

'I keep pressing him for jobs-'

'I bet you do,' Alicia said with a lascivious grin.

'But...' Mai shot her a weary look. 'But... the world just doesn't need the Ghost Squadron at the moment. Bryant has several other crews. We're special, obviously,' she grinned. 'He saves the... top... jobs for us.'

'You mean the hard jobs,' Cam said.

'He's had a few hard jobs lately,' Alicia put in.

Mai shook her head. 'Damn it, child,' she said. 'Will you give it a rest?'

'Only if you fight me.'

'You still looking to get your ass beaten again?'

'Again? I don't think so.'

Mai seemed to let it go. She fixed Drake with a stare. 'So, to answer the question professionally – no, there is no fresh news from Bryant.'

Drake didn't let it foul his mood. They all needed downtime. They just didn't like theirs to stretch into endless days. A few minutes later, their food arrived, and they all tucked in. They ordered a fresh round of drinks, which Drake started on with gusto. The banter revolved around who had the best TV 'face' for a while.

'Well, it's clearly me,' Kinimaka told them. 'I am from Hawaii, after all.'

'What the hell?' Drake said. 'I'm from Yorkshire. What's wrong with that?'

Dahl pretended to choke on his food. 'A runt from the devil's country does not look good on the box.'

'It's not the devil's country. It's God's-'

'Whatever.'

'I don't think any of us look good on TV,' Cam said quietly. 'It's wrong.'

'With your boxing skills, you could make a living as one of those cage fighters,' Alicia said. 'If you ever wanted to.'

Cam turned to Shaw and gave her a hug. 'Oh, I don't want to.'

Alicia shook her head. 'You two still clapping cheeks at every opportunity?'

Cam looked away. Shaw laughed and shook her head. As a couple, they were only just getting started. Drake envied them a little.

'And I've fought in enough cages,' Cam said abruptly, referring to his past. 'I never want to go back there.'

Alicia nodded, saying nothing. She was fully aware of Cam's past. She looked around the table, gauging everyone.

'Obviously,' she said. 'I'm the perfect candidate for a TV "face". The best looking and the one with the most charisma.'

This time, Mai did choke on her food. Dahl looked nonplussed. Even Drake took a deep breath. Could you imagine, he thought, *Alicia* being the mouthpiece of their team? He shuddered.

'What's the problem?' Alicia asked.

Drake steered the conversation around to some other topic. They finished their food and sat back as the waiter cleared the table, ordering yet another round of drinks. Drake was about ready to start on the shots. They all expected a long, messy night. Around them, the small restaurant buzzed with conversation. There were couples and threesomes and another large group near the front window. Darkness pressed up against the glass, a darkness shot through with streetlight. People passed the windows, heads down, on their way to somewhere unknown. Drake watched some of them, wondering where their lives led them.

At that moment, Hayden got a call. She stared at the screen, frowned, and then answered. The conversation stopped. They all watched as Hayden finally sighed and then shook her head. 'No comment,' she said.

'Press?' Kinimaka asked.

Hayden nodded. 'They saw us on TV. Want an interview.'

'Shouldn't Bryant's office be fielding these calls?' Kenzie asked.

Hayden shrugged. 'Yes, but you know the press. They have a way of wheedling through the red tape and finding things out. It's their job, after all.'

Alicia and Dahl ordered desert. The others didn't bother. Drake ordered a round of shots. They would split the bill equally at the end. One good thing about being out of the country on missions most of the time was that your bank account tended to be healthy when you got back, purely because you weren't using it.

They sat back, ate and drank, and enjoyed each other's company. It was good to be together, to share their comradeship and bask in it. They knew each other better than anyone else on the planet and thought of each other as family. Drake loved their banter, their closeness, the way they thought and worked for each other in the field. There wasn't a better team in the world.

Alicia was merciless in her teasing of Mai. 'So, back to Bryant,' she said. 'Is he still a womaniser?'

Mai pursed her lips. 'He was never a womaniser, and you know it. He was forced to cultivate that persona to gain entry into certain circles. Bryant is a good man.'

Alicia held Mai's gaze. 'I certainly hope so.'

Mai nodded. She was sure. Drake had a massive soft spot for Mai. Of course, once they'd been together. That seemed so long ago now. He and Alicia had been an item for years now.

Just then, another phone rang. Drake cast a glance around the table before realising it was actually his. He frowned, reaching for his pocket.

'If that's another reporter,' he said. 'I'm gonna invite them out here so we can just take care of them.'

It was said with a smile. He checked the screen, saw that it was Karin calling. Karin was one of their oldest friends who now worked at the NSA. Occasionally, she called to check in.

'Hey,' he said, holding the phone up to his ear. 'How's it going?'

'It's not good, Matt. I just found out some rather chilling news.'

Drake gripped the phone a little tighter. 'Chilling? Are you okay?'

'I'm fine. But Clive Ingham isn't. Do you remember him?'

Drake was taken aback. The name rang a faint bell. The restaurant and the faces of his friends receded as he trawled through his memory banks. *Ingham? Clive Ingham?* He frowned, unable to place it properly.

'I don't recall,' he said.

'It should. He was one of your school friends.'

Suddenly, it clicked, transporting Drake back in time for a few seconds, and Clive Ingham's face swam before him. He remembered good times, brotherly banter, staving off bullies. Remembered swapped homework and meals at each other's houses. He hadn't seen Clive since the day they both left school.

'You have bad news about Clive? How the hell would you even cross reference us?'

'You know how the NSA has it's nose in every pie. There's a tonne of information about you in the database, Matt, including where you went to school, when, and who with. It's all there if you look hard enough. I just didn't know how close you two were and thought it prudent to call you.'

'Close,' Drake whispered. 'Real close, though I haven't thought about him in twenty years. What happened?' Drake wasn't sure how to feel in that moment, but a sense of sadness crept over him.

'Well, it's the nature of his death that really hit the headlines,' Karin said. 'It made him stand out to us and run a check. Poor old Clive was robbed, beaten, knifed, shot and then set on fire.'

It appalled Drake. His face twisted in disbelief. 'That's bloody horrendous.'

'My thoughts exactly. I'm so sorry to have to tell you, Matt.'

Drake thanked her and hung up. Even though he hadn't seen Ingham in decades, the news and the nature of his death still pierced him deeply. Drake had nothing but good memories of the man.

Alicia laid a hand on his arm. 'Are you okay?'

Drake briefly related the news. A pall fell over the table, throwing a shadow over their night. The rest of the conversation was subdued, with Drake not really taking part. He felt guilty because he hadn't kept in touch with Clive, because he'd almost forgotten his boyhood friend. *Christ, I couldn't even place his name.*

It upset him more than he imagined it should and, soon, he was leaving the table, deciding to walk the few blocks back to the apartment where he and Alicia were staying. Drake said his goodbyes, rose, and left the restaurant.

As he went outside, darkness closed in.

CHAPTER FIVE

The Devil's Reaper, Rhona King, slipped into a black Donna Karan dress and then into a pair of brand-new, pure white ASICS trainers. The dress was because she always dressed up for big occasions – whether that might be orchestrating or watching murder, mayhem, or madness. The trainers were for practicality. She was almost alone. There was no need to stand on any ceremony. She had earned the right to do whatever she wanted. The Donna Karan felt good against her skin, the trainers felt comfy.

A perfect combination for her to watch and direct the next kill.

The murder of Clive Ingham had gone very well. She was pleased. The only real witnesses were the actual murderers, and they were too stupid to know who had actually hired them. Rhona was far removed from that situation. The nature of the murder had already caused a press tidal wave. *Fantastic,* she thought.

She made her way from her bedroom to her operations room. Once inside, she took the time to pour herself a glass of expensive champagne, and then take a few sandwiches from the fridge. Again, it was practicality over form. The champagne was a luxury, the sandwiches a necessity. She sipped the champagne delicately and walked over to her chair.

'You appear ready to do murder,' a voice said.

Rhona looked to the corner of the room. Her own protégé, Vicius, sat there. Vicius was young, tall and thin as a rake, wiry like a blade. His hair was unkempt, his fingers always moving. He had been her protégé for about eighteen months now and was learning her world better than expected. He was one of those sorts that would never get overconfident despite all his experiences, and she liked that.

'It is time for the second death,' she said, unable to keep the smile from her face. 'And I have organised it so that we can watch every precious minute.'

'Do you think Kitano and Drake have any inkling yet?'

Rhona thought about it before answering. 'No. One death won't alert them.'

'It may raise their antennae.'

'Let us hope so.'

She settled herself in her seat, checked her watch. The time was almost at hand. The screens were always on and currently showed a hodgepodge of images. Nothing important. She sipped more champagne and then bit into a sandwich. She sat back.

Showtime. The screens coalesced into something more comprehensible.

The man, last name Akana, exited his pleasant house in Hawaii and walked along his usual route to work. He never drove; always walked. Akana didn't know it, but there was an eight person team on him, and that was just for starters. They knew his daily route off by heart. This eight-person team all had body cameras. They were following him, waiting for him, watching him from across the street. The Devil's Reaper got the entire show in real time.

Akana left his driveway, started walking down the street. He passed under palm trees and alongside parked cars, looked up at the blue skies and took it all in. He was a large, broad-shouldered man wearing a thick coat despite the early morning Hawaiian heat and carrying a small bag that probably held his lunch. The man was bald, his neck bore a simple blue tattoo. As Rhona watched him walk, she saw several of her people running to get into better positions.

The result was the perfect show for her. She watched, sitting back, sipping champagne, as the whole scenario played out.

Akana crossed the road on a whim. An approaching car honked at him, but Akana ignored it. He didn't even look up. Akana was a carefree soul, a laid-back surfer-dude by all accounts who spent every dime he earned on fun things. And who could blame him? Life was for living, and you couldn't take it with you.

Rhona watched intently.

'I like how you've created the show.' Vicius said.

Rhona waved him to silence. 'Just watch,' she said.

Akana reached the other side of the street safely and then continued on his way to work. He sauntered, as they knew he would, looked around at everything as if trying to take in all the delights of the outside world before having to enter the dim haunts of an interior office. Akana was an outdoorsy person and Rhona could tell, just by looking at him, that he loved it. She also knew he worked at a second-hand car dealership and spent most of his day pushing paperwork in some small dingy office.

The dealership was but a ten-minute walk away,

but Akana would make it last. He'd set off almost an hour early. Which, Rhona knew, he always did.

Akana reached his local coffee shop. Rhona had people stationed outside and inside. Akana smiled at one of them, walked on past, oblivious. He went up to the counter, greeted the female barista by name, and started to chat her up. He had an easy way about him, a way that made the woman smile. She was probably used to it, though. Akana did the same thing every morning.

Akana did his best. The barista took his money and ushered him down to the other side of the bar where his drink would be deposited by another woman, who Akana instantly started to chat up. Rhona saw his problem with women now. He wanted to try all of them.

Coffee in hand, Akana left the shop and strode immediately into the one next door. This was a pastry shop, and Rhona watched as he bought a large croissant from the young man behind the counter. Akana was pleasant to this server too, though he didn't take it any further.

Again outside, Akana slowed down even more. He sipped the coffee and picked bits of the croissant off, stuffing them in his mouth as he sauntered. He appeared to be enjoying himself.

'Right on time,' Vicius said, leaning forward.

'He never deviates,' Rhona said.

'How long have you been tracking him?'

'Since I took the job. Weeks ago.'

'You're saying he's done exactly the same thing for weeks? Exactly?'

Rhona saw a teaching moment. She turned briefly in her chair. 'Understand,' she said. 'That this business is very fluid. Yes, things can change in a heartbeat, but in planning properly, and using observation techniques, we can predict what a target will do. And don't forget, if something makes him change routine today, we can always come back tomorrow.'

'He has no idea,' Vicius said with a smile.

'Exactly. Proper planning means you hold all the aces. Do you see?'

Vicius nodded. She turned back to the screens.

Akana continued to amble along, pick at his croissant and sip his hot coffee. Rhona watched cameras focused on his front, his side, and his back. He was under total surveillance and had no clue. He cut through a park, sat for five minutes to watch the world go by. Here, he finished his croissant and threw the wrapper in the bin. At the expected time, he rose and continued on his way.

They were close now.

Akana left the park, smiling to himself. Rhona allowed herself a brief grin of pleasure. This was all going very well. Akana did not know he was living his last moments on earth. She watched his face, saw the contentment there. He was about to die, and the only reason... that he had once been good friends with Mano Kinimaka.

Akana walked back across the street, eliciting another honking horn. He waved at the car easily, unperturbed. It occurred to Rhona then that a car accident might have worked just as well, but then maybe not. In a car accident, you had to sacrifice someone to the cops – the driver. It wasn't always the best way to go. She'd have to explain that in more detail to Vicius at a later date.

Akana was nearing his death. Rhona sat forward,

champagne clasped in her hand, forgotten. She watched, hardly breathing. Akana walked along the street, shops to his right, the quiet roadway to his left. The camera people all backed away, creating a space between them and Akana, not wanting to be caught up in the chaos. Even so, they kept filming, capturing the scene for the Devil's Reaper.

Nearing work, Akana still strolled. Even now, he would be four minutes early. He passed by a bus shelter, looked in the windows of a grocery, and then passed by a building that was fronted by three stories of scaffolding. Akana passed under the planks and iron tubing, as he always did.

Seconds later, there was a dull thud. Akana looked up. The scaffolding groaned and creaked and shifted and then came crashing down on top of him. Akana didn't have time to move a muscle. One second he was staring up watching the mass shift, the next it was descending on top of him in an almighty crash. Rhona saw scaffolding plummeting down like an avalanche, timber and metal surging to the ground. It hit hard, crushing Akana easily, and a great cloud rose, billowing into the sky.

This was always a significant moment for Rhona, followed by a stab of despair. On the one hand, weeks of planning had come to beautiful fruition. On the other, the hunt was over. The kill was done. Fair game was dead.

Akana hadn't stood a chance against her.

'Very nice,' she said, still watching the camera feeds. 'Who's next?'

CHAPTER SIX

Karin Blake sat at her desk, in a large compartmented office, on the second floor of the enormous NSA building in Maryland. This was where she worked these days. It had been a long time since she ran with Drake and the team, but the memories of those days were still fresh. The army training, the fieldwork. The close brushes with death. Karin still wasn't sure if she preferred hands-on work, or office work, but she was damn sure the office was a safer environment, despite her getting kidnapped recently.

Karin was fine now, well recovered. She had thrown herself into work, got through the bad days without too much trauma. As an NSA analyst, and a good one, she still tried to help Drake and his friends where she could, and usually managed to hide her assistance in the form of some other, relevant search or to bury it in paperwork. She would always help Drake out.

Which was why she had rung him the other day, and used NSA resources to learn what had happened to his friend, Clive Ingham. Ingham had been the unfortunate victim of a horrifying murder in L.A. Karin had found the link to Drake, or rather the computer had flagged it. Days had passed since then. Nothing else had happened. Karin was grateful for it.

She sat back, reached for another file and another job. Some other morsel of intelligence to analyse. As she opened the file, there was a beep from her computer and a red flag started flashing.

Intrigued, Karin reached forward and clicked on the red flag. A new screen came up. She frowned. The screen showed a live news report of a man in Hawaii who'd been killed in a bizarre accident. A mass of scaffolding had fallen on him, instantly killing him as he walked to work. It was a terrible tragedy of course, but that wasn't why the database had pinged Karin.

The reason was because, many years ago, the man had been associated with Mano Kinimaka.

Karin frowned, pressed another button. Before he joined the police force, Kinimaka had known this Akana well. Acquaintances always had to be logged on the system, and Akana had been a big one of Kinimaka's.

She looked into the death. Yes, it appeared a load of scaffolding had collapsed on the unfortunate man, crushing him underneath. He hadn't stood a chance. It was an accident. Karin sat back and narrowed her eyes.

Accident?

It was certainly a coincidence. But Clive Ingham, Drake's friend, had been murdered. This Akana hadn't. It was a stretch to tie the two together.

Karin felt a prickle of anxiety creep down her spine. She didn't like the coincidence. It looked innocent, but then...

... most things did until they suddenly weren't.

She clicked a few more buttons, learned a little more of Akana's death, and then went back to Ingham's. She leaned nothing new. The deaths clearly weren't linked. A murder and an accident. One in Los Angeles, the other in Hawaii. Completely different scenarios. There wasn't anything for her to go on.

Karin sat back, still wondering. She decided to let the deliberations percolate, rose and went to the kitchen to pour herself a well-stewed coffee. It wasn't great, but it was all they provided. Once poured, she stood there for a few minutes, drinking it and nodding to a few colleagues who sauntered in. Dressed smartly, like her, they too went for the monstrous coffee and pulled a variety of faces when they took a sip. Like her, they made do. Eventually, usually when it was down to the dregs, someone put on a fresh pot.

Karin slipped out of the kitchen area. She made her way back to her desk. She had scribbled the names, Ingham and Akana, on her pad, and they stared up at her now as if trying to tell her something. Karin pondered what the hell it could possibly be.

Nothing.

Or everything.

She sighed and sat back down. This was impossible. You couldn't make a connection where there clearly wasn't one, no matter how hard you tried. The only link here was that both men were old friends of members of the Ghost Squadron.

Time passed. Karin banished the uneasy thoughts from her mind and got on with her work. Eventually, she packed up for the day, logged off, still uncertain. She left her desk, left work, and drove home. Once home, she showered, made herself some dinner and sat on the sofa to eat it with a tray balanced on her lap. She cracked a beer, enjoyed the smooth taste. Nothing happened. Karin couldn't quite stop thinking about Ingham and Arkana, even as she watched one of her favourite TV shows. Her flat overlooked a main road, and the rumble of passing cars eventually lulled her to sleep right there on the sofa. She woke herself about one in the morning and shuffled off to bed, where she tried to reclaim sleep.

The next morning, she returned to work.

It was waiting for her as soon as she switched her screen back on.

The next red flag.

She blinked; her mouth falling open. What was this now? She ran for a coffee, unable to function without one close to hand, and sat down, started tapping away at the keys. The screen flashed. She clicked on the red flag.

A woman had been killed in a terrible accident. The woman's name was Stephanie Quan. She was a teacher living in Atlanta, but had once been a CIA agent. Stephanie had quit that life when it didn't agree with her, getting out as fast as she could. Now, she had a good job, a happy family life, two cars, a mortgage, and a husband who sold garage doors for a living. Only this morning, she had arranged to buy a dog, probably to surprise her two young kids.

And now... everything had changed.

Stephanie went to her local gym that morning as usual, getting in a workout before she drove off to her job. She used the rowing machine, the cross trainer and the treadmill before moving on to the weight training machines. This was her usual routine, the same thing every other day. Stephanie had done it for years.

Today, however, the weight machine had malfunctioned. The wires holding the weights had snapped, resulting in them wrapping around

Stephanie's neck and decapitating her. Police reports stated the wires were frayed, but, as yet, there was no actual sign of foul play. Pending further investigation, the death was being treated as an accident.

Stephanie Quan had worked alongside Hayden Jaye when she was at the CIA.

The two had been firm friends, coming up through the ranks together. They had stayed friend's right until the day Stephanie left the agency. After that, there had been no more contact, but the fact of their friendship was a matter of record.

Karin read it all again in disbelief. Stephanie had died just a few hours ago. So now they had firm, old friends of Drake, Kinimaka and Hayden, all dead, two accidentally and one murdered.

Karin had already been suspicious. This was too much. Someone, it appeared, was targeting old friends of the Ghost Squadron. Surely, she thought, it couldn't be coincidence. Not three of them.

Someone was trying to get some attention. And they were trying to hurt the Ghost Squadron in the process.

Why?

It was a natural question to Karin's mind. The question she should ask before she reached out to anyone. The answer, she knew, couldn't be anything good.

Karin picked up the phone.

CHAPTER SEVEN

Matt Drake was lying atop Alicia Myles, enjoying himself, when the phone rang. They were on the black leather sofa and it was three o'clock in the afternoon.

Alicia's hand shot out to grab the ringing phone. She said huskily, 'Drake's just beating around the bush. Can you like... ring back in two and a half minutes?'

Drake frowned, 'Hey...'

Karin's voice stopped them in their tracks. 'Sorry, guys, but I think we have a major problem. I need your attention.'

Drake climbed off Alicia and sat down beside her on the sofa. He felt odd, chatting to Karin naked, but didn't have a lot of options.

'What problem?' he asked.

'Three people have now been killed,' Karin said quickly. 'Your old friend, Clive Ingham, murdered in Los Angeles. Kinimaka's old friend, Akana, accidentally killed in a scaffolding collapse in Hawaii. And now Hayden's old friend, Stephanie, killed in a gym accident. That's three in four days.'

Drake sat forward, nakedness forgotten. 'Accidents?'

'Supposedly. But three old friends in four days is a hell of a coincidence.'

Drake thought so, too. 'Could they not have been accidents? We've known people before who could make murder look accidental.'

'That we have. And it's the existence of those kinds of people that worry me. Maybe someone is trying to get your attention. Maybe someone is trying to hurt you by killing them.'

'And maybe the murder and accidents are the precursor to something big,' Alicia said.

'Precisely.'

Drake started moving. He said, 'We're gonna meet up with the others. This is a conversation for everyone. I'll ring you back as soon as we're all together.'

Karin agreed, and Drake hung up. They got dressed, contacted the others, and arranged to meet immediately at Hayden's house. Fifteen minutes later, they were gathered together and once more listening to Karin as she brought the others up to speed. Soon, they were sat back, thinking, staring at each other and wondering what to do with the new information.

'It could be coincidence,' Dahl said, ever practical.

'Unlikely,' Kinimaka said, still in mourning for his friend.

Hayden looked equally shocked at the news Karin had brought them. 'Obviously, I haven't seen Stephanie in years,' she said. 'Not since she left the CIA. But our friendship was probably on the record. Everything is.'

'There could be a powerful entity committing these murders,' Mai said.

'Subtle,' Alicia said.

'Yes, but forceful,' Drake said. 'Are they trying to grab our attention? Or is this some evil game of revenge?'

'It's hardly a game,' Hayden said.

'Not what I meant, sorry.'

'I know, I know,' Hayden rubbed her forehead. 'I'm just in shock, that's all.'

'The question is, what do we do next?' Dahl stood up and went to pour himself a coffee.

'Yeah,' Kenzie said. 'With an invisible trail, which road do you take?'

'Invisible trail?' Cam questioned.

'We have nothing,' Kenzie explained. 'We do not know who's commissioning these murders, if anyone. The trail is cold. Its...' she went silent.

Drake looked up at her. 'What?'

'Well, it's not entirely cold, I suppose,' Kenzie said.

Drake listened to Dahl sipping his drink. It was the only sound in the room for a while. 'What do you mean?' he asked, eventually.

Kenzie addressed the phone that lay on the table in front of them. 'Karin. Did they catch anyone for the murder of Clive Ingham?'

Drake felt a stab of guilt on hearing the name. He leaned forward.

Karin was silent for a few moments, then came back on the line. 'They arrested two men for Ingham's murder,' she said. 'They're both currently in prison, pending trial.'

'There's your trail,' Kenzie said.

'You think we could get access to them?' Drake asked.

'With Bryant's and Karin's influence, yes,' Mai said.

'You think two thugs in Los Angeles are gonna lead us to the person behind all this?' Dahl asked incredulously. '*If* there is anyone behind all this?'

'Do you have a better idea?' Drake snapped.

Dahl held up a hand. 'To be fair, there is no better idea. The other two deaths are being looked at as accidents. Apologies. Of course, I'm worried about my old friends now.'

Drake thought of several rejoinders to that, but didn't have the heart to speak any of them aloud. He couldn't get the old image of Ingham out of his head. He broke off for a few minutes, walked around the room, grabbed a coffee, looked out the window. Drake sighed, feeling helpless. What more could he do?

Nothing for Ingham. He felt guilt, but knew that guilt was misplaced. He also knew that whoever was behind all this wanted him to feel that guilt, wanted him anxious, off his game.

'You think they're coming for us?' he suddenly asked.

'Who?' Alicia said without thinking.

'The person behind all this. The mastermind. Clearly, we've pissed someone off.'

'During our travels, we've probably pissed everyone off,' Hayden said drily.

'I can contact the prison where these two men are being held,' Karin's voice came through the speakerphone. 'Speak to the governor. The authority will sound better coming from the NSA. Also, I could drop Bryant's name and area of business.'

'You think that would get us access?' Drake asked.

'I don't see why not. The prison has no agenda in *not* letting you in.'

It was a good point she made, Drake conceded. It was a long way from here to LA, and he hadn't wanted to make a pointless journey.

'The problem is,' Dahl said. 'What do we do next? I mean, could other old friends be in danger?'

Karin spoke up quickly. 'I need a list, and then I can treat this as a proper operation. I might have to farm it out to another agency, but I can try to get protection for your old friends.'

Drake thought about that. Did he have any other old friends? Sure, he had acquaintances, but real friends? And there were some people he'd knocked about with that he couldn't even remember their names.

'I have a long list,' Kenzie said. 'It may be worth getting in touch with the Israelis.'

'Definitely,' Karin said. 'I can facilitate that.'

Alicia looked at Mai. 'You have any friends, old Sprite?'

'I have family,' Mai said seriously. 'And there's Hibiki, and a few other cop friends. Yes, this person could hurt me.'

Alicia reined it in, sitting back. 'So we're headed for L.A., then?'

Drake turned away from the window, regarding the room. 'It's our only lead. Our only way in. Maybe these two thugs know something about who hired them.'

'And if nobody hired them?' Dahl said. 'Or they won't tell us?'

Drake sighed. 'Then, I fear, this will all escalate.'

'They killed Ingham as part of a mugging,' Karin told them. 'That's the official line. That's what the two perpetrators have said. They haven't elaborated on why the murder was so extreme. And there were more than just two people involved. They haven't caught the others yet.'

'So maybe these two know nothing at all,' Dahl sighed. 'Maybe they really are actually just thugs.'

Drake started reeling off names. Not many, just a

few he remembered from the old days. Most importantly, he gave her the name of Michael Crouch, a good friend to them all. Drake had no idea what Crouch was up to these days, but he did know the man deserved any protection he could get. Especially at the hands of so deviant a murderer.

It took the team a while to come up with a list of names. It would take Karin a lot longer to get them protection. By the time they were done, they were mentally exhausted, and feeling far more anxious. They realised they potentially held the life of death of dozens of people in their hands. Not only that, but if they missed someone off and that person died...

It didn't bear thinking about. They were in a twisted predicament here. Their enemy had engineered it.

When they were done, Karin signed off, and Hayden was already looking for flights. 'We won't wait for Karin to get us clearance,' she said. 'We'll go right away. Hopefully, clearance will come through before we land.'

They rose and made ready to fly to L.A. They packed a few bags, added a change of clothes, a few other items. It was a short list. Drake said little, still dwelling in a past that involved Clive Ingham and an old friendship.

Three deaths so far. He couldn't shake the feeling that they were just getting started.

CHAPTER EIGHT

Drake and the others breathed a sigh of relief when the plane's tyres squealed as they hit the LAX tarmac. Turbulence had plagued the flight and, where Dahl had been snoozing and lightly snoring, Drake had been gripping the armrests and sat up ramrod straight. He made a point of waking the big Swede before the next round of turmoil, but Dahl just let the jiggling of the plane lull him back to sleep. Drake swore at him.

They caught a large Uber from the airport and headed for the prison. Apparently, the California Department of Corrections and Rehabilitation operated thirty-four prisons across the state, but the one they wanted was a solid hour's drive from LAX, and that was in the light traffic of early morning.

The team stayed quiet for most of the journey. They had delayed their flight of last night, not wanting to arrive in the early hours and be forced to grab a hotel. This appeared to be the best option. The Uber driver didn't speak good English and stayed quiet during the entire trip.

Soon, they were pulling up in the prison's parking area. The Uber shot off. Drake stood for a moment, regarding the grim façade. It was a blocky edifice, punctuated by dozens of windows that were all probably offices. They all walked up to the doors and headed inside.

The interior was bright and air-conditioned. It reminded Drake of a hotel lobby. They approached a long, curving desk and nodded at the uniformed man seated behind.

Hayden took point. She told the guy why they were there and waited. They had received confirmation from Karin during the flight that they had been given a special dispensation to visit the prisoners. The guy tapped away at his computer for a while and then disappeared through a back door. Drake and the others all took seats. When he returned, the guard beckoned towards Hayden.

'Three of you,' he said. 'No more.'

Drake looked from face to face. Who would be best to interrogate the two prisoners? Definitely not Alicia. Kinimaka was the other old law enforcement type, and maybe Kenzie or Dahl, too. Of course, he wanted to be in there himself.

'Mano and Drake?' Hayden was by his side.

'Sounds good to me,' he rose and started off before anyone could say anything.

The trio followed a guard along a wide, white panelled corridor with doors leading off to all sides. They passed through a locked gate and then another, coming at last to several sets of interrogation rooms. It was into one of these that they were ushered. The guard came with them.

'You will have time to question Jon Messenger first. You will have time to question Kedar Petrie afterwards.'

'Sounds good,' Hayden said.

Drake remained standing as Hayden and Kinimaka sat down. The guard departed, leaving the room otherwise empty. Drake and the others waited. Minutes later, the internal door opened, admitting two guards and the prisoner. The man had long, lank, black hair and an unshaven face. His eyebrows were big and bushy and crept along his forehead like giant slugs. His face was harsh, the lines looking like they'd been etched by a chisel. He lumbered along, moving slowly, and deposited himself in the single chair with a weary sigh, as if he was exhausted.

'Jon Messenger,' one guard stated and then backed out of the room. Drake, Hayden and Kinimaka were left alone with the prisoner.

They introduced themselves and asked if they could ask a couple of questions.

'Might as well,' Messenger said in a deep, bored voice. 'Everyone else has.'

'You killed Clive Ingham,' Drake said flatly.

Messenger shrugged. 'If you say so.'

Drake felt his hands curl into fists, but Hayden laid a hand on his arm. She fixed Messenger with a steely gaze.

'Can you tell us why you did it?'

'Needed a smoke. Dude had a vape.'

That was actually untrue. Ingham hadn't used a vape, Hayden knew. She decided to call the man out.

'Not true,' she said. 'Listen to me. You're going to jail for a very long time. Nothing can change that. But if you answer my questions, I can make your stay a little more comfortable.' She spread her hands wide. 'Or not.'

Messenger showed interest for the first time, looking up at her. 'Maybe you should explain that.'

Kinimaka raised a hand. 'She means talk to us, asshole, or we'll crush you.'

Messenger sighed, bored again. 'I don't need that kind of shit. Perhaps the men should stay quiet and let the pretty lady talk.'

'We know you killed Ingham to order,' Hayden said quietly.

Messenger's eyes narrowed. 'What are you talking about?'

'Someone told you to kill Ingham,' Hayden said. 'Maybe the job was commissioned. What can you tell us about that?'

Messenger squinted. 'Ingham was a stupid dude in the wrong place at the wrong time. I don't even know what commissioned means.'

Drake stared at the man, wanting to hurt him. Maybe attending this interview had been the wrong option, after all. It hadn't occurred to him properly that he'd be coming face to face with Ingham's murderers.

'I mean,' Hayden said. 'That somebody paid you to kill Ingham. Somebody purposely ordered the hit on that man. I want to know who that was.'

Messenger stared at her as if weighing her up. His carved face didn't move an inch. The slug-like eyebrows remained in place. 'And if they did, what exactly did I get out of it? I'm stuck in here.'

Drake thought that was an excellent question. 'It's not like you expected to get caught,' he said.

Messenger shrugged. 'Shit happens. I go to jail, do my time, I gain respect in the gang.'

Hayden jumped on to that. 'What gang?'

But Messenger shut her down. 'What can you do for me, pretty lady?'

Drake shuddered for Hayden, but knew she could take care of herself. 'Like I said,' she told him. 'We can make your life more comfortable.'

'How? I'm gang affiliated in here.'

'You have a commissary, right?'

'You gonna top me up?'

Hayden nodded. She hoped he would accept because, truth be told, there was nothing else she could offer this man.

'A few treats would be a nice thing,' Messenger said.

'Which gang are you with?' Drake asked.

'The 12K Boyz.'

Drake hadn't heard of them, but then he wasn't exactly au fait with local gang culture.

'Thanks,' Hayden said.

'Not anything you couldn't find out from one of the guards,' Messenger growled.

Drake shifted. 'Does that mean you're not going to help us?'

'How about this?' Messenger said. 'Go fuck yourselves.'

Hayden tried cajoling some more, but Messenger wouldn't be budged. The man appeared confident in his decision, in his environment, willing to accept his lot. Maybe the brief line he'd dropped about doing his time and being better respected by the gang was on the money.

In the end, they got rid of Messenger and went to the next interrogation room. Already waiting for them was Kedar Petrie, a clean shaven whippet-thin man with a jaw that could cut timber. His teeth were yellow, his eyes bloodshot. He looked weary, downtrodden.

Hayden went through the same spiel, hoping for a different reaction.

'You're gonna pay me for information?' he asked.

Drake saw that as a good sign. He nodded. 'Right into your account. You'll be the richest man in here.'

Hayden narrowed her eyes at him as if to say: "not damn likely", but he'd said it now and couldn't take it back. Petrie already had a hopeful expression on his face.

'Are you a member of the 12K Boyz?' Kinimaka asked.

'Sure. How'd you know?'

Hayden didn't answer him. She said, 'Who told you to kill Clive Ingham?'

'What did Messenger tell you?' Petrie looked suspicious for the first time.

'He told us everything,' Drake lied. 'But we need you to corroborate.'

'Hell,' Petrie said. 'It's no big secret. And, to be honest, it's pretty damn obvious. I mean, who the hell do you think told us to kill Ingham?'

Drake was slightly taken aback. Were they looking at this the wrong way? It didn't seem obvious to him. 'Maybe you could tell us,' he said.

'The leader of the gang,' Petrie looked at them as if they were stupid. 'Our boss. The man who runs 12K.'

Now it was obvious, and pretty clear cut. Drake knew they couldn't have guessed anything like that, though. They needed it to come from the horse's mouth.

'What's the name of the gang leader?' Kinimaka asked.

'Anyone can tell you that. It's Raul Ramirez.'

'And he's the top dog?'

'That's him.'

'The man who gave the order to murder Clive Ingham?'

'Who?'

'The man you murdered so vilely,' Drake said. 'The reason you're in here.'

'Oh, him, yeah, Ramirez told us to do it.'

They were done with this asshole. As he asked for a value on his commissary, they had the guards escort him out of the interrogation room, then made their way back to the rest of the team. It was Cam and Shaw who stood up first, asking for information. Hayden and Drake gave it to them straight.

'We're looking for a gang boss named Raul Ramirez. He gave the order to kill Ingham.'

'A gang boss?' Cam breathed. 'That could be problematic.'

'You mean getting close to him, trusting him not to kill us, gaining admittance to his incredible presence... all that kind of shit?' Drake said. 'Won't be a problem.'

'We're gonna need firepower,' Dahl said.

Drake nodded. 'You got that right, mate.'

'Karin will provide,' Hayden said. 'Like the CIA, the NSA has drop boxes and safe houses in many places. Especially places like L.A.'

'You think she can get us access?'

'I certainly hope so. Otherwise, we're buying weapons on the streets.'

'Any ideas how we're gonna get close to this Ramirez?' Kenzie asked.

'The hard way,' Alicia said.

CHAPTER NINE

Karin directed them to a shared agency safe house in L.A. where they stocked up on weapons. Drake and the others went for trusty Glocks and many spare mags, knowing they couldn't take anything bulkier, as they were still working on civilian streets. They chose knives and a Bluetooth comms system.

All this time, Karin was busy doing the legwork.

She investigated the 12K Boyz, contacted the local cops and tracked down the right department that would deal with them. She spoke to a couple of cops, got talked at, advised, and finally found out the pertinent information. All she really needed to know was where their base of operations was.

'Green Meadows,' she explained. 'That's where the 12K Boyz has a HQ. It's one of the most dangerous neighbourhoods of L.A., so watch yourselves. You're talking 30,000 people living in a 2.2 square mile area which is struggling with gang violence. You won't be contending with just the 12K Boyz in there.'

Drake thanked her. They finished getting ready, pulling rucksacks and filling them with provisions. No need to get hungry or thirsty on a job. The last thing they required was a car or two, and at this the station leader balked.

'Come on, guys,' he was a short, hairy man who, for some reason, was constantly clad in a bullet-proof vest with the letters FBI emblazoned across the front. 'I can't let you go into Green Meadows with a couple of pool cars. We'd never see them again.'

'You mean us?' Alicia asked him archly.

'Nope. I definitely mean the cars.'

Hayden leaned on him, spoke to him all about inter-agency cooperation. It wasn't often the NSA asked for help, but this was one of those times and he was going to have to cough up. The guy looked like he was warring with himself, trying to make a decision.

Eventually, he caved. 'Do it,' he said finally. 'Parking area across the street,' he held out two pairs of keys. 'For God's sake, bring them back in one piece or the commander will have my ass.'

Fully loaded, they left the safe house, found the cars and started towards Green Meadows. The L.A. traffic was stop-start, thick and slow-moving. They had an address from Karin and programmed it into the sat-nav. Using police records, they got photos of Raul Ramirez and spent some time studying his face. They wanted to recognise him easily. According to Karin, the 12K Boyz were one of the smaller gangs with a combined membership of just a few hundred. Nevertheless, they were considered well organised and violent, not to be messed with.

It was mid-afternoon by the time Drake and the others cruised past the address they'd been given. They wasted no time scoping out a place to park from which they could observe the entrance and then settled in to wait.

The HQ of the 12K Boyz was fronted by a two-pump gas station with a small shop and an extensive building attached. The front door appeared to be a rickety glass affair, past the shop and halfway down the building. There were lots of windows with drawn blinds and several dumpsters standing outside. The exterior was neglected. Rubbish had piled up near steps and there were a few cars parked haphazardly all around. When a new car arrived, it didn't slot in to a space. The driver just seemed to abandon it and head swiftly into the building. Drake and the team settled in to wait and to watch, to get a feel for the comings and goings.

Drake watched as a random car filled its tank. He was hungry, so grabbed a sandwich from a pack and started munching. He also grabbed a bottle of water. Soon, his example set the others off, and they were all eating and drinking.

Alicia, sat in the passenger seat, was the one who abstained. In the car with her, was Drake, Cam and Shaw. There wasn't a lot of conversation in the cramped confines of the car. Alicia kept her eyes on the front door of the HQ.

They started coming up with names for the regular visitors.

'There goes Bill again,' Alicia said on seeing a muscleman with a beard and a tight t-shirt running from his car to the door. 'Carrying a plastic bag probably full of dope.'

'And there's Fred,' Shaw said, nodding at a man carrying a duffel bag no doubt crammed with money. 'He's gotta be the strong arm of the gang. Look at all the heavies in the car.'

Afternoon passed into early evening. The activity increased. They weren't just observing; they were scanning for entry points too. The more the merrier. So far, they'd only found the front door.

'I'm going for a walk,' Mai said suddenly through their comms system.

Nobody had to remind her to be careful. The sight of gang members coming and going, guns and knives in obvious sight, was enough to put them all on guard. The gang members appeared secure in their environment. They didn't check around to see who might be watching, didn't scan the area for cops or feds, just carried on with their business, even carrying some of their product in plain sight.

Mai took a cursory walk around. She crossed the road to the gas station, went into the shop. She took a slow walk around the block. Twenty minutes later, she was back in the car.

'You can feel the danger out there,' she said. 'It's a loaded neighbourhood. We're not gonna get anything done in the light.'

They continued to watch as the shadows grew longer. Drake was happier as the night advanced and the heat lessened. He didn't know what the temperature was inside the car, but it was bordering on ridiculous. They had cracked a few windows, but it didn't seem to help that much.

Full dark came. Still, they watched. Depressingly, there had been no sign of Raul Ramirez. They saw Fred and Bill a few more times and a loner they nicknamed George. This George was a skinny bald guy in his twenties who seemed to run everywhere. He left his gold Buick Le Sabre running, entered the front door running, exited it running. The guy was in one hell of a hurry.

More hours passed. The activity around the building increased. They realised George appeared on the hour, every two hours, and it was with that knowledge that they finally came up with a plan.

In the early hours just before dawn, the activity lessened. Now, it seemed, was a gangster's time to sleep. But as they hoped, George kept on coming.

It was Mai who they tasked with the operation. She cracked open a door and exited her car just ten minutes before George was due to make another running appearance. She glided across the road, slipped into shelter, and made her way close to the place where George always parked. Drake, watching her, could barely discern her from the shadows all around. There were plenty of overhangs, and high roofs and close buildings to provide the shadows. Mai just knew how to blend easily with them.

Mai crouched in the dark, her eyes watchful. She listened to the noises, watched the faceless windows in front of her. There was no motion at them, she saw. The gang members never came close. She didn't like to think of the activities going on inside the building and wished they had enough people to put an end to them. But there were dozens and dozens of gang members, maybe a hundred or more. They just didn't have enough personnel.

She waited patiently, counting down the seconds until George was due to make his appearance. Right then, there was a commotion around the front door. A man came out, his neck in the grip of another, bigger man. The two tussled for a moment and then the first man was thrown to the ground. The second drew a gun on him.

'You heard what I said,' the man grunted. 'I can't work with the shit you bring me. Get better product.'

The man on the ground held up his hands, staring at the gun. 'Sure, boss,' he said. 'Whatever you say.'

The man was allowed to scramble to his feet and walk away. The second man covered him every second with the gun, shaking his head. He muttered, ducked back inside the front door.

Forty seconds later, George turned up.

Mai uncurled herself from the shadows. She waited until the car came to a stop; the door cracked open, and George jumped out. George was already in full flight, but Mai was able to dart around the front of the car, grab him by the collar and haul him back. George squealed in shock, too stunned to struggle. He landed on his ass, looking up.

Mai hauled him to his feet and dragged him back into the shadows.

'What are you doing?' George asked incredulously.

Mai understood his shock. There weren't many people brave enough to abduct a gang member outside his HQ door.

'Information,' she said. 'That's what I want.'

George shook his head at her. 'Go to hell.'

Mai had confronted many young men in such a way. She ended up knowing that the only real way forward was to grab something they treasured. She did that now and started to squeeze. George's eyes bulged.

'Ow,' he said. 'Please don't.'

Mai didn't relent. 'Raul Ramirez,' she said. 'Where does he hang out inside this building?'

George flinched as she applied even more pressure. He was biting his tongue, standing on tiptoe as he tried to cope. 'If I tell you, they'll kill me.'

'They'll never know. And guess what happens if you don't tell me?'

Mai felt safe, wrapped in shadow. It was her natural habitat. She'd been trained at an early age to use the darkness, to embrace it, to twist it's depths for her own means. Now, it suited her; it worked perfectly to compliment her. She used its many facets, worked well in it. George was putty in her hands; she was able to manoeuvre him wherever she wanted him to go. Another reason she had decided to crush his nut sack.

'Please let go,' he whimpered.

'I want the layout of the HQ, and I want to know where Raul Ramirez stations himself. Got it?'

George nodded, then groaned in pain. He looked at her, clearly expecting her to let up on the pressure. When she increased it, he groaned again.

'Oh, God, all right, all right,' he quickly explained the layout to her, which seemed to comprise three large rooms where dope and pills were packaged and lots of side rooms where other operations were undertaken. Some of the minor bosses had their offices there, too. Raul Ramirez had a corner office at the far end of the building, a place he rarely left. Ramirez even had a bed set up in there, and a nearby kitchen and dining room. Mai saw this new information as a major problem.

How the hell were they going to get to Ramirez?

'Who else goes inside, and when?' she asked. 'Apart from gang members.'

'Our informers,' he said, and then to her surprised look. 'People we have placed in rival gangs. Hookers. Some cops on the quiet. Salespeople, trying to sell us alternative product,' he shrugged and then winced. 'I can't think properly.'

Mai thought about it. Maybe they could pretend to be hookers to gain entry. Maybe they could pose as salespeople. But those ideas were fraught with danger. They couldn't exactly just tag along with a load of hookers, and they'd have to find some product to sell to act as salespeople.

'Come with me,' she said to George.

To be fair, he didn't have a choice. Mai walked him further into the shadows, towards the back of the building. George walked as best he could, groaning all the way. Mai, feeling like a bit of a sadist, let up a little, but warned him not to try anything.

'Show me,' she said. 'You say Ramirez has a corner office? Where is it?'

George pointed. 'That one. It's the only corner room.'

Mai clasped her other hand around his throat. 'You'd better not be lying to me.'

'I promise. But listen, I show up at the same time every day, every few hours. I'm rarely late. They're gonna be wondering where I am.'

Mai realised the kid was right. She let him go, dusted him off, straightened him out. She smiled. 'It's our secret,' she said. 'You don't mention me. I won't let it slip that you spilled all the beans. Don't forget.'

She let him go, watched him walk awkwardly to the front door and enter. She stayed in the deeper shadows, enjoying their solace. They now knew where Raul Ramirez slept, ate and worked.

How could they make it work for them?

Mai waited until all was silent, until nothing moved, and then made her way through the shadows back to where they were parked.

In her ear, the others chatted about what she'd learned.

CHAPTER TEN

The night was still fully dark, but it would soon get lighter. The timing would be tight, but the Ghost Squadron decided to act immediately, rather than to have to wait another twenty-four hours. Ten minutes after Mai returned, they were exiting their cars and crossing the road, checking their weapons, and searching for the shadows. Mai led the way as they crept softly through the darkness until they were stationed close to Ramirez's office, able to look up at his windows from their crouched positions.

'We make this quick,' Drake said. 'Shock and awe. There are too many enemies inside, so we get in, get the information, and then get out as quickly as possible. We set?'

They all nodded. They rose in the dark and approached the nearest window. Kinimaka reached up and tried to slide it open. No such luck. It was locked from the inside. No option. Kinimaka used a crowbar to break it open, making lots of noise.

They jumped up to the sill as the window collapsed, faced with a drawn curtain. Drake pushed it inside. The room he saw was large. It contained a desk, a chair, a single bed in the corner. Ramirez was lying on the bed, staring at him in shock, trying to blink the sleep from his eyes. There was a gun lying next to him on the nightstand.

Ramirez reached for it.

Drake leapt into the room, drew his own gun, and covered Ramirez with it. He shook his head. Ramirez's hand froze three inches from the butt of his gun. His eyes were wide, questioning.

Drake ran towards him.

At the same time, the door to Ramirez's room flew open. Two women raced in, both wearing skimpy night dresses. They looked confused on seeing Drake, and even more shocked when the rest of the Ghost Squadron started jumping in through the broken window.

'Don't move,' Alicia told them. 'Just stay in that corner.'

They complied, not a threat. Drake turned to Ramirez, thinking this had gone far better than expected.

And then there was a commotion at the door. Drake looked over to see three armed men rush into the room. Dahl, Kenzie and Cam were on them swiftly, tackling them and fighting for their guns. Ramirez took the opportunity to scoop his gun up.

Drake dived at him.

He hit the man hard under the chin with the top of his head. Ramirez grunted. Drake rammed his own gun into Ramirez's ribs.

'Drop the weapon,' he breathed.

Ramirez didn't listen. He was used to giving the orders. But he couldn't bring his gun to bear, couldn't aim it at Drake. The Yorkshireman jabbed at Ramirez's throat, then bent the man's wrist back almost all the way. The gun dropped to the floor. Ramirez gasped.

Drake didn't waste a second, knowing Dahl and the others were dealing with the guards. 'Clive Ingham,' he said. 'Your men robbed him, beat him up, knifed and shot him, and then set him on fire. I want to know who you were working for. Who asked you to do that?'

Near the door, Dahl elbowed a man in the throat. He grabbed a gun and broke the fingers that held it. He grabbed his opponent by the skull and then rammed that skull into the doorframe. The owner simply slithered down the frame all the way to the floor, folding in half.

Cam threw stunning punch after punch into his opponent's midriff. Bones broke. The man, still with his gun arm free, was in too much agony and shock to bring his weapon to bear. He collapsed and then went lights out as Cam concentrated on the top of his skull. The gun fell away.

Kenzie took on the third guard. He already had his gun raised, forcing Kenzie to dodge out of the way. A shot went off. Not good. Everyone in the building would hear it. But it was just one shot. Maybe they wouldn't act on it in this nest of murderers and drug dealers. Kenzie kicked out, striking the man in the stomach. She grabbed the gun arm and broke it, hearing the terrible snap of bone and the man's high-pitched shriek. He fell to his knees. She was still holding the broken arm. She lifted it. Her enemy turned very compliant, offering his face up to her. She smashed him full in the nose and then across the temple. He crashed limply to the floor.

Drake was face to face with Ramirez as Alicia, Hayden and Kinimaka crowded around. Hayden reiterated what they wanted.

'Who ordered the killing of Clive Ingham?'

'You will die here today,' Ramirez spat at them.

Drake didn't doubt it, unless they hurried the hell up. He smashed Ramirez in the mouth with the barrel of his gun, breaking teeth. 'Answer the fucking question.'

'Fuck you.'

Right then, one of the docile women started screaming and rushed forward. In one hand, she held a gleaming knife. Drake saw no real threat in her capability and left the problem in Alicia's hands. The Englishwoman turned with a sigh, waited until the attacker got close and then just smashed a front kick into her abdomen. The woman, in mid-strike with the knife, folded into a heap of agony. Alicia relieved her of the weapon and then turned back to Ramirez, shaking her head.

Drake broke more teeth. Ramirez spat them back at him. He jammed his gun up under the man's chin.

'Last chance,' he said. 'Tell us now.'

'Like I said...'

Ramirez snarled up at him, eyes afire with hatred. The man was big and tattooed, bald and with cauliflower ears. He wore nothing but a pair of boxer shorts, and Drake couldn't see a patch on his body that wasn't covered in ink.

Drake had an idea. 'Get ready to burn this place to the ground,' he told Hayden.

She nodded, turned away. Suddenly, Ramirez was struggling, trying to sit up. 'Hey, wait, wait,' he said. 'This is my business. What the hell are you going to do?'

'You heard me, mate.' Drake's accent was thick as the stress built.

'What?'

'I'm gonna order this place burned to the ground,' he said. 'Right now.'

Dahl, at the door, was suddenly in a gunfight. Bullets flew at him, and he ducked out of the way. Kenzie hid behind a plaster wall. At any moment, a bullet could fly through. Dahl picked off his opponent with the next shot but was sure more were coming.

'Hurry it up,' he growled.

Drake nodded at Hayden and Kinimaka. 'Burn it,' he said.

They turned, heading off to grab imaginary flammable cannisters. Ramirez yelped and struggled. Drake let him sit up.

'No,' he yelled. 'You can't. We'll never recover. Business is hard enough as it is. Damn you!'

Drake smashed him across the side of the face with the gun. 'This really is your last chance, mate.'

'Go fu-' Ramirez began, spitting blood.

Drake hit him again. 'Yes, we know.'

'We got the gas,' Hayden said from out of Ramirez's eyeline.

The leader of the 12K Boyz tried to sit up. Drake elbowed him down, keeping him there. 'Do it,' he said to Hayden.

'No, *no!* Wait. You can't do that. What do you want to know? *What do you wanna know?*'

Drake held his gun close to the man's face. 'Weren't you listening, mate? Who ordered the killing of Clive Ingham?'

Ramirez's face went through myriad changes, his expression strained, anxious, his lips trembling. He wanted to tell them, needed to tell them, but something huge was holding him back. Something he couldn't quite get past.

'Please...' he said.

'Who ordered the killing?' Drake insisted.

Right then, there was more gunfire. Ramirez looked hopeful. Dahl saw a plaster chunk explode beside his head. Kenzie ducked to the ground as bullets whizzed past. Both returned fire, and the gunfire abruptly cut off. There were groans from Ramirez's men.

Ramirez cursed. 'I have dozens of people here,' he spat. 'Why can't one of them do something?'

'They're trying,' Alicia said. 'We're just too good.' She glanced over at Hayden. 'You ready with that petrol... umm, gas?'

'Ready.'

Ramirez bit his lower lip until it bled. He stared up into Drake's eyes as if begging him to just walk away. Drake waved the gun.

'All right,' Ramirez said finally. 'We're the 12K Boyz. You can't tell anyone what I'm about to tell you. *Anyone.* It would get us all killed and then there'd be the deaths of hundreds on your conscience.'

Drake grunted. 'All we want is a name.'

'Okay, okay. It's Alvarez, okay? He's a boss man. Runs at least half a dozen gangs in L.A., including the 12K Boyz. He has an enormous mansion in the Hills. Lives it up like a fucking movie star. Guy's a whacko, but he's the go-to man. We get our direction from him.'

Drake acted instantly. They had the information they needed. He smashed Ramirez into unconsciousness, gave the order to leave through the comms and then started running. The team turned, covering each other, and headed for the windows, jumping through and out into the night. Outside, they quickly turned, still covering each other, and ran for the shadows, creeping away. The skies above were just starting to lighten, but there was enough darkness left to shield their movements. As they ran past the front doors of the building, they saw no movement. Ramirez's men were probably still wondering what was going on, maybe even tending to Ramirez.

In silence, the Ghost Squadron raced back to their cars.

CHAPTER ELEVEN

The team were spent, weary as they could remember, but they had no time to lose. The knowledge that someone was targeting their friends, and maybe ultimately them, spurred them on. They returned to the cars, left the area quickly, and found a twenty-four-hour fast-food restaurant parking lot in which to stop. Famished, they left the cars and entered the restaurant, ordering at the counter. Soon they were seated with white and yellow wrappers all over the table, tucking into juicy burgers and picking at seasoned fries. They drank their cold drinks through straws and discussed the case. Still early, they had the diner to themselves.

'Alvarez,' Hayden was speaking into her phone and munching at the same time.

'Sorry?'

Hayden swallowed. 'Sorry, it's a gang boss named Alvarez. He has a place in the Hollywood Hills, a mansion.'

Karin could be heard speaking on the other end of the line. 'Let me look at that and come back to you.'

Hayden hung up. Karin was on the case. Her database was endless, and if anyone could find Alvarez, it was her. They went back to eating, relaxing, and taking their minds off the danger they'd just been in. The attack on Ramirez's place had been high risk, but it had paid off. Things could so easily have gone south.

Before they'd finished eating, Karin was back on the line.

'Hey,' she said. 'Alvarez is a big player. Far larger than Ramirez. The guy's right, though. Alvarez runs a lot of gangs in L.A., tries to stay apart from the action by living in the Hills, uses a lot of middlemen to liaise with the gang leaders. He's known to the local cops, to the FBI. I have a lot of info on him.'

'He's the next part of the puzzle,' Drake said. 'He knows who's targeting our friends.'

'It's going to be really hard to get close to him.'

'Do you have an address?' Kinimaka asked.

Karin reeled it off. They also got a description of the man. They finished eating, tidied up, and left the diner, returned to their cars. By now, the sky was fully light and an early dawn was rising over the swaying palm trees to the west. Already, it was warm, a balmy seventy degrees. Drake guessed it was going to be a hot one.

Soon, they joined the flow of traffic along Franklin Avenue and then Cahuenga. Drake saw the famous Mulholland Drive twisting off to his left. They did a bit of bumper to bumper traffic before coming to an off ramp where they could head directly towards Alvarez's mansion. Here, though, the roads were narrow and twisty and there were cars parked street-side. Their progress slowed. Drake found he was staring through the gates of lots of houses, trying to see the properties within, marvelling at their beauty and wondering how they all appeared so different. The sat nav told them they still had another thirty minutes before they would reach Alvarez's house.

There was a man selling coffee at the side of the road. Alicia made them stop for a cup and then they were all purchasing it, fortifying themselves for what was to come. They continued up the twisting roads, heading deeper and deeper into the Hills. They passed canyons and lookouts and houses perched on cliffs, houses with stilts.

When they came to Alvarez's place, they cruised past slowly. They saw locked black, iron gates, a winding driveway and, beyond that, a white mansion with two wings. From the brief view, they could tell Alvarez had a lot of guards hanging around, but their guns weren't on show.

Drake was searching the surrounding area, looking for somewhere from which to observe the house. At first, he couldn't find anywhere, but then spied a little parking area up a switchback to the left, from where they could possibly get a better view. He directed them up to it and then started rummaging in his bag.

Came up with a monocular spyglass and fitted it to his eye.

They started observing the Alvarez house from both cars.

Drake saw a wide, clean mansion with dozens of windows looking out onto a green, grassy sward that had a fountain for a centrepiece. The front door was a double wooden affair with huge handles and a massive fake door knocker fashioned in the shape of a wolf. Guards wandered the grounds, walking aimlessly it seemed but taking in the entire property on their ramblings. There were no guards by the front gates, just a slew of CCTV cameras. Drake sighed upon seeing them.

'The place looks as tight as a drum,' Dahl said through the comms.

'Unfortunately, yes,' Hayden said.

'There's always a weakness,' Drake said. 'We just have to find it.'

'The other bad news,' Cam said. 'Is that they can see us as easily as we can see them.'

Drake had thought them pretty secure up here. Now, he took a step back from his need to question Alvarez and reviewed their position. Yes, they were stationed in a gravelly switchback, alongside a house and near a wooden fence, but if someone looked up here, they could easily be seen. And Alvarez's guards would soon get suspicious of two new cars overlooking their property. Drake cursed. Cam was right. They were going to have to move. He got out of the car, looked around.

'There's nowhere else,' he said. 'No other vantage point. We need eyes...' he cursed again.

'Get back in the car,' Dahl told him. 'You're even more conspicuous out there.'

Drake complied, settling in his seat. He put the monocular to his eye, gazed at Alvarez's mansion once more. 'Any ideas?' he asked.

'We need more time to reconnoitre,' Hayden said. 'Twenty minutes just isn't enough.'

'Drive away,' Kenzie said. 'We're too exposed up here.'

They started their engines and proceeded to drive away. Drake had seen one of the guards staring at them already, so it wasn't a moment too soon. They drove carefully away from the mansion until they could find a place to park, then pulled over to the side of the road. They sat in silence for a while, thinking.

Using the comms, they threw ideas around.

'Infiltration?' Mai suggested.

'Hard to do without a proper recce,' Hayden said. 'We don't know how many guards he has, where they're stationed. The security systems he has in place. Rotas. Possible civilian presence. We'd be going in essentially blind.'

'It's a dangerous situation all round,' Drake said. 'Sometimes you have to just do it.'

Hayden, in the same car, turned to stare at him. 'There's dangerous, and then there's reckless.'

'Can you think of a better idea?'

'I can,' Shaw said. 'We'd just need a little luck.'

Drake blinked at her. 'Care to elaborate?'

'We're gonna need Karin.'

Many hours later, they were standing in a glaring white marble hallway between two Doric columns, looking up a curving marble staircase that led to an expansive second floor. They had their bags on their backs and were staring, a little nonplussed, from side to side.

'So this is ours?' Alicia said, standing totally still.

'For a week at least,' Hayden said.

'You're welcome,' Shaw said.

'I'm not sure I like it,' Alicia said. 'It's too neutral. It's a soulless, anonymous chunk of pretentious marble architecture.'

Drake stared at her. 'Jesus, love, did you eat a dictionary?'

'It's not personal. It's the opposite.'

Drake agreed, but they weren't here to settle down. They were here for one reason only. To spy on Alvarez.

On hearing Shaw's plan, Karin had also agreed they'd have to get lucky, but she'd gone away to do her best. An hour later, she was back on the phone, telling them she had indeed had some luck.

There was a property overlooking Alvarez's mansion that was for rent.

Using her considerable pull, Karin had got the real estate agents to organise an immediate occupation. Between her official capacity and some cajoling, and using the NSA's credentials to bypass the red tape, they had hired this house for a short time. Hours later, they were stepping inside, and now they were wondering what the hell they should do with all the vast space.

'First things first, a good shower,' Alicia said.

Drake stared at her. 'What. The. Fuck?'

She grinned. 'I'm joking,' she said. 'Let's go get set up.'

They all climbed the marble staircase, found the front-facing rooms, and considered what they had to work with. Their new house didn't overlook Alvarez directly, but it had good side views of the gardens, front and rear, and the main building. They couldn't see the main gates, but they could see the winding drive and the front door. They stood away from the windows, using their eyeglasses. After a while, Dahl proposed they should take shifts. This was going to be a long observation.

They settled in. When night fell, Drake decided they should order in from Uber eats. He went around with a notebook and a pen, getting everyone's orders, and then made a phone call. Fifty minutes later, their food arrived, bringing with it a mouthwatering smell. Those tasked with watching Alvarez's house ate where they stood. The rest of the team found a kitchen and sat down around a breakfast bar and a table.

'This is kind of surreal,' Mai said. 'Sharing a house.'

'I'm the best companion you'll ever have,' Alicia told her.

'So long as you don't creep into my bedroom at night.'

'I can't promise that.'

'She watches me sleep,' Drake said, hiding a grin. 'It's unnerving.'

Alicia stared hard at Mai.

'Go away, Taz,' the Japanese woman murmured. 'You can't upset me.'

'But I enjoy trying.'

They ate some more, settled back. The eatery had sent over a crate of beers too, so they cracked open those and sat back. Of course, they would all have to sleep in their clothes for a while, but they'd faced worse.

'Does this place even have six bedrooms?' Alicia asked.

'You assume you're sleeping with me?' Drake smiled.

'I do.'

Drake shrugged. 'We can always fit another in if we have to.'

'Dahl?' Alicia said with interest.

'Piss off.'

The night passed slowly. They organised themselves into shifts. Those observing the Alvarez house jotted everything down in a notebook – the guards shift patterns, the comings and goings, any sightings of Alvarez himself or people connected to him. Karin had provided them with a list of known contacts. The next morning, Drake rose and took his turn, soon familiarising himself with the processes. During his four hours, all he saw were the guards wandering around and a delivery van. Alicia sat beside him, complained constantly of boredom. She wasn't a sitter, entirely the opposite.

The morning passed, and then the afternoon. They were getting quite familiar with Alvarez's routine. He didn't do much, ate in a lot, received visitors in big black SUV's with chrome grilles. He had a staff, maids and at least one cook they'd seen taking a smoke outside. There were others too, a few men in suits who clearly worked in the house. They saw several cars being washed and a man tending the grounds. There was no sign of Alvarez himself.

Another evening went by. Still, they watched. Still, they ordered in. Another night was spent tossing and turning on unfamiliar beds. The next day dawned, and their watch was unrelenting. And still, there was no sign of Alvarez.

Drake, watching, was wondering if Ramirez had given them the right information when the front door opened and the man himself came out. He was wearing a white shirt and jeans and he came out to greet a visitor, clasping the man by the hands. Clearly, this was an important caller. Alvarez disappeared back inside the house, but at least they'd established that he was on site.

More time passed. Another day. They watched and waited, becoming increasingly anxious because all their surveillance was telling them just one thing: they couldn't access the house without absolute risk and a potential bloodbath.

It was a little after seven on a Friday when they finally caught a break.

Alicia and Drake were watching through their cyeglasses, looking forward to the end of their shift when they could eat. There was a sudden flurry of activity around the garages. Guards rushing back and forth. Then one of the garage doors started opening. A large SUV was driven out and taken right up to the front door. Drake and Alicia were on their tiptoes. Drake quickly jumped on to the comms.

'Get ready to move,' he said. 'We may have something here.'

In the background, there was the sound of the team starting to rush around.

Drake watched as the SUV's doors opened and then several guards gathered around. A second SUV was brought up behind the first, this one filled with guards. Drake was already sure Alvarez was about to come out, to *go* out. What else could all this activity be for?

Sure enough, the figure of Alvarez exited the house and started walking down the steps towards the first SUV. He climbed in the back.

Drake and Alicia whirled and started running.

CHAPTER TWELVE

The Ghost Squadron ran for their cars.

Already positioned the right way, they just had to climb behind the wheels and make their way through their own gates, out into the roadway. By the time they were ready, Alvarez's convoy had set off. Drake, behind the wheel of the first car, gunned it in pursuit, then had to slow down as they quickly caught up along the twisting road.

He slowed, allowing some space between vehicles. Alvarez's convoy made its way down the hill, then along a dark canyon, back up another hill, and finally to an on-ramp. They followed a highway for ten minutes, allowing themselves to mingle with traffic and hopefully allaying any suspicions the guards in the cars ahead may have. When the lead cars turned off the highway, Drake followed. He could see Dahl driving the second car in his rearview mirror.

They continued for a while. Drake recognised some roads. He saw a sign for the Sunset Strip, another for Hollywood Boulevard. They were cutting through the heart of L.A. Drake settled back to see where they were being led. The good news, the best news in long, boring days, was that Alvarez was away from his fortress like house.

They drove through the night. Streetlights and the blazing glow of shops and restaurants lined the way. Other cars veered across the road from all directions, making progress difficult, but it was just as hard driving for the cars ahead.

Finally, both of Alvarez's cars slowed as if they were stopping. They pulled off the road into a parking lot. Drake, in traffic, could see the sign of the establishment they were about to grace.

'Club Allure,' he said. 'Crap, they've come to a bloody strip club.'

'A high class one,' Alicia pointed out the Bentleys, Rolls Royce's and G-wagons in the car park and the suited men on the door with their top hats and tails.

'You'd best stay outside then,' Mai told her.

'Don't you worry. I'll fit right in.'

They took their time pulling into the parking lot and parking up. Alvarez slid out of his own car surrounded by guards and then waited for the other car's contingent of guards to surround him before moving forward. Drake took a head count.

'Seven,' he said. 'He's well protected.'

They watched Alvarez walk up to the front doors of the club, in front of the waiting line of people, and get instant admittance. The doors were red leather, studded and, when opened, showed a plush interior. Drake and the others knew Alvarez would be at his most vulnerable inside the club, and quickly exited their vehicles and made their way to the front door.

Now, they encountered the long line.

Mai didn't waste a second. She took out her phone and called Karin. 'How quickly can you set me up on a fake ID and website as an exotic singer?'

'Ten minutes,' Karin told her. 'That's my bread and butter.'

'Call me back when it's done,' Mai said.

Kenzie blinked at her. 'What's an exotic singer?'

'Someone who sings in strip clubs.' Mai shrugged. 'At least, it is now.'

Eight minutes later Karin rang back to say she was ready. She gave Mai the website address and texted her a link, and also gave her some social media pages that she'd quickly set up. Armed with the new identity, Mai approached the doormen with her phone in her hand.

Drake was a step behind her.

'Mai Kitano,' she told the men, smiling. 'Could you let us in? I'm an exotic singer with a big following on social media and could really promote your club.'

The doorman squinted and then looked closely at her phone. 'I like it,' he said. 'Is this you?'

Mai nodded. Drake assumed Karin must have worked wonders with a few pictures of Mai and some deep fakes.

'Are you singing here?' one of the other doormen asked.

'If they'll have me,' Mai touched his arm flirtatiously.

'What about you?' the first doorman turned his attention to Alicia. 'Do you sing?'

'Oh, I do a lot more than sing.'

'Care to show us?' the second man said.

'Maybe later.'

The flirtatious banter with the doormen did the trick. Soon, they were making their ways through the doors into the upmarket gentleman's club. Inside, it was cavernous, all strobe lights and smoke and poles. Loud music pumped through a loudspeaker system. A mass of people gyrated on the dance floor or sat in their seats watching the pole dancers. There was a large bar to the right, six people deep, and a couple of bartenders working their socks off.

Drake and the others made their way through the crowd. Drake turned and shouted above the noise. 'Gonna have to split up. He's in here somewhere.'

'No, we don't,' Alicia said. 'He's right there.'

She nodded ahead. Drake blinked and then turned to look. In front, threading through whirling men and women, were Alvarez and his seven goons. They were unmistakable, nudging people aside as they went, carving a swathe through the throng. Drake nodded, surprised, and then followed.

Straight through the dance floor they went, heading for the other side of the club. The noise, the flashing lights and the smoke was an assault on the senses. As they passed the poles on their raised dais, the women reached out for them, asking for money. Drake saw men dotted around too, also revolving around poles, and assumed this was an equal opportunity club.

They followed Alvarez to a far corner where, not surprisingly, there was a free booth. Alvarez settled himself on a plush sofa, arms spread across the back, and crossed his legs, puffing on a fat cigar. His men arranged themselves beside him and around the booth, facing the club and forming a barrier. Soon, a waitress came over to take Alvarez's order. Drake saw Alvarez lay a fat wad of cash on the table.

They had crossed the dance floor. There was nowhere else for them to go except straight for Alvarez. Drake saw his guards' hidden weapons. They couldn't start anything obvious here in this nightclub.

Alicia dragged him to the left, towards a booth. Four of them managed to slide in there. That left Mai,

Cam and Shaw to pretend they enjoyed dancing so that they could stay relatively close to Alvarez. It wasn't a pretty sight.

Drake pretended to sit back and relax in the booth, monitoring Alvarez and his men. At first, nothing happened, but then the drinks came to the criminal and then the women came. Two leggy blondes and then a brunette were vetted by the guards and then allowed to get close to Alvarez, sitting close so that he could put his hand on their legs.

'Asshole,' Alicia murmured.

'One we have to get closer to,' Drake said. Both of them were having to shout to be heard over the pounding music.

'Just keep watching. Something will come up.'

Drake made a disgusted face and turned away. The club was rocking, people twisting and turning on the dance floor, men and women circling the silver poles. Several danced in cages that hung from the ceiling, swaying to and fro. Swirling lights illuminated the chaos. Drake saw a mixture of every ethnicity, an exultant mix of like-minded men and women. Many of them carried drinks in their hands and some, he saw, even danced around their handbags, transporting him immediately back to the days when *he* used to frequent nightclubs.

Alicia tapped him on the shoulder and yelled in his ear. 'Heads up.'

Drake focused on Alvarez's booth. A tall, dark-haired woman had approached, passed through the guards and was now leaning forward, whispering something in Alvarez's ear. The gang leader nodded, smiled, and then rose to his feet. The dark-haired woman took his hand. She led him away from the table and toward a side booth that had a heavy curtain pulled across. The woman pushed through the curtain, taking Alvarez with her.

'That's a private lap dance if ever I saw one,' Drake shouted.

Alicia nodded. 'This is our chance,' she yelled and then rose to her feet. Mai and Kenzie got up with her. Together, the three women set off on a roundabout route towards the private booth.

Alicia led. She circumvented the row of guards by pushing through a pack of people standing behind them. The private booth was part of a row ahead. She turned quickly to the others, nodded.

'Fast and sweet,' she said with a slight grin.

'Just how we like it,' Kenzie said.

The three women reached the curtain, hesitated, looked at the guards. None of them were watching too closely. Alicia pushed on the curtain, went through.

She raised an eyebrow. It was a big room, and the two were alone. Alvarez sat with his back to a wall whilst the dark-haired woman, now nude, gave him a sensual lap dance. Alvarez's eyes were closed and, at first, he didn't register the newcomers. Alicia, Kenzie, and Mai fanned out.

The woman stared at them, alarm in her eyes. Alicia put a hand to her lips. Then she motioned for the woman to get off Alvarez and move away. She walked forward, bent down, and put her hands on Alvarez's knees.

'Hey dickhead,' she said, leaning forward. 'Wanna dance with me?'

CHAPTER THIRTEEN

Alvarez jerked upright, eyes flying open.

Alicia shot forward, throwing a hand out to cover his mouth. She rammed her knees into his crotch, balancing on the edge of the chair. Alvarez's eyes now registered some pain. Alicia locked on to them and shook her head.

'Make a sound and I'll strangle the life out of you,' she said, placing a hand on his throat.

Alvarez's eyes bulged.

Alicia kept it as quiet as possible. 'I'm gonna ask you a question,' she said. 'Honest answers mean you get to stay alive. Dishonest ones lead to pain. Get it?'

Alvarez tried to spit at her. She increased the pressure on his throat until he calmed down. 'I will kill you, you sadistic bastard,' she said. 'I'd love to.'

Behind her, she knew Kenzie and Mai had her back. Mai was keeping the lap dancer calm.

Alicia leaned close to Alvarez's right ear. 'Talk to me,' she said. 'Who ordered the hit on Clive Ingham?'

Alvarez's face betrayed surprise and then fear. He shook his head, murmured into her hand. Alicia pulled it away slightly.

'Hel-' he started to yell.

Alicia slammed him in the nose with her palm. All

of a sudden, Alvarez appeared to be crying, and looked very startled. He clammed up instantly.

'The next one will break it,' Alicia said, still gripping his larynx.

Alvarez betrayed his fear and disbelief by staring around wildly. Clearly, he couldn't believe he was in this situation, a few dozen steps away from his seven-strong guard, and yet under threat of injury and death.

'Answer the question,' Alicia growled.

She started when a guard thrust his head through the curtain. 'Call for you bo-' he began, and then boggled in disbelief. He held a phone in his hand.

Kenzie reached out, grabbed his jacket, and dragged him inside. The guard stumbled, but recovered quickly. Kenzie smacked him in the mouth, saw his lips mash and blood flow. Hoped it would prevent him from crying out. It did, for now. She then did the next best thing, grabbing his throat with one hand and punching him in the stomach with the other. All this time, the guard was not pliable. He twisted and punched out, caught her with a blow across the chin which she ignored even though it made her stagger.

Another guard popped his head through the curtain. 'Boss?'

Mai leapt at him. Alvarez was cackling as best he could. Mai caught hold of the guard's long hair and yanked him into the room, making sure the curtain closed behind him. Before he could utter a sound, she bent him over and kneed him in the nose, breaking it, then pushed him back upright and jabbed him in the throat. His hands went straight to the point of impact and he retched, but he couldn't utter a sound.

Kenzie still had her guard by the throat, wrenching him back and forth. She delivered punches to his temples, to his chin, trying to knock him out. The guy was on the back foot, but still struck out, aiming punches at her abdomen. Kenzie ignored the punches, ignored the pain, just concentrated on trying to knock him out as silently as possible.

It was a tough, soundless struggle. The women wrenched the men from side to side, hands on throats, trying to keep them quiet. They fought almost in one position, just moving viciously from side to side. Alicia stayed on Alvarez, unable to let him speak. She could only watch. The lap dancer was curled up in the corner, sobbing.

Mai gripped her opponent hard, leaning on him and squeezing his throat. The guy struggled, but was weakening rapidly. Already, he was on his knees. She bore down on him, her grip unbreakable.

'Do it so he can see,' Alicia snapped. 'So he sees what could happen to him, and how defenceless he is.'

Both Mai and Kenzie heard. They fought harder, increasing their grips and blows until both guards were wilting, on their knees, eyes closed. Neither Mai nor Kenzie let up, delivering crushing blow after blow and choking the life out of them. It was silent, and it was harsh and implacable. Mortal combat. Both Mai and Kenzie ended up standing over their downed opponents as Alvarez watched.

Alicia now jabbed her fingers gently against Alvarez's larynx. 'Talk,' she said. 'Or I will kill you.'

'You are asking me the worst question,' Alvarez breathed.

Alicia hadn't expected that. 'What?'

'The worst question. The person you speak of is terrifying.'

Alicia blinked at this scarred, hard man, this leader

of multiple gangs, this crime boss. He was terrified even thinking about what she had asked him. His eyes were wide with fear.

'You know, don't you?' she said. 'You really know.'

Alvarez shook his head. 'I can't. She will utterly destroy me and my family.'

She?

Alicia increased her grip on him. 'You would rather die here, now, at my hand? Give yourself a chance.'

Alvarez closed his eyes, uttered a whimper of despair that shocked Alicia. He seemed like a broken man.

'You will tell us everything,' she pressed.

'I will tell you a story,' he said. 'A story about the Devil's Reaper.'

CHAPTER FOURTEEN

'They call her the Devil's Reaper,' Alvarez began. 'But her real name is Rhona King. She's probably in her early thirties, maybe thirty-five. She grew up hard in some European shithole, I don't know where. But her parents died young, and she jumped through foster care for a while...'

'How the hell do you know all this stuff?' Alicia asked.

'The Devil's Reaper uploaded her own exhaustive bio to the Dark Web. That's how she started off.'

'Go on.'

'She went between homes, caused chaos, ran away, ended up in juvie. Made a name for herself in all the wrong ways. She was eighteen before her feet touched the ground, and then she had nowhere to turn, nowhere to go. There was an altercation with an aid worker, and she was suddenly being sought by the cops. When Rhona applied herself, though, on the few occasions when she enjoyed her life, she always did well in education. They called her a delinquent, but she was actually just badly misunderstood.'

'Why is she called the Devil's Reaper?' Alicia asked.

'Don't you know? Rhona King is the prodigy of the Devil.'

Alicia narrowed her eyes at him. 'You're kidding? You mean *the* Devil? The contract killer who... died in the desert?'

'That's him. That man was an artist, a true–'

'Get on with it,' Alicia grunted.

'There's a myth about how he died, you know,' Alvarez went on. 'A dark myth almost as black as Rhona's heart. He was lured under false pretences, dragged to his death by a deceitful team, shot in the back, strangled by a stranger's wire. He met an untimely death, murdered by cowards, in a hostile scrap of land where nothing grows.'

Alicia was astounded. It was all she could do not to tell him that *her* team had killed the Devil and to speak up for them. Instead, she said: 'The Devil was a human piece of shit who would kill hundreds of innocent people just to fulfil a one-hit contract. He was the lowest scum of the earth.'

Alvarez shrugged. 'Then you will probably feel the same way about Rhona. She has carried on his work, right where he left off. She's been doing it for years and has amassed a powerful reputation, maybe even eclipsing the Devil's own. When you deal with the Devil's Reaper, you deal with true evil, true cold justice and true perfection. She is the epitome of revenge.'

'Somebody's revenge,' Alicia said.

'Yes. Whoever can find and afford her.'

'So she reaches out for people to do her jobs?' Mai asked.

Alvarez nodded. 'She has a shortlist of people she considers worthy,' he said proudly. 'I am on that list.'

'And she ordered you to kill Clive Ingham?'

'She employed me, my talents. She pays well. I am grateful to help.'

Alicia couldn't get into the deep depravities betrayed by his words. She didn't have the time. 'What more can you tell us about this Devil's Reaper?'

'She stepped right into the Devil's shoes when he died, took up the slack and made it appear as if nothing had changed. Never missed a beat. People, dark people, respected her for that. Obviously, the man trained her well, but it takes a special kind of person to just step into another's shoes and carry on. Rhona is special. If you're looking for her, I recommend you just kill yourselves right here and now.'

'Keep talking,' Alicia urged him. 'Make it quick.'

'She has midnight black eyes and full red lips.' Alvarez shivered. 'Wears expensive clothes and trainers and has dozens at her beck and call. She has her own prodigy too, a youth named Vicius, who she's training to be just like her. That's all the personal shit I know from the Dark Web. I've heard dark stories, though... stories of how she treats her lovers.'

Alicia swallowed. 'How's that?'

'Do you know the Praying Mantis? Yes? Just like that. She draws them in, uses them, spits them back out and then disposes of them. The Devil's Reaper has no living ex-lovers. Do you understand?'

'I think I get the picture.'

'Such respect,' Alvarez shivered. 'There is nobody else alive like her. Please never tell her where your information came from. It is not just my life you will be taking.'

'You haven't answered the most important question yet,' Alicia said.

Alvarez sniffed. 'Which is?'

'*Why* did this Devil's Reaper want you to kill Clive Ingham?'

'You think she would tell me that?' Alvarez looked aggrieved.

Alicia assessed him closely, read his body language. 'Yes,' she said. 'I do.'

'You're very good.' He stared at her as if noticing her for the first time, giving Alicia a creeping feeling.

'Why Ingham?' she asked.

'She has a big contract,' Alvarez said. 'She's working for someone who has a score to settle, a terrible score. Don't ask me who that is, because I just don't know.'

'What do you know?'

'Only that she told me she was working for this third party to engineer the total suffering of the team who murdered her mentor. That team, she said, included Mai Kitano and Matt Drake, and others. Those were her exact words- *to engineer the total suffering*. I love that.'

Alicia sat back, stunned despite herself. The Devil's Reaper was working for an unknown entity who wanted to make her entire team suffer.

'After the suffering,' she said. 'What comes next?'

'Oh, if it helps, she told me her ultimate goal was to murder everyone. Just the kind of thing she likes. This time, there doesn't have to be any covertness about it. In fact, she was told the messier the better when it comes to the key players.'

Alicia checked that both Mai and Kenzie were listening. She couldn't keep the shock from her face.

'Are you a key player?' Alvarez asked softly, insightfully, and with a growing smile on his face. 'Because... if you are...' he laughed. 'I'd start running. But, hey, you've still got time. You're not gonna die anytime soon. The Devil wants all your friends first.'

Alicia was too stunned to act. She sat back, thinking

hard. Then, collecting herself, she grabbed Alvarez by the throat. 'One last question,' she said. 'Where do we find this Devil's Reaper?'

Alvarez guffawed, his voice sounding odd with her fingers squeezing his throat. 'Are you crazy? You really think she would tell me? I don't know where she is any more than I know your name.'

Alicia saw the truth of it in his eyes, and in his words. The Devil's Reaper would never reveal her whereabouts to the likes of him.

The guards on the floor were coming around. Mai and Kenzie knocked them back into oblivion. Alicia regarded Alvarez.

'You've been useful,' she said. 'But now we're going to have to part ways.'

'What is that supposed–'

She struck out, smashing him in the temple, knocking him out. Then, quickly, the three women turned to the still-crying lap-dancer.

'Why haven't the other guards come to investigate?' Mai asked her.

After a few sniffles, the woman said, 'Other things happen in here as well as lap dancing. They only disturb if it is important.'

Mai nodded. 'Got it. Look, wait here for a few minutes and then leave. Don't say a word. The quieter you are, the better off you will be.'

And then the trio quietly slipped back through the curtain, made their way past the guards, alerted their friends, and headed for the exit. Armed with information, Alicia didn't know where to look when Drake glanced at her questioningly.

'Have we got a story for you,' she managed.

CHAPTER FIFTEEN

Drake drove for a while, listening to Alicia talk.

It was stunning, disturbing stuff. Everything centred around this new player – the Devil's Reaper, and even that person was working for someone. An unknown entity. Obviously, someone they'd pissed off hugely during the last ten years or so.

Drake drove aimlessly for a while. It was dark, and the city of Los Angeles was alive with night crawlers, people partying through the night. They walked the streets, played on the sidewalks, nipped in and out of the clubs and pubs and restaurants. They lit up the darkness with their enthusiasm, their zest, and life. Drake drove the first car, Kinimaka the second, and they eventually decided they were going to have to stop at a hotel. No way were they returning to the house that overlooked the Alvarez place.

Decision made, they found the first decent place en route and parked up, walked through the lobby and got themselves a slew of rooms. It wasn't too late yet, only ten-thirty, and they decided to hit the bar and talk about what they knew.

They found a far corner, ordered drinks, and sat back, sipping them slowly. Alicia recapped what she'd already told them and the knowledge that they were up against a formidable opponent who really wanted to hurt them for several reasons. Rhona King was a force to be reckoned with.

'What happens next?' Shaw asked.

'We go after the Devil's Reaper,' Drake said. 'That's exactly what happens.'

Alicia held her drink up, glass sparkling under the lights. 'Amen to that.'

'But that's not the first thing we have to do,' Dahl said. 'And it's even more imperative now that we know what's happening.'

Drake looked inquisitively at him.

'Rack your brains,' the Swede said. 'For any friends you might have missed. Young or old. Think hard. You could save someone's life.'

Drake nodded. Dahl was right. Their friends, old and new, came first. The obvious ones were safely protected, but he wondered about other older acquaintances. Who might know about those?

They knew about Bryant, their boss, and Mai's boyfriend. They knew about Kono, Kinimaka's sister. Knew about Mai's sister and her best friend. Kenzie had a family in Israel who were being protected. Cam had no one. Alicia recollected a few old friends from her army days, who were being looked after. She also had her Gold team to worry about and made calls to all of them. The team she frequently joined would be high-value targets on the reaper's list. Hayden had had friendships in the CIA. Torsten Dahl had numerous associations with members of the Swedish special forces, not to mention his family, who were all being protected. Shaw also had several friends who required attention. They sat for a while, brains on fire, trying to come up with anyone they might have missed. The trouble was – what would you really call an old friend?

The answer today was – anyone you were on record with as being close to.

They all came up with a few more names and emailed them immediately to Karin. By then, they were dog tired and forwent the night's promised pleasantries discussing the Devil's Reaper and grabbed some much needed sleep.

Drake and Alicia hit the sack together, falling almost immediately into a deep slumber. Six hours later, they were both wide awake and staring up at the ceiling.

'She's coming for us,' Alicia said.

'A vengeful blast from the past,' Drake said.

'Funny how the evil old bastards never really go away.'

'You're referring to the Devil? The Blood King? The Blood King's son and now this protégé, the Reaper. Somebody once said that evil never dies. I think they were right.'

'Every day,' Alicia said. 'We're surrounded by evil. Everyone is. Most people just don't know how prevalent it is.'

'That's because there's people like us around, fighting it.'

'Until it spills over and everyone gets affected.'

In a glum mood, they slid out of bed, got dressed, and made their way downstairs. They breakfasted with the others, passing small talk for a while, until they were done and could go to the quiet lobby, hot coffee and tea mugs in hand. Here, they called Karin and put the call on speakerphone.

'What have you got for me?' she asked.

'First,' Drake said. 'Are you safe? What precautions are in place for you?'

'I'm fine. I'm practically living in the office. Working and sleeping here. Nobody's getting in, believe me. But there's a watch on my apartment too. And they check my car regularly.'

'Listen,' Mai said. 'We have some news for you.' And she went on to explain to Karin everything they knew about the Devil's Reaper and her mission to destroy the Ghost Squadron.

'That's just nuts,' Karin said. 'A crazy story. I've never heard of a Devil's Reaper.'

'Neither had we until last night,' Kinimaka said.

'I got your email, by the way. I'm getting protection in place for these extra people.'

'Hopefully that will thwart her,' Hayden said.

'It might turn her attention towards us,' Shaw told them.

'And then she might show her hand,' Dahl said hopefully.

'If anyone can find information on the reaper,' Drake said. 'It's the NSA.'

'I'll get on it.' Karin signed off.

They were counting on her. Drake then called his old friend, Michael Crouch, and tried to pick his brains, but Crouch hadn't heard of the Devil's Reaper either. They tried Hayden's CIA contacts, Kinimaka's too, and asked them to start a search. Kenzie got on the phone to Israeli intelligence. All of a sudden, there were several agencies worldwide working on trying to harvest information about her.

Drake sat back, sipping his hot coffee. 'What more can we do?' he asked.

'I hate sitting here twiddling my thumbs,' Cam said. 'I want to be up and at it, punching someone.'

Drake nodded. 'We all feel the same, mate. Trouble

is, at the moment, we have no one to punch.'

Cam cracked his knuckles and looked around, as if seeking an opponent. It occurred to Drake right then that if the Devil's Reaper were to walk right through the door at that very moment, guards in tow, she wouldn't stand a damn chance.

'We'll get through this,' he said. 'And no one else will die.'

'The reaper is a ghost,' Kinimaka said. 'How're we gonna catch a ghost?'

'Well, we are the Ghost Squadron.' Alicia tried to lighten the spirits.

Mai bit her lip. 'Even if we get info on the reaper,' she said. 'We still don't know who's behind it all. Ultimately, that's who we need to catch.'

'Agreed,' Drake said. 'And only the reaper will have that information.'

'Maybe, maybe not.' Dahl wiggled his hand. 'The reaper seems kind of chatty.'

Drake agreed with a nod. There was no telling who she might have conversed with, and they weren't even close to getting near her yet. He sipped more coffee and sat back to await Karin's call. They spent some time in conversation. When the phone rang again, all hell might break loose.

And then the phone rang.

CHAPTER SIXTEEN

Karin immediately started searching the NSA databases for anything relating to the Devil's Reaper.

Fully expecting a slew of information to start scrolling across the screen – as usual – she hunted with confidence, sipping a coffee and munching on a muffin. It was odd then when the words *The Devil's Reaper* returned no results. Karin sat back, frowning. She tried again. She opened all the databases and retried. Shocked, she expanded her search a little further to *The Devil*.

And now a hundred – a thousand – hits were returned. Most of them referred to the mad assassin they'd hunted and killed. She didn't have time to read them all, but got the general gist. When she tried to add the word *reaper* to her search, again she had no luck.

Were the Ghost Squadron being duped?

Was there actually a Devil's Reaper? Did she even exist?

Karin was at a dead end. If there was a Devil's Reaper, she operated so far in the shadows that even the NSA hadn't heard of her.

What to do next? Karin read snippets of information about the old Devil himself. She had to fight not to get lost in the flow of it. At one point, she came across a note that said he had *two* protégés. That was a bit off, but it was just a snippet in a cascading flow of information. Maybe the protégé had a protégé. It was entirely possible.

Karin took a moment to leave her desk, walk over to the kitchen and, since she had decided to abstain from the bad coffee, grab a cup of tea. She made it, took it back to her desk, sipped the hot beverage. The break solidified something in her mind.

The reaper lived in the shadows. There was only one US agency that lived in the shadows.

Karin knew someone who worked for the CIA. Knew him well. A guy named Daniel Robbins who worked close by. The CIA had more resources in the shadow-world, especially abroad. They might well have secretive information they hadn't shared with anyone.

Karin, now at her wit's end, made the call. Daniel Robbins answered on the first ring.

'Yeah?'

Karin went through the pleasantries before getting to the point. 'I need your help.'

'Oh, yeah? That might cost you.' Robbins liked her, she knew, but he was a bit of a sleaze with it, never knowing when to ease up.

'Can you help me or not?'

'Depends what you can do for me.' He laughed.

Karin shook her head. 'We may get to that if you lighten up, but, listen, this is life or death serious shit. I'm out on a limb here, and my friends are in grave danger. I've exhausted my options and think the CIA might be able to help.'

'Must be serious if you've exhausted the NSA option.'

'Have you ever heard of a contract assassin called the Devil's Reaper?'

Robbins was silent for a while. Then, he said in a quiet voice. 'No, never.'

'You suddenly don't sound like yourself, Daniel.'

'Sorry. I... I'm thinking. You want me to look into this person?'

'I really do. And as quickly as possible. The fate of my friends really depends on it. Please, Daniel, I need you.' She laid it on thick.

'Can we get a drink later tonight?' Robbins rallied a little.

'Sure, I don't mind that. So long as I'm not still at work.'

'Give me an hour.' Robbins ended the call.

Karin sat back. She busied herself with background work, running checks, looking for associates, anyone linked to the Devil. It was grunt work, and it yielded no results. An hour passed. No word from Robbins. Tension already infused her and now she felt it ramp up a notch. She was hugely conscious of Drake and the team under fire, facing an implacable enemy who just wanted to make them suffer. She checked her watch. Another half hour flew by. Still no word from Robbins.

Finally, the phone rang. He was an hour late. Karin quickly scooped it up.

'You're late,' she said.

'Crap, woman, I hope you're not this impatient in everything you do.'

'Do you have anything for me or not?' she couldn't help the harshness in her voice. It was born of anxiety.

'I contacted all of my euro resources. I called Italy, France, the Czech Republic. I worked damn hard for you, Karin.'

'Thank you,' she said, thinking that she really needed results.

'The Devil's Reaper exists,' he said, settling into a monotone. 'She's a prodigy of the Devil, that old killer we now know a lot about. She walks in his footsteps, takes on the hardest contracts. Makes murders look like accidents. Kills dozens to get to one. She is actually one of a kind.'

'What do you have on her?'

'Not a lot. She works at the highest level. We don't even know who uses her, though we have a few ideas. She's literally the most wanted. She's high on every agency's wish list that knows she exists, but remains a mystery. Nobody's ever got near her.'

'You're saying everyone thinks grabbing her is a lost hope?'

'You get to that stage when you've been chasing for years.'

'She will make a mistake. They all do. In fact, I think she's made a mistake taking on the job to destroy my team.'

'Your team?'

'Figure of speech. If anyone can beat her, they can.'

'But you sound desperate.'

Karin bit back a retort. 'My team thrives off information. But they need a place to start.'

'You know as much as we do. She works with the darkest of the dark, always in shadow. We don't even know where she operates from. The jobs attributed to her are many, and probably too numerous to be true. Do you remember that ferry that sank in Greece last month?'

Karin said that she did.

'That was attributed to her. Apparently, the Greek

minister of finance was aboard and had been blocking several big business initiatives. The new minister of finance has already given the go ahead for them all.'

Karin thought about it. 'Could be coincidence. You can't lay everything at her door.'

'And that's where *she* thrives. She doesn't want you to believe she exists. Then, she strikes.'

'You sound like you admire her.'

'Not what she does. Not the way she operates. But she's a smooth operative at the top of her game, make no mistake about that. Another example... eight men died in a boating accident just nine weeks ago. Three of them owned a firm that has since been broken up by big pharma, a firm that was challenging them at the highest level.'

'You can't accuse everyone.'

'We're not. But there are patterns. She could easily do a big job every month.'

'And despite all that, we do not know who this woman is?'

'Not a damn clue.'

CHAPTER SEVENTEEN

Rhona King, the Devil's Reaper, lounged in her office, surrounded by screens. She wasn't sitting in the main chair, from where she orchestrated her kills. Instead, she was reclining on a plush, red leather sofa in the corner, feet drawn up, a glass of sparkling champagne in her hand. She wore a short black Gucci number. Her long, elegant legs were bare. The big guard standing in front of her didn't dare stare at them.

He was terrified of her.

Just as she liked it. She stretched out now, daring his eyes to wander. When they didn't, she let him off the hook.

'Tell the cook to send snacks. Sweet chilli nuts. Red chutney and crackers. A truffle or two. I feel the need to celebrate.'

The guard, armed with two handguns and wearing a bullet-proof vest, nodded. She watched him walk away and sipped her champagne. So far, everything she touched had turned to gold. It was a great reason to celebrate.

'I am invincible,' she said into the air.

She had three close bodyguards. They were always fully armed and wearing body armour, always on alert and ready to act. They'd been trained to the max, perfectly capable of taking several attackers out at once. The most important part was – they feared her. That was how it should be, Rhona thought. The hired help scared of the boss.

She could wipe them or their family's off the face of the earth in just one day. They knew that. And yet, for the money, they continued to work for her. That thought made Rhona run back over all the close associates she'd destroyed through the years.

There had been a few. Terry, the sous chef, had almost poisoned her with his awful choice of good ingredients. She had sent him home in disgrace, made sure a fire rampaged through his row of terraced houses that very night and that his family was caught in the flames. Then there was Jane, her driver, who had inadvertently caused an accident whilst Rhona was in the car. This accident brought unwanted attention to Rhona and, although she had handled it, Jane had to be punished. And so she was. Beaten up and left for dead that very night by a notorious gang. Jane died later in the hospital from her injuries.

But all that was immaterial. It didn't bother Rhona one bit. She made sure her staff found out, though. It helped keep them in line. And once you worked for the Devil's Reaper, there was no going back.

She stretched out now, looked up as the snacks appeared on an enormous silver platter. There was another glass of champagne, too, which she appreciated. The platter was placed down on a low oaken table and then the server backed out of the room, eyes down. Rhona reached out for a handful of crackers.

Vicius wasn't with her today. He was "practicing" in another room. Rhona had never been able to simulate what she did. Her teaching had always been real, hands on. So they identified a few low-level targets and let him loose on those. It made for excellent entertainment and, if it went wrong, the blunder never really hit the headlines. Vicius had practiced hundreds of times this last year alone.

Rhona ate and drank. She luxuriated in her brilliance. She had everything she wanted. A select group of clients. Freedom to murder as and when she wished. A network to make it happen flawlessly. The Devil might have built it, but she had developed his dream into something incredible, something he'd be proud of.

Rhona's thoughts turned to Mai Kitano. She drew her legs up, ate a handful of nuts, and watched one of the monitors in front of her. Using a remote, she brought up the footage of Mai and her team getting all the plaudits for stopping London's nuclear explosion just a few weeks ago. To be fair, Mai and none of her colleagues looked happy with the attention. But they got it anyway. And now, Rhona knew what Mai looked like. She knew her enemy so well. Drake and the others, too.

Though she would never admit it, she was grateful that the Tsugarai had come along with this mission. She'd never really had closure since her mentor's death but had not been able, professionally, to do anything about it. Now, whilst working for the Tsugarai, she could kill two birds with one stone. And it didn't matter if the Tsugarai were to inadvertently back out now. That wasn't how she worked. Once she was locked on a target, nothing would stop her from completing her mission.

An alarm sounded. Rhona, happy to work with the

slight fog in her brain caused by the champagne, rose to her feet. She smoothed the little black dress down. At this stage of the latest operation, she was happy that her expertise wouldn't be needed. Those on the ground would do all the work.

This would be a good one. She was going after one of Mai's old friends.

She seated herself behind the key bank of monitors, watched as her major players got into position. She saw the soon-to-be victim, a woman named Akari, with bleached blonde hair and wide eyes and a cheerful smile on her face. Akari was walking down her driveway towards her car that was parked at the side of the road. As usual, Rhona had people everywhere, all with cameras, so that she could take in the full magnificence of the kill. Rhona saw two other figures following along behind Akari.

Cops.

They were her escorts. By now, Rhona knew, Mai and her team were aware of what was happening. They had made calls to all their old friends, arranged protection. That was a shame, but it was still something Rhona could work with. Cops were always stretched thin, and could only spare so many people. On Akari, they had two men.

Rhona watched them, noting their complacency. They didn't look left and right, didn't check the car, didn't stop her from walking out into the road. Of course, her team had reconnoitred all this over the last few days. They knew how good the cops were.

And they would never see their deaths coming.

Akari wore torn blue jeans and a white jacket. She had an expensive pair of bright white Balenciagas gracing her feet. Rhona liked her style. Yesterday

DEVIL'S REAPER

they'd been Christian Louboutins. Akari, it seemed, spent all her money on chic footwear. She approached her car, slowed down, obviously in her own headspace as she prepared to drive the brief journey to the television studio where she worked. Akari didn't look around, didn't check the street. The cops should be doing that for her.

They gave it a cursory glance.

Now, all three of them climbed into the car, the cops going one upfront, one in the back. Akari turned the vehicle on and then waited for a break in traffic. Rhona watched as several of her minions followed in their own cars.

The cameras stayed on the woman.

Akari drove efficiently, her blonde hair standing out clearly through the window. She turned left off her street and followed a wide road with far less traffic, closing in on her destination. Rhona leaned forward. It wouldn't be long now.

The other cars backed off, now wanting to get involved in what was to come. This gave Rhona a clearer view of the events as they unfolded. She saw Akari driving conservatively down the street, saw the open road to all sides, saw the approaching tanker as it barrelled out of a side street. She watched as it adjusted its course slightly, moving at top speed, marvelled as it closed so rapidly on its target.

Akari and the cops didn't even see it coming. Or maybe they did, Rhona reflected. Either way, there was no course adjustment to the car, no sign of it trying to get out of the way. The tanker crashed into it from the side, sliding through the metal like butter, smashing through the doors and the seats and the people inside. It destroyed the car utterly. Air brakes squealed a little too late. A steering wheel was turned after the damage was done. Akari's little car stood no chance at all.

Rhona knew the driver of the tanker would go to jail, and so did the driver. He had done this for his family, so that they would live in peace and comfort for the rest of their lives. It had been a no brainer for him. The man was already dying.

The various cameras took in the entire scene. Akari's car was shoved along, wrapped around the front of the tanker. People walking by started screaming, took their phones out, called the police. The assholes among them started taking pictures instead. People came out of their stores, their offices, stopped and climbed out of their cars just to look. A few ran to the scene of the accident, hoping to help.

Rhona had seen enough. The attack was successful, as she'd known it would be. She watched a little while longer as the cops started showing up, saw the blue lights, laughed to herself. Another job well done.

Mai Kitano would hear about it soon enough.

Rhona had a list, and that list was almost exhausted. The list contained the names of the people she wanted to kill before she moved on to the Ghost Squadron proper. Just a few more to go. Some of them were well protected, but she hadn't failed yet.

She wouldn't, ever fail.

Who was next?

Rhona looked up as Vicius came into the room, gliding softly through the door. She raised a glass at him, signalling her victory. He gave her the thumbs up, signalling his own. He grinned, smoothed his hair back with a sweep of his hand. Then, still grinning, he made his way across to her and made a motion.

Rhona pulled her chair out.

Vicius sat down on her lap and nestled his head in the crook of her neck. He hugged her. He was happy. Rhona nuzzled the top of his head and sat contentedly, joyfully, staring at the bloodshed.

CHAPTER EIGHTEEN

'We have a new strategy,' Karin said.

Drake sat up straighter, listening hard. Around the table, the others all leaned forward. So far, it had been all bad news. This was different.

'What do you have in mind?' Hayden asked.

Drake glanced around the lobby. There was a businesswoman in an orange dress seated nearby, just crossing her legs, another wearing a black dress to the right and looking up as a waiter charged her credit card. A man with a white shirt sat further away, tapping on a tablet that he held in one hand. It was busier than he would like, but he didn't think anyone would be listening in.

'Talk to us,' he said.

'I'm using the CIA,' she said. 'We're going-'

'Wait,' Hayden said. 'You're using the CIA? That just doesn't sound right.'

'The NSA has no records regarding the Devil's Reaper. And I know a guy in the CIA.'

'Don't get in too deep,' Hayden warned.

Karin didn't answer that straight away. Finally, she said. 'I'm in pretty deep. I'm taking him out for dinner.'

'Just make sure he knows where he stands,' Drake

said with steel in his voice. Where Karin was concerned, he'd always felt a little like a big brother.

'I will,' Karin said. 'Anyway, we've decided on a new strategy. We're going to track down the reaper using her own best clients. It's a sound plan.'

'It would be if we knew who they were,' Kinimaka said.

'Well, that's where the CIA comes in. They have a file on the reaper. It's pretty thick. They like her for dozens of hits, if not hundreds. A traffic pile up in Madrid. A helicopter malfunction if Tokyo. A riot in Amsterdam. Two men killed whilst attending a football match. It goes on and on.'

'Where has all the information come from?' Mai asked.

'The CIA has been aware of the reaper for years. Before that, they were aware of the Devil and knew he had a protégé. Obviously, she's very good and has a solid network around her, preventing anyone in law enforcement from getting too close. To many people though, she's still a myth.'

'I once knew a man who was considered myth,' Drake said wistfully. 'We put an end to him and his bastard son.'

The others nodded, steel in their expressions. Karin went on. 'The hierarchy in the CIA don't fancy her for half the jobs. They think she's an easy scapegoat, someone to blame when their people can't figure out who the real culprits are. They're... short sighted.'

'That's a mild way of putting it,' Alicia said.

'So how do we find the reaper through her best clients?' Hayden steered the conversation back around.

'We find out who they are to start off with. The

same people who believe in the reaper have made a shortlist of the bad guys they believe she works for. The most prominent of those assholes is the Allegri family, a big crime outfit operating out of Italy. They believe she's done at least a dozen jobs for them. Many low key, just bumping off rival crime lords, but they clearly use her like their favourite takeaway.'

'How does this help us, though?' Kinimaka asked.

'The boss of the Allegri family is a man named Emiliano Allegri. He can give you a way to contact the reaper.'

'Direct contact?' Shaw asked.

'Yeah, draw her out. Try to arrange a meet. Whatever works. If you can nab Emiliano and get him to talk, you can get to the reaper.'

'And what's stopping him from warning her afterwards?' Cam asked, a little naively.

'Fear of what she'll do to him if she finds out he blabbed,' Dahl said grimly. 'Everyone's terrified of the reaper.'

'You mentioned she'd done quite a few jobs,' Hayden said. 'Are the Allegri family our best choice?'

'They're the most obvious,' Karin clarified. 'The ones were certain of. The others… not so much.'

Drake sat back, breathed deeply, and surveyed the room. No one had taken an interest in their conversation, and he hadn't expected them to. The business men and women had departed. People milled far away, around the reception, and crossed the lobby with their heels clacking or their soles creaking.

'You want us to nab the head of a crime family living in Italy?' Kinimaka said. 'That's quite a coup if we can pull it off.'

'On home soil too,' Hayden said. 'I agree with Mano.'

'We've accomplished far harder tasks,' Mai said.

Drake was thinking the same thing. There was nothing they couldn't do. 'If that's what it takes...' he said.

They got the Allegri family's details, then ended the call with Karin and spent some time searching for and booking flights. It happened that the first flight out was in just a few hours and, if they hoofed it, they could make it. They left the hotel in a hurry, called a large taxi, and headed for the airport at double time. Once there, they flew through security and then ended up with a couple of hours to spare airside. Drake didn't enjoy cooling his heels. The weirdest thing of all was having a look around Duty Free with Alicia. It felt surreal. Here they were hunting for the Devil's Reaper, trying to save their friends and colleagues from terrible deaths, racing for Italy as fast as they could, and yet they were forced to kill time wandering around an airport and visiting the various shops. Drake didn't like it, and found it odd when Alicia told him to loosen up. Shouldn't it be the other way around?

Finally, their flight was called. They walked to their gate along the bright, shiny hallways, queued to get on the plane with hundreds of others, and slid into their economy seats. Drake didn't like it. Maybe Bryant could have got them some military transport, but Bryant was playing everything low key at the moment. He was still under protection. With nothing else to do but accept his lot, Drake buckled up, waited for the plane to take off, checking the length of the flight to Italy, sighing, and then sitting back.

'If you're pissed off now,' Alicia leaned over and whispered to him. 'Wait until they serve dinner.'

It was a long journey, interspersed with turbulence,

bad food, and alcohol. Drake didn't drink too much, but had enough just to take the edge off. When the pilot announced they were about to start their descent, Drake gripped the armrests thankfully. Every second in flight, he thought, was a dangerous second wasted. Their plight was already desperate.

The plane touched down lightly with a squeal of rubber on tarmac. Then came the dreaded shoving and inching up the narrow aisles, surrounded by people. They soon cleared customs and then had to wait for Dahl's bag to come through the carousel. They had checked it so that they could bring their comms system through.

'We should rent two cars,' Hayden said as they waited. 'Not leave anything to chance.'

And so, as soon as they'd grabbed Dahl's bag, they sought the rental area of Milan Malpensa airport and found out that the journey to Milan was about thirty miles. The drive to Allegri's neighbourhood was a little shorter, as the crime king lived on the outskirts of Milan. They piled into two cars and started on the forty-five minute journey, taking care in the heavy, crawling traffic.

It was ten p.m. in Milan and, after some debate, decided there was nothing they could do that night. They drove until they were close to Allegri's address and then found a hotel. It was a backstreet affair, lit with a romantic air that was completely lost on the travellers. Spent from the air travel, they found their rooms, their beds, and were asleep even before they'd remembered to set their alarms.

But the next morning, they were ready.

CHAPTER NINETEEN

Morning dawned in a fiery blaze of sunrise.

Drake saw it through a curtained window, slid out of bed, showered, and dressed. Soon, they were downstairs, breakfasting, and trying to come up with a way of getting close to Emiliano Allegri, the crime family's boss.

'Start with a good old-fashioned recce,' Dahl said. 'Get the lay of the land.'

It was the simplest and most obvious thing to do. The first thing they did was visit a safe-house, the address of which was provided by Karin, and tool up with various weapons. Then, they were in their cars and headed for the address Karin had provided them. It was a bright morning; the sun blazing down. The local traffic was light for now. Kinimaka drove Drake's car with Hayden, Cam, and Shaw in the back seat. They followed a long road, made a couple of turns and then found themselves on a winding, tree-lined avenue. They followed the white lines for a few minutes and then looked to the left as they saw they had reached their destination.

Allegri's home was fronted by a long, black, fiercely spiked, iron fence through which could be seen the walls of a house. Drake saw a statue and then an outer courtyard around which stood several long archways, all leading to an inner courtyard. This was reached through another gate, currently open, through which Drake could see the main house proper, a white, rendered four storey building with leaded windows and a massive front door. The grounds were studded with trees and lined by high hedges and other vegetation.

Drake turned his attention to the personnel. On their first drive past, it was hard to make anyone out. The roadway was busy, but they could slow down and take a good look on their second journey past. There was no one by the front gates, nobody patrolling the inner driveways. Perhaps this was for aesthetic reasons. Drake wasn't sure, but when he got a look through to the inner courtyard, he saw a load of black suited bodies and could tell that some of them carried guns.

The traffic was thick, and the front of the property unmanned, so they decided on a third and fourth drive by. They grew accustomed to the area. Clearly, though, they couldn't keep driving by the place and had to observe it over time, so they tried to identify a place where they could stop.

'Buildings across the street,' Kenzie said through the comms. 'Can't we just do what we did in L.A.?'

'We can try, but I doubt lightning will strike twice,' Hayden said. 'Besides, the buildings are lower over there. We won't be able to get a good look at Allegri's grounds...'

'I'll get Karin on it anyway,' Shaw said and took her phone out.

'That's about the best we can do,' Drake said, pointing.

Across from the Allegri mansion, there stood a large car park that was currently half empty. It had spaces right at the front that looked straight down Allegri's property and would give them a good view of the grounds, the driveway, and the front of the house. Drake directed Kinimaka to head in that direction and soon they had parked up and were getting the lay of the land.

Drake settled back in the passenger seat. Ahead, he could see two rows of passing traffic. Beyond that stood the Allegri house and all its comings and goings. Drake knew this was going to be a long job. They sent Cam and Shaw out to look for breakfast and started to watch the house.

Hours passed. Kinimaka and Drake in one car, Dahl and Hayden in the other, had the best views as they were in the front seats. Cam and Shaw came back with paper bags full of croissants and other pastries and cardboard trays full of coffee. Drake waited for his to be passed around and then tucked in, even finding a miniature tub of butter and a plastic knife which he put to good use.

They could only watch the movements to and from the house. Karin came back to them, informing that there were no buildings they could move into and sent them a photo of Emiliano Allegri. They saw a delivery van enter the property and then a normal car, its driver dressed like a medic. Maybe there was someone on the property who needed to be visited by a doctor. They didn't see much else that first morning but, around lunchtime, there was an abrupt shift in activity.

Guards appeared at the gates, and walking down the driveway. Two black cars started along the winding road, the sun blazing down on them. Drake and the others watched closely, knowing their vantage point was well concealed by the amounts of passing traffic and the fact that the car park was almost full.

The two car entourage wound up the driveway and then approached the gates, which opened on electric motors, slowly. Soon, the cars pulled out into the flow of traffic, passing right by the car park. Through an open window, Drake got a clear view of Emiliano.

'Go,' he said abruptly. 'Follow them.'

And so it began. The first trip led them to a restaurant where Emiliano exited his car surrounded by bodyguards, found a quiet table inside, and proceeded to eat a pasta-based meal. It was decided that Cam and Shaw would eat at the same restaurant and report back, and they returned with a bland story of Emiliano scarfing down his meal with a couple of glasses of white wine and chatting up one of the waitresses with long black hair. Apparently, Emiliano was quite pushy with her, but was still brushed off.

It wasn't gold, but it was at least a tad of information. Every little helped.

Next, before going home, Emiliano visited a downscale apartment block. The Ghost Squadron sat and watched as a young woman poked her head out of a door, smiled, and then beckoned him inside. The diversion lasted for an hour and then Emiliano was back, soothing down his tie, a smile on his face. He had left two men standing outside the door to the house. Now, they followed him back down to his car where other bodyguards smoked and waited. Emiliano climbed in and they were soon on their way.

'Clearly, he likes the ladies,' Alicia said.

The surveillance continued. Emiliano was driven

back to his house by two p.m. and everything went quiet for a while. At four p.m., the entire retinue reappeared, once again carrying Emiliano to some important place.

Drake and the others followed at a discreet distance, using the thick flow of traffic to remain out of sight.

This time, Emiliano went to a glass-fronted gym. They were able to send Dahl and Kenzie in as a couple pretending to be looking for a free trial and watch as Emiliano went through his various exercises. They returned later to say he struggled with the weights, seemed to enjoy the cross trainer, and hated the treadmill. Once again, he tried to chat up several women and even appeared to succeed with one. They definitely exchanged numbers, Kenzie said with a shudder. The woman was half his age, she also pointed out.

But it was a weakness, and a good spot. They later followed Emiliano back to his home and by then it was rush hour. They got parked again and watched for quite some time as the shadows grew longer. It became clear that Emiliano wasn't planning on exiting again that day. Still, they couldn't risk it. They stayed in place until late and then went back to their hotel for a much-needed evening meal.

The next day, it all started again.

Surveillance was boring, Drake knew that. It was all about gaining information, any snippets or titbits that they could later weave together. It could be anything, but they had to observe a target over days, not hours.

They waited and waited. Again, they sent someone out for breakfast. This time though, they were premature. Emiliano made an early appearance, and they had to leave Cam and Shaw behind, stuck at the pastry shop. They followed Emiliano to a café and watched as he smoked and ate and drank espressos. He had grabbed an outside table. It was almost comical to see his bodyguards take most of the rest and refuse any sort of foods or beverage. Many of them, in an unprofessional manner, had their hands on the bulges of their guns, as if hoping for action or trying to appear tough. Drake shook his head at them.

'Losers,' he said.

During breakfast, Emiliano again tried to chat up the waitress, and this time grabbed her wrist as she turned to leave. She shrugged it off gently but firmly and turned away, leaving a sad Emiliano pouting after her just for show. Once she'd gone, his face hardened.

When he'd finished, Emiliano snapped his fingers and was ushered back to the car. The bodyguards were everywhere, preventing anyone from approaching him, even those ambling past. They stopped shoppers and business people in the street, making them walk the long way round.

A quick trip back to the mansion. Cam and Shaw were waiting in the car park. Now, it was the Ghost Squadron's turn to eat breakfast, and they were all famished. They ate and compared notes.

'So we have four places he seems to eat or visit regularly,' Hayden said, munching. 'A gym. A woman in an apartment block. A restaurant, and a breakfast eatery. I'm assuming regularly because they all seem to know him, to tolerate him, and he seems comfortable in his actions. And that's just two days. We need to keep watching.'

'The restaurant was big,' Cam said. 'Maybe we could nab him there.'

'It's a possibility. How many guards did he take with him? Did he visit the restroom?'

'Two and no,' Shaw said.

'Hard to plan a mission hoping for a stroke of luck,' Kinimaka said. 'We stay on point.'

And "point" was their observations, their surveillance. With no choice, they spent another day at it. According to Karin and the CIA, this guy was their best route to the reaper. They had to work the mission as best they could.

Today, Emiliano visited a small diamond shop where they couldn't gain entry without arousing suspicion. Through the window, Hayden and Kinimaka, posing as a couple, noticed several beautiful, sparkling diamonds in display cases and even more dazzling women behind the counter. Emiliano was fawning over both, and then they were forced to walk on by so as not to appear conspicuous. Emiliano returned a little while later with a small white bag and a smile. Perhaps he'd got another number.

Again, they visited the apartment block. This time, two women answered the door and ushered Emiliano inside. The crime boss spent what Drake was sure was a pleasurable two hours in there before making a dishevelled reappearance and then being driven back to his mansion. Then it was lunch time.

The day flew by as they followed Emiliano around. That afternoon, he visited a couple of boutique shops and then the same restaurant as the day before. He was quite the creature of habit. Today, a different waitress got his unwanted attentions and she, again, ignored them. Obviously, they would be wise to him there if he tried it every damn day. But Emiliano had no shame and later tried to attract the attention of a well-dressed blonde woman when her husband had gone to the toilet. That didn't work out for him either.

Emiliano made one other trip that day. He went to a swimming pool, where his bodyguards watched him swim for an hour.

Another day passed with a similar routine. And then another.

Finally, they were ready.

Drake addressed them all in the lobby of their hotel. 'Everyone know what to do?' he asked.

'First,' Alicia said. 'We all need our little black dresses.'

CHAPTER TWENTY

Emiliano hadn't visited his favourite restaurant the day before, so they took a measured gamble he would today.

Alicia, Kenzie, and Mai were already seated at the bar. They had been waiting across the street until Drake called to tell them Emiliano had set off, and then they entered and took seats to look as though they'd been there since opening time. They lined the drinks up, started talking loudly, made it appear as if they were the centres of their own universes.

Fifteen minutes later, Emiliano arrived.

The women were dressed to impress, wearing knee-length, tight-fitting dresses that they'd purchased for the occasion and high heels. Their hair was styled, and Kenzie at least had a little makeup on. The others hadn't bothered, saying it was a step too far. But they had made sure they would be in Emiliano's eyeline. Now, it was just a matter of waiting.

Emiliano took his usual seat. Less than five minutes later, Alicia heard him say to one of his guards. 'Go buy their drinks.'

The man appeared, offered to pay for them, and pointed out Emiliano, who held up a hand. They gave him the universal cheers salute with their glasses and radiant smiles, laughing as though they weren't exactly sober. As expected, Emiliano invited them over to his table, giving them an expansive wave.

'Won't you join me?' he asked obsequiously. 'I do hate being alone.'

Alicia led the way, grabbing Mai's hand and pulling her along. They all took seats around the table, facing Emiliano, and thanked him again for their drinks.

'You're not local,' he said. 'Are you on holiday?'

Alicia nodded, told him they were on a break from their boyfriends and trying to find as much Italian sausage as they were able. Emiliano looked so shocked she thought she'd messed it all up by being too blunt and he would blank them, but he managed a smile and a quick recovery.

'Does anything strike you on the menu?'

It wasn't the best rejoinder he could have made, Alicia thought, not even that good. She held the four-page menu up in front of her and took a moment to scan her surroundings, scoping for Emiliano's bodyguards. There were just two in evidence, standing a discreet distance away, though she knew more were on hand near the cars. For all intents and purposes, they had Emiliano to themselves.

So far, so good.

They chose their food and ordered. They laughed at Emiliano's jokes. Luckily, they were seated on the opposite side of the table to him, so didn't have to endure any touching, as they'd observed him doing to other women. He talked non-stop, mostly about himself, explaining that he was an importer/exporter, a wealthy business executive, an animal at the top of his game.

'What do you do for fun?' Mai asked.

'I talk to beautiful women,' Emiliano gestured expansively.

Alicia did an internal eye roll. 'Do you meet lots of beautiful women in your job?'

'Not as many as I'd like to,' Emiliano admitted. 'But then a day like today comes along and it's all worth it.'

The women smiled, laughed, let him compliment them some more. They talked about the champagnes they loved, the art they'd seen, the jewellery they loved. They were careful to name drop the very brand Emiliano had purchased yesterday.

'Well, I can see that you are not only beautiful,' Emiliano said. 'But also women of great taste. Here, let me buy you more drinks.'

He kept topping them up. Alicia lost count of the number of drinks she downed, and even with her robust fortitude, she was getting a buzz. Not only that, Emiliano's jokes were becoming slightly funny. She knew it was past time to act.

At that moment, however, their food arrived. She was forced to stop talking and start eating, downing forkfuls of pasta. On the plus side, Emiliano shut up too, and they could adjust their ears to something more tuneful for a while – like the growl of passing cars or a blaring horn. Alicia put her head down and didn't look up until she was finished.

Emiliano was watching her. Again, he topped up her drink. 'Here, have some more.'

'Are you trying to get me drunk?' she laughed. She was finding it very hard not to revert to her normal character, who would, by now, have choked him on his spaghetti and meatballs.

'Perhaps I am.' He was currently topping Kenzie's glass up. 'What are you like when you're drunk?'

'Oh, I can do wonders with balls,' Alicia said.

Emiliano almost choked as he sipped his drink. 'What?'

'I'm a party organiser. I find I do my best work after a few glasses of the good stuff.'

'Ah, I see. That makes more sense.'

'Although, I must confess, the drink does kind of lower my inhibitions.'

'Really?'

Alicia leaned forward. 'Fancy taking this conversation somewhere more intimate?'

Emiliano gave her a wide smile. 'My home is but a ten-minute drive away.'

'Oh, I'm not going to your home, Emiliano. I'm not that drunk or stupid. You're a good customer here, as you say. Surely they have a quiet room we could use, or a restroom?'

Emiliano stared at her, and she gave him the suggestive eyes. Briefly, his eyes flickered towards his guards. To be fair, Alicia had expected him to leap at the chance. The reticence was a surprise.

'You're forthright,' he said to cover his caginess.

'Well, I'm an Englishwoman on holiday.'

Emiliano wasn't exactly jumping for the bait. Mai finished her drink and held her glass out. 'I don't mind sweetening the deal,' she said.

Kenzie remained silent, probably thinking that three women throwing themselves at him might make the Italian suspicious.

Emiliano's eyes were wide, his mouth open. He bit his lip, trying to keep the excitement from his face. He looked past them, towards the restrooms.

'Both of you?'

'Why not? You only live once.'

'Oh, my god...' Alicia sensed Emiliano was a reserved man, always in control, but it seemed to have deserted him now. She saw him start to rise.

Yes.

'Damn it,' he said suddenly and sat back down.

'What's wrong?' Alicia frowned.

'My men would have to come with us. They aren't allowed to let me out of their sight.'

Alicia affected a light laugh. 'You're joking, right? The last thing I want is your men watching us.'

'I agree. But, because of the work I do, I need a constant bodyguard. They won't allow it.'

'Can't you tell them to wait for a few minutes?' Mai said. 'Surely they don't accompany you to the restroom?'

Emiliano hung his head slightly. 'They do.'

Alicia gave an incredulous laugh, still working her hardest to get the crime lord alone. 'You're tuning us down to be with your men?'

'I'll rent us a hotel room?'

Alicia made herself look annoyed. It wasn't hard. 'Damn it, Emiliano, you're spoiling our fun.'

She felt desperate. She looked ravishing.

'They could stand outside the door,' Mai said with a distasteful smile on her face.

Now it was Emiliano's turn to frown. He studied their faces. 'You don't give up easily, do you?'

Mai shrugged. 'Like she said, we're on holiday. I know what I want.'

Emiliano looked longingly at the restrooms, but then turned towards his guards and gave them a little wave. When they came over, standing behind him, he said, 'These ladies were just leaving.'

Alicia assumed an irritated look. She pushed her

plate away and rose to her feet. Mai and Kenzie did the same.

'I'm immensely disappointed,' Emiliano said, still regarding them suspiciously.

'You don't know what you're missing,' Mai mouthed at him.

And Alicia bent close to his ear, close enough so that the guards moved in Emiliano's direction.

'You lost out big time, my friend. Me and Mai there... we love ourselves a big, old Italian sandwich.'

Emiliano twitched. Alicia turned away from the table, leaving him behind, and her friends followed. They said nothing, just walked away. They kept on walking until they were sure none of Emiliano's guards were following them.

Then they returned to the cars.

Drake and the others looked up expectantly as they approached. 'Get some?' Drake asked.

Alicia gave him the finger, but it was obvious from their faces that they came with a wedge of disappointment.

'We failed,' Kenzie told them as they gathered around the cars. 'Emiliano wouldn't go for it.'

'I'm shocked.' Drake looked at them. 'What the hell is wrong with him?'

'It wasn't that,' Alicia said. 'The guy was just too wary. Wouldn't go anywhere without his guards and losing them was the whole bloody idea.'

'All dressed up for nothing,' Mai sighed.

'More importantly,' Dahl said. 'What do we do next?'

'I don't see any alternative,' Drake said. 'We have to swipe him from the street.'

CHAPTER TWENTY ONE

In failure, they returned to the hotel. They went to the restaurant, sitting around glumly. Alicia, Mai and Kenzie watched them all eat, and then they started to drink. After food, they returned to their favourite seat in the lobby and sat around, studying each other, all waiting for someone to speak.

'It's not ideal,' Hayden said finally. 'Far from it. And we're not used to losing-'

'I don't think my chicaneries have ever failed before,' Alicia sighed.

'Nor mine,' Mai said glumly.

'Forget that,' Drake said. 'The guy's clearly more disciplined than we gave him credit for. Remember, he's the head of a crime family. It's what we do next that's important.'

Dahl nodded. 'And what's that?'

Drake started talking. He went on for a while, explaining his plan. Around them, people came and went, wandered back and forth. Sometimes, they had to keep their voices low. Other times, they could speak freely. Together, they made plans for the next day.

By midnight, they were back on course, or as close to it as they possibly could be. They retired to bed and were up early the next morning, even before breakfast was served. They were out the front door and driving their cars well before dawn.

They needed to drive the route that Emiliano would take, check for dangers, cover every angle. They could leave nothing to chance.

As far as they were able.

They made several recces, walked the streets, found a place with minimal exposure. With hours still to go, they found food and drink and took a break. Soon after, they were at it again, figuring out a way to get close to Emiliano Allegri.

'I'm dreading the next call from Karin,' Kinimaka said. 'This part of the mission is taking up so much time.'

Drake felt the same, but knew there was no other approach they could make. 'We have to get close to this guy. He uses the reaper all the time.'

'I got close to him,' Alicia murmured. 'Didn't work.'

'Today will work,' Hayden said. 'It has to.'

'There's still a lot of chance involved,' Dahl said. 'I'm not big on chance.'

'Suck it up,' Drake told him. 'We're out of options.'

'Oh, I get that. Doesn't make it any easier, though.'

'Is this absolutely the best plan?' Shaw asked. 'It could get us all killed.'

'It's kill or be killed,' Drake admitted. 'The Allegri family is a serious outfit. They're well protected. This will take all our skill.'

Cam cracked his knuckles, always ready for action.

The team looked at each other as best they could. There didn't seem to be a lot more to say. They were about to challenge a serious crime family on its own soil, take some of them out of the game, engineer a stand up fight in the street.

'All this to get to the reaper,' Drake said. 'She's making us do this. Our friends... they're still under protection all around the world. They're being hunted, and so are we. The reaper won't stop.'

'If only we could find out who's actually behind it all,' Mai said. 'Who's pulling her strings.'

Drake nodded. 'Maybe Emiliano can tell us.'

'Oh, I hope so.'

'The problem is,' Hayden pointed out. 'Now that she's been let loose on us, she won't give up. Even if we get to the person or people behind all this, we still have the reaper to deal with.'

'That's just hearsay,' Kinimaka said.

'But it's also probably entirely true,' Hayden said. 'The reaper works that way. Always completes the mission. That's what the Devil used to do, remember, and she is his protégé.'

Kinimaka inclined his head. 'I guess you're right.'

'One way or another, we will deal with the reaper,' Drake said. 'We have to. She's committed too many heinous acts. We just can't let her continue to work the way she does.'

'I worry about the next phone call,' Kinimaka reiterated.

Drake found his eyes glancing inadvertently at his phone. He, too, was worried. If he saw Karin's name come up on the screen, he couldn't imagine what he would do. Now, though, he decided a few words through the comms would work best.

'People,' he said, his accent thick. 'We're all out of options. This is our only chance with Emiliano and the Allegri family. Stick with it. Be at your best. Let's not let the reaper get away with more murders. This could be as hard as anything we've ever done, but we have to get through it. Work fast, work well, and we'll succeed. They'll be blindsided, in shock. That should give us a few minutes to snatch Emiliano. It's our last chance to end all this.'

In his car, the others nodded. Through the Bluetooth system, there were words of acknowledgement, of encouragement.

As a team, they were ready.

'Bring it on,' Dahl said.

CHAPTER TWENTY TWO

Mid afternoon was bright and without a breath of air. Cars and other vehicles choked the main roads. The route to Emiliano's mansion was thick with traffic, but not where Drake and the others waited.

They checked their watches. Emiliano should be here in just a few minutes.

Of course, this was all dependent on the crime lord keeping his gym schedule, but he hadn't wandered off it so far, and they had no reason to believe he would. Drake sat at the wheel of the first car, Dahl the second. Their hands gripped the wheel, white knuckled. They were about to cause chaos.

They waited down two dark alleys a few hundred yards apart. Out on the street, Cam was the spotter. The young man was leaning against a wall, head down, pretending to scroll through his phone but keeping a sharp eye out. When he signalled, they would act.

Seconds passed. Then a minute. The tension inside the car ramped up. Drake watched Cam intently. There could be no mistakes this afternoon.

A man on a scooter drove by. Someone walked past the far end of the alley, pushing a pram. Still, they waited. Bright light spilled all over Cam.

And then he looked up, raised his right hand to smooth down his hair.

They're coming. All is clear.

Drake yelled out that they were a go and then slammed the accelerator pedal into the floor. The engine roared. The car shot forward, exiting the alley and cutting crossways in front of Emiliano's SUV. Drake brought it to a sudden stop. From further back, Dahl's car also shot out of an alley, cutting off Emiliano's rear path, the Swede's car stopping just at the back of Emiliano's second car.

No time to waste. Drake and the team threw their doors open and leapt out of the car. They drew their weapons and started shouting, ordering Emiliano's guards to lay down their weapons. As if in answer, the doors of both enemy cars were being thrown open. Men were lunging out, guns in hand.

Drake fired first. Now they would have to be even quicker. The sound of gunshots would be reported. His first bullet snagged a man in the wrist, made him cry out and fall to the floor. The man following him tripped over him and also went down. Drake's next bullet destroyed the car's windscreen. A man was jumping out of the front passenger seat, already firing even though his gun wasn't properly aimed. Drake shot him in the chest. All around, his team was taking out the guards, dropping them as they exited the car.

Something similar was happening behind where Dahl and his team were also firing on the exiting guards. They shattered the window glass and peppered the metal, saw guards go down in a hail of bullets. They ran forward, shooting, trying to see into the car and tag a guard before they got tagged.

Together, the Ghost Squadron launched a daring, reckless, coordinated attack. Their targets were at a disadvantage, but only as long as they remained in the cars.

They piled out. Drake was rushing forward, trying to get a better angle. A guard dived out, gun extended and then rolled across the ground, ending up at Drake's feet. Drake kicked him in the face, seeing a better way of taking him out of the action than killing him. The man went unconscious and stopped moving.

Drake peered into the car.

The driver was aiming a gun at Hayden. Before he could fire, Kinimaka shot him through the head. Blood exploded inside the car. Drake spied Emiliano on the back seat. The crime lord hadn't moved. He looked calm, angry even. Drake waved his gun at the man.

'Out. Now.'

Emiliano glared at him, but started to move. Drake guessed two minutes had passed since the start of the attack. So far, he had heard no sirens. Looking around, he saw no one in the street either, which was perfect. Dahl and the others had now taken cover behind their own car as the guards fired back.

Hayden and Kinimaka rushed to help with that.

Drake waved his gun in Emiliano's direction. This was all going too well, he thought. And of course, that was when it all went wrong. The man who'd fallen out of the car before rolled over and aimed his gun up at Drake. The Yorkshireman had a millisecond to get out of the way, dodged left and fell to his knees. Despite the jarring pain, he aimed his gun and squeezed off a shot just as his enemy did. The bullets screamed past each other in flight, both missing.

Drake fell on the man and smashed him in the head with his gun. The guy's skull rocked back and hit the road surface. Drake then fired a point-blank shot into his stomach. He looked up. A knee connected with his face, almost broke his nose. One of the men he'd wounded had staggered to his feet, but had lost his gun. Now, he threw himself on top of Drake, flattening him to the ground. Drake's gun was caught between them, stuck. The man head-butted him, blood flying. Drake struggled underneath his bulk, couldn't bring the gun to bear. It was only when the man started punching that he found a bit of space.

He rolled left and right, trying to escape. His enemy was bleeding on him. Drake punched out with his free hand, stunned the man by striking at his temple. There was the cessation of movement, and then Drake rolled him off.

Shot him in the chest.

He leapt up, turned back to the car. Emiliano was still sitting in the same place, observing the action with the same expression.

'Your men are dying,' Drake said. 'Order them to stand down. Save their lives.'

Emiliano looked forward and then turned to look behind. He said nothing. It was only when Alicia reached in to drag him out of the car that he spoke.

'You!'

'Yes, I have that effect. I really need to talk to you, asshole.'

She pulled him out into the street. Drake took stock of the situation. It looked like there were two or three guards hiding behind the second car, exchanging gunfire with Dahl's team. That was the extent of Emiliano's protection. Drake grabbed hold of Emiliano.

'Quick like we said.' He started pulling the man towards their own car.

It was just him and Alicia with Emiliano. The others had gone to help Dahl's team. As Drake swept his eyes over the scene, he saw another guard taken out. Right then, the other two guards threw their guns away and stood up, hands in the air.

'Don't shoot.'

Emiliano started shouting, cursing them, threatening their families. Drake swiped him across the mouth to shut him up. Dahl told the men to stand next to a wall and glanced around at Drake.

'Are we ready?'

Drake nodded. They all flew towards their cars. And then Drake heard another car speeding down the road.

Damn, all we needed was-

But this wasn't just another car. It sped right up to the rear of Dahl's car. A back door flew open and a large man carrying a massive machine gun climbed out. Drake didn't recognise it, but it was so heavy it needed a strap that ran over the man's bulging neck.

'Fuckers!' he yelled in thickly accented English and opened fire.

At first, Drake almost froze in shock. What the hell? Then the training kicked in and he was grabbing Emiliano, throwing him down to the ground. Scenarios blasted through his head. Maybe one of the guards had called the attack in. Maybe they said Emiliano had been ambushed and killed. They hadn't had a clear view of the battle.

So the heavies had sent in the worst of them.

The noise of the machine gun was monstrous. Bullets chewed through the air. Drake kept as flat to the floor as possible, grinding Emiliano's head into the ground. Alicia was just behind him, also flattened. Their car shook and juddered as bullets smashed through it, holes appeared everywhere. Bullets hit the far side and tore all the way through, exiting just above Drake's head. All he could do was look underneath the car.

Glass rained down on him from broken windows. Currently, the gunner was aiming high at door level. Soon, he would think to lower his train of fire towards the floor. Drake could also see Dahl's group lying prone in front of Emiliano's first car. They were grouped together, a deadly gathering just waiting to be picked off.

'He's alive!' Drake thought to shout, hoping to be heard above the clamour. 'Your damned boss is alive!'

But there was no reasoning with the shooter. He didn't let up. Probably couldn't hear anything except the stentorian sound of gunfire in his ears.

Drake wriggled under the car, took aim. It was a tough shot, because he had to avoid Dahl's team in the process. He steadied himself. Above him, the car rocked to the impact of high velocity bullets.

Drake opened fire with a full mag. His first two bullets missed because of the angle. His enemy never shifted, deaf to any kind of return fire. Drake's third and fourth bullets, fired almost simultaneously, struck the shooter in the meat of the thigh, staggering him. Instantly, the shooting stopped. The gun's barrel now pointed at the floor as its owner started yelling.

Dahl was on his feet in a millisecond, gun in hand. His first shot blew the top of the machine gun shooter's head off.

In the aftermath of the madness, Drake hauled Emiliano to his feet and gave him a shake. 'What the fuck, man?' he yelled. 'I mean, what the fuck?'

Alicia grabbed Emiliano and started hauling him towards their car. Dahl and his team raced for their own car, ignoring the driver of the new vehicle as he just sat there, his hands on the wheel. As one, the Ghost Squadron jumped into their cars.

Turned them on and roared off, prize to hand.

CHAPTER TWENTY THREE

They drove Emiliano to an abandoned lot, driving through a pair of rusty, hanging gates and then lining the cars up alongside each other. The whole place was overgrown, weeds everywhere sprouting up through the cracks in the surface, a brown hedgerow leaning dangerously to the side as if on its last legs. It was a large, square space, and it held a kind of silence, an isolation from the world and everything that bustled around it.

Drake turned to Emiliano. 'We want information,' he said. 'And we want it fast. How fast determines if you live.'

'I will tell you nothing.' Emiliano's face was hard, his eyes flinty.

'We know who you are,' Alicia also turned. 'A prick of a crime boss who thinks he rules the world. So listen to me, mate. We're here to show you *we own you*.'

'And you were willing to throw yourself at me to have a brief word.' Emiliano laughed.

'Believe me, you wouldn't have lasted a minute alone with me. I'd have had you singing in thirty seconds.'

Emiliano scrunched his face up at her. Drake had

had enough. His friends' lives were on the line and this wanker was pulling faces at them. He threw open the car door, jumped out, and then opened Emiliano's door, dragged the man out by his collar. Threw him to the ground. When Emiliano hit the concrete, Drake knelt on his spine.

'If you're gonna get out of this in one piece,' he said. 'I suggest you answer all our questions.'

He grabbed Emiliano's right hand and, to prove he was serious, bent one of the fingers back until it snapped. Emiliano gave a little shriek. Drake roughly spun him around so that he was lying face up.

'What do you want from me?' Emiliano sobbed.

Drake was livid. Friends had been murdered. Other killings were probably being planned. And this guy used the reaper all the time to do his dirty work.

Drake stepped on his chest. 'We're looking for the Devil's Reaper. We know she works for you. And don't lie to us, Emiliano. If we have to come looking for you again, we'll take down your entire organisation.'

'You see how easy it was to grab you?' Alicia added. 'We can destroy your whole way of life.'

The others were crowding around by now, blotting out the sun for Emiliano. All he could see were shadows, boots, and fists.

'The Devil's Reaper,' Drake reiterated. 'Start talking.'

'Oh, God, you couldn't have asked a worse question,' Emiliano spluttered. 'Ask me anything else.'

Drake put some pressure on Emiliano's chest.

'Please, please, if she knows I told you, she will... will...' he couldn't go on, his voice choked with emotion.

Dahl bent down and punched Emiliano in the

mouth. Teeth flew, blood poured. Dahl growled point blank in his face. 'We're way beyond that. She's killing our friends. Tell us how to find her right now.'

Emiliano brought his hands up to his face. 'Please.'

Drake was about to punch him again when Mai reached out a hand to stop him. She leaned forward and grabbed Emiliano by the chin, making him look at her.

'There's no way out of this,' she said. 'Nobody's gonna save you. You're ours now, for as long as we want. This is your chance to make it quick.'

'Quick?' Emiliano's voice was garbled because of the pressure of her hand. 'Please don't kill me.'

Emiliano wasn't exactly tough. More like a mollycoddled, overprotected baby, Drake thought. If they pressed him hard now, they might break him.

'Don't worry about the Devil's Reaper,' he said. 'You should worry about us.' And he reached down, grabbing another of Emiliano's fingers.

'No, no, *no*.' Emiliano jerked his hand away.

'Answer the damn question then.'

'I can't even remember the damn question.' Emiliano showed a little spirit.

Drake didn't reward him for it, and he didn't mess around. Another finger snapped and Dahl drove his boot onto Emiliano's ribs, breaking at least one. The man wheezed and curled up, coughing into the dirty concrete. His face was white, covered in blood, and stretched in a rictus of pain.

'Fucking crime bosses,' Alicia snarled. 'Happy to order their henchmen to maim and strong-arm and kill. Happy to lord it over those with far less. But when you put the pain to them, they squeal like a baby.'

'You're a murderer,' Mai said. 'A criminal. A

parasite. You think the world's gonna miss you? Think again.'

The Japanese woman jabbed his broken rib, then concentrated a double strike to the ribs on the other side of his chest, breaking two more. Emiliano started crying.

'Tell us all about the Devil's Reaper,' Drake said. 'How do you contact her? How does she help you? Why does she do so much for you? I want everything.'

Emiliano coughed and then moaned in pain. 'Please, no more. I will talk. But you don't tell her I told you. You don't tell her!'

Drake gave him a little slack. 'Agreed.'

Emiliano, in the middle of the city of Milan, close to a bustling pavement and a well-trafficked road, among millions of people, saw only the dark ring that they created. He heard vehicles rolling by, the laughter and chatter of men and women, the cries of birds. He heard it, but he couldn't associate it with freedom, with everyday life. Emiliano was caught in Hell, and the only was through was to be forced kicking and screaming all the way.

'The Devil's Reaper trusts us. We gave her her first jobs after the Devil was brutally murdered. We trusted her, saw something in her. She has worked for us ever since, never failing, never slipping up or erring. Not once. She is the most formidable creature in the world.'

Alicia put a boot close to his throat. 'Actually,' she said. 'That'd be me. But go on.'

'She never fails. You can rely on her to always come good. Yes, it takes time, but we've come to accept that. Her kills are sublime.'

Drake wanted to kill him there and then, wanted to

rip his heart out. But he held off, knowing they needed all the information he could give.

'We use her regularly, all the time, actually. She always has a job on for us, though she's extremely busy.'

'What kind of person is she?' Mai asked.

'I don't know her personally. I've spoken to her at length, though. She's forthright, flirty, tells it like it is. She's witty, intelligent, sarcastic. Knows exactly what she's doing and what she's saying. She has her own protégé, a man called Vicius.'

'Someone else to worry about,' Drake said.

'Or split wide open,' Kenzie growled.

'She is a reliable, honest, trustworthy woman,' Emiliano went on, still creased up in pain, grunting often. 'Yes, in a shady line of work, but still a diamond.'

'Where is she?' Drake asked. 'I want an address. And how do we contact her?'

Emiliano laughed and then started coughing, gripping his ribs. 'I have no idea where she is. She wouldn't disclose that information for obvious reasons.' He tried to laugh again and then gave up. 'And our way of contacting her has never changed.'

Finally, they were getting somewhere. Drake shook the man as he stopped talking. 'Go on.'

'She has a man. His name is Jarell. He, too, is a ghost, but I know how to get in touch with him. You give the job to Jarell. He passes it on to the reaper.'

Some headway at last. Drake thought they were one step closer to the most elusive enemy on the planet. 'Who is Jarell?'

'A player. A major player. He's connected in his own right. Dabbles in everything. Obviously, his reputation is enhanced by being the gateway to the reaper.'

'Is that what he's known as?' Mai asked. 'The gateway to the reaper?'

Emiliano nodded painfully.

'Jarell leads to the reaper,' Dahl said. 'I do like the sound of that.'

Drake wasn't finished with Emiliano. 'Now keep talking,' he said. 'Explain how we contact this Jarell.'

'Not difficult. He owns a nightclub in Milan. All the right people frequent it, if you know what I mean. Celebs. Supermodels. People like me-'

'Get on with it,' Hayden urged him.

'You go into the nightclub and you find him. You talk to him. It isn't easy. You need to convince him you're right for the reaper, a good client. He will test you. The only way forward is to pass the test.'

'And then what?' Kinimaka asked.

'Then? Well, he will give you a contact email where you can submit your request. The reaper may then be in touch.'

It sounded plausible, and it was a way forward. Perhaps this Jarell would have a clearer idea of the reaper's whereabouts, Drake thought. They had to get close to him, to trick him into believing they were the real deal.

Once again, he leaned into Emiliano. 'Which nightclub?' he asked.

CHAPTER TWENTY FOUR

Kono Kinimaka hadn't seen her big brother in a few years now. She had instead been getting on with her life, moving from place to place, even getting pregnant. Kono had delivered a healthy baby and taken a year off work before diving back into her career once more. She loved her life, loved every aspect of it.

Now, she was a single mother. The father of her baby was no longer in her life, having decided he would prefer to be with a dance instructor in San Francisco. Kono didn't sweat the loss. Someone that shallow, that selfish, that self-centred, wasn't the right person to be raising her child, anyway. She moved on, made a new life.

Now, she worked six days a week as a model. She made good money, could hire help to look after her baby whilst she went to work. She had a pleasant apartment, a newish car, didn't have to count the pennies. Kono figured she'd carved out a decent existence for her and her child.

All she needed now was to keep at it, keep earning and saving, looking after and connecting with the baby. These were formative years. They were tough years, but they were magical too.

That was one reason her brother's new intrusion in her life had been so hard to bear.

Somehow, Mano had got himself into big trouble. That trouble had spilled over into Kono's life so much that now she had to cope with bodyguards. There were two cops watching her apartment, watching over the baby and the sitter, and two cops on her. They were following her now as she drove, trying to stay behind her.

It was a bind. Kono hated the restrictions it caused. Her babysitter was spooked, too. Kono hoped she wouldn't lose her. This kind of attention put a strain on everything.

Kono was driving to work in stop start traffic. The day was bright, sunny, but windy. A gale buffeted the side of her car, rocking it. She pulled up to a traffic light, engaged neutral, and then just sat there, worrying about the cops back at the apartment and behind her. She didn't know their names, didn't know if they were any good. Why were they here? A message had come from Karin stating that they were necessary, but hardly anything from Mano. When the man-mountain called her, he had begged her to accept the protection, told her it was all about life and death. Of course, she had listened to him, accepted it, told him not to worry.

She didn't even know why.

Now, as she waited, her gaze drifted to the black leather bag in the passenger seat. It was full of the clothes they wanted her to wear at this afternoon's fashion shoot. Yes, they would provide a few outfits, but Kono liked to bring her own too. It felt more professional. And, regarding that, Kono was getting quite a name for herself on the fashion model circuit.

She'd been asked twice already to attend reviews in Paris and London. Lucrative jobs. So far, Kono had turned them down because of the baby, but she couldn't continue to turn them down. If she did, the offers would dry up and then she'd be back at square one. Kono needed to find a way to balance the job and her home life.

A husband would be useful.

She snorted aloud at that. It wasn't what she was looking for. Her gaze drifted again to the black bag, her mind going over its contents and hoping she had packed everything that she needed.

Among the assorted items was a puffball mini skirt, a backless halter top, a black minidress, stone wash low-rise jeans, a faux leather jacket, a bikini and mesh lace up top, and others. Kono had quite the collection and always came up with something surprising. The photographers loved her.

She patted the top of the bag, her bag of tricks. She glanced in the rear-view mirror, saw the cops sitting two cars back. Suffice to say, they enjoyed being present at the photo shoots as much as anyone. But they didn't get distracted. They were good at their jobs.

Kono had come to respect them through the last week. They both possessed a dry sense of humour and seemed to enjoy making her laugh. Considering they were there, interrupting her life, it wasn't too bad.

One of them waved at her now, seeing her eyes in the mirror.

Kono shook her head. The lights changed. She moved off, bumper to bumper with the car in front. There was a guy still sauntering along the crosswalk, she saw, getting honked at by a few cars and giving them all a dirty look, as if he was invincible. A man on a bicycle whizzed past him, just missing slicing him in half.

Kono crawled along. Today's studio was called Jaded, and was a twenty-five minute drive, twenty if she walked. It wasn't funny. Kono hated being late, and the current slow pace was killing her. She wished she could leave her car behind for the cops to drive back.

Inch by slow inch, they moved. Kono watched the mirrors, looked through the side windows. All around was a sea of pedestrians going about their business. She loved to people watch and, in this situation, there wasn't a whole lot else to do. She saw men and women in their business clothes, others in rags, saw the housewife dressed up to the nines and the young mother pushing her pram. It was a typical day, even for Kono, as she crept towards her photo shoot.

Kono arrived, parked her car and waited for the two cops and then they walked in together. It was a large room with a domed ceiling and huge gilded windows. It looked elegant, and that was the idea. A few period pieces stood here and there, an old chest of drawers, a wardrobe, a dark cabinet. In contrast, on the other side of the room, a beach scene had been laid out in front of a green screen. Kono saw heaps of sand and a bucket and spade and even a beach ball. She nodded. She had been told what to expect. Facing the beach scene currently was a bearded man holding a serious-looking camera. He waved when he saw Kono enter the room.

'You ready to get started?'

Kono waved back and nodded. 'Ready when you are.'

'We'll do the beach shoot first.'

Kono knew what that meant. She unhooked her backpack and walked behind a screen. She slipped out of her jeans, shirt and underwear, pulled on the required branded bikini, and walked over to the beach scene. The man with the camera was ready and started directing her. Not that, by now, Kono needed any direction. The other people on set got on with their jobs, pottering around. Kono posed and let the guy take his snaps, then changed into another bikini, and then three more. An hour passed.

The two cops stood around and drank coffee, grazing over a food bar that had been laid out in one corner. They seemed happy enough, but kept their eyes on the doors and occasionally walked over to the window to survey the street outside. Kono got on with her job.

Around midday, a man entered the room. He was dressed in a long black coat, and his eyes roved furtively. He had short hair and moved with his hands in his pockets. Kono, standing in a red bikini with the beach ball balanced on one finger, noticed him straight away and frowned. When she did, the photographer looked up.

'I didn't ask for a sad face, Kono.'

The cops had also noticed the man. They started towards him. Before they reached him, another man entered the room, hot on the heels of the first. He also wore a long coat and had his hands in his pockets.

The cops sped up.

They weren't fast enough. The first man pulled his hands from his pockets, revealing that he held a compact Smith and Wesson handgun. The second man did the same. They dodged to the side and aimed.

They started shouting a slogan, something about protesting against the company Kono was working for. The first man opened fire, shooting a hole through the beach scene. The bullet buried itself in the sand. Then the second man opened fire, his bullet smashing into the camera that the photographer held, jerking it from his hands.

Still, they shouted their protests at the tops of their voices.

It was surreal. Madness. Kono couldn't believe what was happening. She froze as the gunshots pounded the air. The two attackers were rushing forward now, closing the gap between them.

What the hell was happening? She'd never seen anything like it. These people were protesting against the brand by shooting the place up. Really? It didn't feel real...

It isn't real. They're here for you.

In her mind's eye, she saw it playing out. How she would catch a stray bullet. How she would die, and the men would swear it was an accident. But there was no cover on the beach set, there was no cover in the room.

She fell to her knees. The photographer was also on his knees, hands over his head, screaming and holding his injured hand. By now, the cops had reached the two shooters.

The cops fell on them, grabbing for their weapons. Kono couldn't just stay there. She rose to her feet, backed away. The cops and the gunmen tussled. A gun skidded across the floor, but it was one of the cops' guns. All four men were on their knees now, struggling hard.

Around the room, people were huddled in fear. There was nowhere to go, nowhere to hide. A man and a woman were padding towards the exit door, trying to look innocent. Kono yelled at them.

'Get your phones out. Call the cops!'

If she'd been able to, she would have done it, but there was no room for a phone in this particular bikini. Still, she backed away.

The cops fought valiantly. One fell to the floor, looked up into the barrel of a gun, then tripped his opponent just as the man fired. The bullet smashed into the floor by his head. The attackers weren't taking any prisoners. Not now. The second man shrugged his cop off and started running towards Kono.

Raised his gun.

Kono threw her hands up, then braced. Maybe she could run at him, take him by surprise. She gathered herself, then stopped as the chasing cop brought down the attacker. The two men went skidding across the polished wooden floor.

The attacker ended up at Kono's feet. She kicked him in the face with her bare foot, hurting her toes. But the man flinched, blinked, looked up at her. She didn't hesitate to kick him again.

Her foot stung.

The man lashed out, grabbed her ankle, and pulled. Kono ended up on her ass, banging down beside him. The man lunged at her. By now, the cop was back in the fight. He threw himself at the attacker, leaning on his gun arm and trapping the weapon. Still, it went off; the bullet scurrying across the floor and slamming into a far wall.

Kono kicked out with her heel now, slamming it against the man's nose. The cop threw punches into his kidneys. Still, the attacker did not relent. His face was red and bruised and bleeding, his eyes wide, his stomach being pummelled – but he fought on.

Kono smashed her heel again and again into his face and head. Around her, the support staff broke for the door. Someone had called the cops. There were sirens close by. Kono was sitting near the attacker on the ground when he looked up at her.

'You... got... lucky.'

But he still held the gun and was trying to push the barrel back in her direction. The cop, sweating and panting, fought hard. Kono scooted across the floor, away from the gun's line of sight.

Another gunshot shattered the room. Kono flinched. A bullet had passed not eight inches from her head, shot by the first attacker who had flung his cop off. Now, though, that cop was back on him, still struggling.

Kono was torn between wanting to run and wanting to help the cops. She wasn't a runner, couldn't bring herself to just abandon the two men who were trying to save her life. The only other man in the room now was the photographer, curled up in a ball on the floor.

Kono used all her strength to kick the second attacker as he lay on the ground. This helped the cop take control of him, wrench the gun free and then climb on top. The cop smashed him in the face several times until he was half-unconscious, then turned towards his partner.

Kono was already on it. She raced across the room, and as the two men struggled upright, used her momentum and force to kick the attacker heavily between the legs. He collapsed on his face, unable even to groan. Kono felt pain race from her toes to her brain and wondered if she'd damaged her foot.

But the guy was now out of the fight. If she'd hurt

herself, it had been worth it. There was another noise at the door and several cops ran in, all with their guns out. Kono waved at them, shouted that they'd got everything under control.

The cops raced into the room, fanning out, and took control of the two attackers. Kono's own cops rose to their feet, dishevelled, beaten, bleeding. They both stood with their hands on their knees, panting, before walking over to Kono.

'Are you okay?' they asked in unison.

She put an arm around each of their shoulders. 'I am,' she said. 'Because of you.'

'Hey, you did your bit. I've never seen a guy kicked in the nuts so hard. You must have crushed them.'

Kono made a face. 'The last thing he expected when he woke up this morning, I guess.'

They laughed, letting the relief wash over them. This close to death, it was good to take a step back and crack a joke. It was how they dealt with it. Kono, seeing a release of the tension on the cops' faces, let the adrenaline fade from her own body.

She was still alive.

But she had come so close. She glanced around the room, saw the photographer still curled up in a ball on the floor.

'Todd,' she said. 'Hey, Todd, you still wanna carry on with the shoot?'

People laughed. It helped relieve the tension still further. Kono figured they were done for the day and now, feeling safe, made her way back over to the screen, which she closed completely. She dressed again and then shrugged her backpack on, walked over to Todd and helped him to his feet.

'You good?' she asked.

'I'm far from good.'

'Hey, we survived. Look at it that way. We're alive and they're going to jail. They'll never do this again.'

Todd nodded. Kono continued to stay upbeat, to try to lift the mood of the moment, even with the cops. She succeeded, to a certain extent, but always, deep in her heart, her worry was for her brother, Mano, and the rest of his team.

CHAPTER TWENTY FIVE

They could hear the nightclub way before they saw it.

Drake wore smart jeans and a shirt. The others were similarly attired, prepared to get into the club that Emiliano had told them Jarell frequented. They had a description of the man, his name, and very little else. Still, if he was the force Emiliano thought he was, Drake thought that would be enough.

The nightclub stretched around a corner of the block, L-shaped. They walked up to a set of steps, looked up at the doormen, and held out their money. They gained entry, stood in the lobby. The music seemed to get louder. Drake gathered himself for the onslaught of noise before they walked through the outer door into the club proper.

They entered through swing double doors. Drake thought he could feel the floor vibrating, see the walls shake.

'You certainly don't come here to talk,' Alicia yelled.

Everyone turned to her. 'What?'

She shook her head. They started forward. In front of them, a twisting mass of people stood around and shouted at each other or just danced. Lights shuddered and shifted and strobed all around, illuminating different parts of the club on a rolling cycle. To the left was a high stage where people danced in the spotlight. A curving bar stood to the right. Drake tried to circumvent the mass of roiling people by heading for the bar.

'Best source of information in the place,' he shouted.

'What?' everyone answered.

They reached the bar, found a space, and leaned over. Here, the noise wasn't as intrusive. Drake beckoned at the barman, who held a finger up. He served three more people before making his way over to them.

'What can I get you?'

Drake held a twenty euro note out. 'Information,' he said.

The guy looked wary. 'What kind?'

'We just wanna meet someone,' Alicia shouted. 'A guy called Jarell. Can you point him out?'

The barman's eyes had widened at the mention of the name. 'He's not hiding,' the guy said, snapping the note from Drake's fingers. 'Jarell does business here. You don't want to meet Jarell.'

Drake frowned. 'That's exactly what we want to do.'

The barman shrugged as if to say: "your funeral", and then nodded at the back wall. 'Jarell hangs out in the third booth from the fire exit. Blue curtain.'

Drake thanked him, turned, and saw that they'd have to brave the dance floor to reach the booth. He sighed, took a deep breath, and ventured into the chaos.

Writhing bodies bent and twisted everywhere. Drake had to duck several times to avoid being swiped by an arm. Hips batted him from side to side. Behind him, his colleagues pushed their way through the throng, taking it slowly. Drake heard Alicia propositioned and heard an appropriate response. It took them ten minutes to get halfway and then another eight to fight their way through. All the time, the music assaulted them and the flashing lights assailed their eyes. It was like being on a glitzy battlefield.

They made their way through, found a line of booths, each with a different coloured curtain. Jarell's blue one was currently drawn halfway across. Drake peered inside. He saw three women and two men. The women were drinking and laughing, shouting at each other and ignoring the men as they had a good time. The men were busy chatting, actually shouting in each other's ears, but the equivalent of whispering in the noisy club.

Jarell had been described as bald, with ebony skin and a muscular physique. He was tall and had one gold tooth. Drake saw him now and moved forward. He didn't have to check with his team, knew they were ready. They'd been working as one for so long now they could just about read each other's minds.

Drake walked to the edge of the booth, leaned over, shouted, 'Jarell!'

The man's head swivelled towards him. 'What do you want?'

Drake was actually surprised to see no security around Jarell. Maybe the man could take care of himself. He saw a sliver of that now as Jarell eased himself into a better position to take action and revealed a bulge at his waistband. The man was carrying.

'Can we talk?'

Jarell licked his lips, looking calm. 'We have business?'

Drake nodded. 'We do.'

'Are you all together?'

Drake nodded. 'Big job,' he said.

Jarell beckoned them into the booth. 'Two of you,' he said. 'Preferably the women.' He laughed uproariously, as if he'd cracked the best joke in the world.

Drake went into the booth with Alicia at his side. The women shifted down and the other man crossed over to the other side of the booth. Drake took Jarell's left side whilst Alicia squeezed past him to the right. Jarell gave her no room to manoeuvre.

'How did you get my name?'

'I can't tell you that,' Drake protected Emiliano despite his misgivings. 'But it will be worth your while.'

'They all say that,' Jarell said, and then took a swallow from his beer bottle. 'I am rarely satisfied.'

Drake leaned towards him, pitching his voice as low as possible so that he could still be heard. 'We want the services of the Devil's Reaper.'

Now, Jarell went still. It was as if the man had frozen. Nothing moved, not his eyes, not his mouth. He didn't even blink. Drake watched his hands just in case they whipped towards his hidden gun.

After what felt like an age, and after Jarell had first stared at Alicia and then Drake, the man spoke, 'Where did you hear that name?'

'We're well connected. You should be able to tell that by the way we found you.'

Jarell put a hand on Alicia's knee, but it wasn't anything lascivious. It was to push her away. 'You must leave.'

Drake remembered Emiliano saying that they

would be tested and that they would have to convince the man. 'We're told you're the man to talk to.'
'Leave now.'
'We've been through a lot to get here,' Drake said.
Jarell reached out to put a hand on Alicia's knee again. She caught his wrist and twisted it hard. 'Be careful,' she said.
'This is not the place for you. I don't know this Devil's Reaper.'
'We do,' Drake said. 'We know of her. And we're very interested in buying her services. And you're the man who can supposedly facilitate that.'
Jarell studied them. Finally, he said. 'Stand up in front of me, both of you.'
Drake thought it an odd request. 'Why?'
'So that you shield me from the rest of the club. So my lips can't be read. I'll take no chances.'
Both Drake and Alicia got up and stood before Jarell. There wasn't a lot of room and the guy had to look up at them. Drake, looking down, tried to focus on the guy's words.
'The person you speak of values her privacy to the fullest. There can be no mistake here, no leeway. I have to trust that you are who you say you are. If not...' he spread his arms wide. 'So who are you?'
Drake gave him a made-up name and a made-up story. He told the guy he'd recently been working for a large crime syndicate who'd ripped him off, that he wanted to extract a little revenge from the boss and that the reaper's name had been proffered as the best in the business.
'It might not interest her,' Jarell said. 'She tends to go for more *interesting* jobs.'
'She can make it interesting,' Drake said. 'The death, I mean. The more interesting, the better.'

Jarell nodded, still looking up. 'I see you're trying to show me you know her and appreciate that. I can try. Give me an email address.'

Drake hadn't expected that, but they had a few they could use. 'Why?' he asked.

'You don't contact me again face to face. We're never seen together again. Do you understand me?'

Drake nodded. Alicia said, 'Don't fuck with us, Jarell. We can always find you again.'

Jarell switched his attention to her. 'I can't promise the reaper will want to know you, to help you. Money definitely isn't her motivation. I can only try.'

Drake nodded, made a show of taking Alicia by the hand, and walked off. He left the email address with Jarell. That hadn't been easy, and they'd done as much as they'd been able. He understood why Jarell was being so cagey. The reaper would want her interests closely guarded. He made his way back to the team.

'Let's get the hell out of this place,' he said.

They went to a hotel, booked rooms, and planned to stay for the night. They ate and drank and turned in. All the time, they monitored the email address they'd given Jarell, but nothing happened. There was no movement from his side.

Drake set an early alarm and woke to check the email address. Still nothing. He wondered how long they would have to wait. But he guessed the reaper wouldn't be so easy to contact and wouldn't feel obliged to send an immediate reply. These things could take time. The team met for breakfast and then started twiddling their thumbs.

'I don't do waiting well,' Alicia moaned.

'Ya think?' Mai said. 'I can hardly tell.'

'Think about all the men you've shagged,' Kenzie told her. 'That should keep you quiet for a few, um, years.'

Alicia gave her the finger, twisting around uncomfortably in her seat. Hayden was monitoring the email address. Kinimaka sat next to her, looking bored. Cam and Shaw had ordered finger food and espressos. Dahl was leaning back, arms crossed, staring at the ceiling. The big Swede looked about as happy as Alicia.

The morning passed slowly. At midday there was a soft chime and Hayden suddenly sat straight up. She blinked at her phone.

'We have an email,' she said.

'Is it concerning Viagra?' Alicia asked. 'I always get those.'

Hayden pressed on it to open it up. She stared. 'No, no, it's from Jarell. Very guarded. No names.'

'What does it say?' Kinimaka asked.

'"Regarding our meeting last night, I would invite you to one more. Tonight at 8 p.m."' she reeled off an address in Milan.

'I'm up for that,' Shaw said.

'It sounds dodgy,' Alicia said. 'Don't speak too soon.'

'And yet we have no choice. If Jarell's gonna be there, we have to be there,' Drake said. 'He's our only link to the reaper.'

Hayden looked at him. 'You're right,' she said. 'We should check this place out early, find a few hiding places. Maybe leave a few people behind. We need to do this right.'

Drake rose to his feet. 'Already on my way,' he said.

CHAPTER TWENTY SIX

It looked like a motorway services, a truck stop and a caravan park all rolled into one. It was a vast area dotted with buildings. A light drizzle drifted through the night and collected on the car's windscreen as they pulled into their destination.

Drake peered through the car's windows. 'What'd he say? Meet where the Albion trucks collect?'

'I see them,' Dahl pointed to the right.

'Pull up right here,' Hayden said.

They all leaned forward as Kinimaka brought the car to a stop in a parking space. To the right stood the large services building containing shops and arcades and fast-food restaurants, lights blazing. Directly ahead was the lorry park, about half full. To their left, the road wound away past a few caravans to a petrol station and then the exit. Drake could now see six Albion trucks lined up side by side, about three hundred yards ahead.

'He could have an army with him,' Mai murmured.

'Whatever it is, we'll deal with it,' Drake cracked open the door.

The drizzle instantly coated his hair and face. He waited for the others to join him, checking his weapon, and then started off. The ground was slick, their footsteps echoing on the concrete as they walked. They spread out, approaching the area with a wide front, watching cautiously on all sides.

Drake saw Jarell almost immediately.

The tall man was standing between two trucks, in shadow, smoking a cigarette. The tip glowed bright red as he drew on it. When Jarell saw them, he stepped forward and flicked the cigarette away.

'What do you have for us?' Drake asked immediately, knowing the others would fan out, scan the area and leave him and Alicia to focus on their primary target.

Jarell blew out a mouthful of smoke. 'I am the gateway to the Devil's Reaper.'

'Yes, we know that,' Alicia growled. 'That's why we're here.'

'She trusts me. She believes in me. As much as anyone can be, I am her friend. Colleague. Confidante. I have an obligation to her.'

'What are you trying to say?' Drake was genuinely puzzled.

'That you can't just wander up to me, drop the reaper's name, and expect an audience. That isn't how it works.'

'All I want to do is offer her a job,' Drake said easily.

'Which is why I haven't killed you yet.'

Alicia's eyes widened. She made an expansive gesture. 'What, *all* of us?'

Drake nudged her, trying to keep it civil. They needed what Jarell could offer.

'You think we don't have facial recognition software in the club?' Jarell said suddenly.

Drake froze. At that moment there came the mechanical click of dozens of guns being unholstered and the shuffle of feet. He saw shapes above, shapes to the side. Figures were standing atop the trucks, pointing down with their guns, and had materialised out of the shadows behind Jarell.

'I don't know who you are,' Jarell whispered. 'But I do know you're not who you say you are.'

'Hey, hey, wait,' Drake said. 'Steady on. I'm just a man trying to enlist your services.'

Jarell regarded him, studying him closely. Finally, he shook his head. 'I don't trust you,' he said and turned to his men.

'Kill them all.'

CHAPTER TWENTY SEVEN

Expecting the order, Drake was already on the move. He threw himself under a truck just as half a dozen weapons opened fire; the bullets grazing the tarmac at his back.

He rolled under the truck, coming out the other side. Already, he had his gun out. Alicia was nowhere to be seen. He assumed she'd done the same on the other side. The high canvas side of an Albion truck now faced him.

Drake heard the thud of boots on the roof above. They were jumping across the trucks, chasing him.

He aimed up, saw movement, fired. The bullet arrowed up towards the dark skies. That should make them more wary, give him a chance to make a move. He stayed quiet now and rolled underneath the next truck, coming up facing yet another Albion truck.

The entire area stood in silence. Drake knew his own team and at least a dozen shooters were in the area. What the hell was happening?

Everyone had gone to ground. They were waiting. A thick tension settled across the night. So many shooters, so many weapons, all prepped.

Drake heard a scrambling sound. Were they coming after him *under* the trucks, too? Quickly, he hid behind a tall wheel, his back to the rubber, and waited. Soon enough, a head and shoulders popped out from under the truck.

Drake broke the overwhelming silence. He shot the guy in the head.

The noise seemed to trigger an escalation of violence. Gunshots rang out across the truck stop. There was the sound of fighting. Drake knew he couldn't stay hidden. He ran down the side of the truck, approaching the rear, looked around. Further down the row, crouched, he could see Dahl and Kenzie returning fire with several enemies. Looking up, he could also see figures creeping across the tops of the trucks.

Drake stepped out, took aim, and fired. Instantly, he dropped two. The others fell flat, trying to present smaller targets. Drake turned his attention to the truck he stood behind, looked up.

A figure was up there, peering down.

Drake rolled, fired. A figure fell off the top of the truck and hit the ground hard with a burst of blood. He didn't move again. Drake now looked under the trucks, trying to gauge which legs belonged to enemies and which to friends, but there was just no way. He did see several dark shapes crawling or rolling towards him.

Catch 22. He couldn't back away because the trucks were covering him from gunfire above. He couldn't stay where he was because the shapes would soon crawl out to confront him. Instead, he ran around the back of the truck to the next one in line.

It was an odd feeling, being alone in the middle of a gunfight. He didn't know where Alicia was, didn't know where his friends were. Drake waited. He saw a shape come up from under a truck, shot it in the chest. Another followed. Drake shot that one, too. There was a noise from above. Drake ducked under the truck just as bullets strafed the ground where he'd been standing.

Thinking fast, Drake crawled quickly to the front of the truck. Here, he was temporarily clear. He used the side skirts and then the bonnet to climb up the truck himself and then slide onto the roof.

Looked across. Saw several men standing upright, aiming down and exchanging fire with his friends. Drake also saw three men leaping across the top of the trucks in his direction.

At the moment, in the dark, they thought he was one of them.

Drake knew he needed to take full advantage of that. He made sure he had a full mag, then dropped to one knee and aimed. His first three shots hit centre mass, taking down the men who'd been leaping across, one of them in mid jump. Next, he targeted the men shooting down at his friends. One took a bullet to the shoulder, yelled out and twisted around. By the time they realised they were being picked off, Drake had taken out another three.

The rest of them hit the roof hard, lying prone and aiming at him, firing, but by that time Drake was already sliding back down to the ground.

He raced towards his friends.

Saw Alicia tussling with a big, meaty dude. The guy had a knife in one hand and a gun in the other and thus couldn't get a proper grip on Alicia. The Englishwoman used the guy's strength against him, letting him fall to his knees before kicking him in the throat so hard she broke something. The guy choked as Alicia turned away.

The others had spread out behind the trucks, some a little way underneath. There was no sign of Jarell. There seemed to be a kind of stalemate in effect. Everyone was carefully hidden, nobody moving forward. Drake knelt down so that he could look under the trucks.

Nobody was under there. All of Jarell's remaining team were on top of the trucks. Drake beckoned at Alicia, Cam and Shaw, and waited until they could get clear to run over.

'We go up,' he said. 'All at the same time. A blitz attack to take them out.'

They nodded, ran to the front of the trucks where they could find easier handholds. They started up at the same time, keeping an eye on each other. Drake found he had chosen a truck atop which several men already stood. He climbed silently, waited, watched his colleagues, hiding just below the top.

Soon, they were all ready.

Drake exploded into action. He leapt up on top of the truck, firing and running at the same time. Two men folded in half, taking bullets to the gut. Another man swung around. Drake ducked under his arm and punched out. The blow landed heavily and sent the man flying into space.

Two more men faced Drake.

They were already aiming their guns at him. He rolled desperately, felt the sting of a bullet passing millimetres from the side of his head, the tug of another on the sleeve of his jacket. They had fired and missed. He came up at the end of his roll, gun up.

He didn't miss. Both men flew off the truck into the night, crashing down to the concrete below.

Drake span, gun aimed, mindful that he might be

able to help his colleagues. Alicia was atop the next truck, tussling with a short, stocky guy. They both had guns in their hands, arms high, and were silhouetted by the sky, two brawling shapes atop the truck. Alicia's figure was brawny and tall, her opponents broad and short. They struggled tremendously, backlit by the night.

Drake ran to the front, trying to get a bead on the next truck where Cam was fighting. The young fighter seemed to be having no problem. His opponent was already doubled up and groaning at his feet. Cam had relieved him of his gun. Beyond that, he saw Shaw struggling similarly to Alicia, but couldn't get a clear shot off.

Alicia pounded her opponent, beating down on him from her higher position. The guy fell to his knees, still holding out. Alicia pulled away, twisted into a spinning kick that almost took his head off. The guy flew to the side and crumpled, not moving. Alicia didn't miss a beat. She knelt, sighted on Shaw's opponent, and fired a single shot that clipped him in the shoulder and sent him flying off the truck into the night. Shaw gave her a thumbs up.

Drake surveyed the area. There were no more bad guys, not up here. He shouted down to Dahl and Hayden.

'You clear?'

'Yeah, clear down here. Mai and Mano are checking the front.'

'Clear,' Mai's voice was heard.

'Where's that bastard, Jarell?' Alicia grunted. 'He ambushed us.'

'Got him.' Mai shouted again. 'He was hiding in one of the trucks.'

'Coward,' Alicia said.

They climbed down from the trucks, reached solid ground, and made their way over to Mai. The Japanese woman had Jarell by the scruff of the neck and was throwing him against the side of a truck. Not enough to immobilise him, but enough to hurt.

'You tried to kill us.' Drake made a show of being furious. Inside, he was actually as cold as ice.

'Kill him,' Dahl growled theatrically. 'Make it hurt.'

'I think I just might do that,' Drake said.

Jarell held up a hand. He was whimpering. His eyes were leaking, nose bleeding. He started stuttering.

'You made a big mistake coming here,' Drake said. 'You made an even bigger one, bringing those shooters with you.'

As they spoke, Cam and Shaw roamed around their perimeter just in case they hadn't cleared it of shooters. They found nothing except dead bodies. Already, there was the sound of sirens in the air. Drake knew they'd have to hurry.

'How do we get to her?' Drake snapped.

Jarell started blubbering. 'I can't tell you, man. I just can't. Death would be the least of my worries. I can't betray the reaper.'

Drake slammed the side of the truck an inch from Jarell's head. 'Do it or I'll kill you.' He let him feel the barrel of the gun.

'I can't betray the reaper,' Jarell sobbed.

Drake fired. The bullet singed Jarell, passing millimetres from his flesh. 'Give me the reaper or the next one's in your brain.'

'Please, please, I can't do that. I won't. Kill me. Just kill me.'

Drake could see it in Jarell's eyes. He would die

before he gave the reaper up. Still pressing, he jammed the gun into Jarell's stomach.

'Give me something or I will kill you.'

'Stop, stop, no wait. I can give you something. I can give you something good.'

Drake eased up with the gun, backed off just a little. 'It better be, Jarell.'

The man was crying, snorting, shivering all at the same time. He couldn't keep still. His knees were shaking. It was Drake's arm that kept him upright.

'I can't give you the reaper, but it can't hurt to tell you the name of the people who hired her to destroy your lives.'

Drake's eyes widened. 'You know who that is?'

'She told me. I don't think it's a big secret. Maybe they want you to know.'

Drake shook him. 'Go on then. Who is it?'

Jarell wiped his face with his sleeve, then tried to collect himself. 'An organisation out of Japan. They were once-'

'Japan?' Mai said, surprised.

'Yeah, that's what I said. They were once all-powerful apparently, a big deal, but are now small fry. Gnats in the grand scheme of things, she said…'

Drake noticed a terrible look dawning on Mai's face.

Jarell went on. 'They're called the Tsugarai. Like I said, small fry, but they want a very big revenge.'

Mai wobbled where she stood, stunned and shocked. Drake put a hand on her shoulder, trying to cover his own surprise. The Tsugarai had hired the Devil's Reaper to do this? He hadn't even thought of the Tsugarai in years.

'Are you absolutely sure?' he asked.

Jarell nodded eagerly, pleased that he had given them something that might save his life. 'The Tsugarai,' he said. 'Without a doubt.'

The name hung in the air, encompassing the Ghost Squadron entirely like a heavy shroud, suddenly becoming the focal point of their lives.

CHAPTER TWENTY EIGHT

Andrea Agneson stepped out of a hot shower and towelled off. She looked around her closet, wondering exactly what to wear. The white trousers might get dirty from where she was going. The black ones weren't showy enough for her. The green ones were quite the opposite. Maybe the blue? Style them with a nice white top and then a small black, glittering Gucci jacket?

Mind made up, she dressed and then checked the time. She was way ahead of schedule. Andrea didn't want to eat – they were planning on getting a bite before the show began. She had a bit of time on her hands.

Andrea couldn't wait to see Nina. The two had been friends for decades, but rarely got to go out together anymore. In fact, this was the first time in half a year that they had got together. Andrea laid back on her bed and thought about the good times. From their time in the army to working as trainee chefs in competing restaurants to meeting their respective partners and spending less and less time together. But the bond never broke. Andrea and Nina were friends for life. It didn't matter how much time they spent apart. When they met, it was as though they'd never been separated.

Andrea sat up then and checked the time once more. She wanted to be early, not late. They had agreed to meet at Cut and Craft, a rather nice steak restaurant in the precinct. After that, they were going to watch a local band perform at a nearby club. They would find a table and listen to the music and talk without stopping. They would laugh and maybe cry and tell all their stories and absently watch the stage and the band. It would be one of the best nights ever. Andrea already knew.

She exited her apartment, locked the door, and then ventured out into the street. Expecting the cold, she was pleasantly surprised to feel the warmth. She set off on the brisk fifteen-minute walk to the restaurant and kept her eyes open, hoping to bump into Nina early.

It didn't happen. Twenty minutes later, she entered the restaurant to find Nina already seated, waiting for her. The two embraced tightly, and Andrea found that there were a few tears in her eyes.

'It's so good to see you,' she said.

'And you,' Nina held her hand. 'It feels like years and yet it feels like just yesterday.'

They caught up, couldn't stop holding hands. Their words seemed to fall over each other. Twice, the waitress appeared to take their order, and they hadn't even looked at the menu yet. In the end, they had to take a breather to order, conscious of the time the band was starting and that they would have to go early to get a good table.

They ordered and drank their sodas and sat back when their meal arrived, two medium cooked sizzling steaks with chips and sauce and veg. They talked as they ate and time passed swiftly and then they had to call the waitress over to pay the bill and exit quickly. Soon, they were outside again, crossing the road to the enormous bar where the band was due to play. They entered through the front doors, spied a corner table, and quickly crossed over to it before anyone else could snag it. Andrea went up to the bar to grab them a couple of pints and then sat back down, still catching up.

To their left, a raised circular platform formed the stage. Currently, there were men and women tuning instruments, running wires across the floor, and messing around with a battered old drum kit. A vocalist was tapping a mic as if trying to get it to work.

Andrea turned to Nina. 'I was reminiscing about the old days,' she said. 'Remember... the army?'

'Those were some days,' Nina laughed. 'We didn't have a clue what we were doing.'

'Still don't,' Andrea said lightly.

The bar started filling up, and soon there was standing room only on the floor. The noise level increased tenfold. Andrea and Nina sat smiling, happy in each other's company. They went up for more drinks, waited for the band to appear. Their table was near the front, giving them an uninterrupted view of the stage.

The night turned. Half an hour later, the band came on and started to play. The vocalist caught Andrea's attention, and she gave him a little wave. Nina laughed, shaking her head. The band launched into their hour long set.

Andrea never noticed the two men pushing their way through the crowd. She heard a few protests, a loud shout, a voice raised in threat. When she turned her head that way, she saw nothing but a sea of faces.

The atmosphere was great. Just then there were more raised voices, a few more shouts. She wondered what was going on.

And turned to Nina. 'Something's happening over there.'

In the end, it was just two stocky men wanting to get to the front of the crowd. They'd bullied their way through the throng all the way from the back of the bar to the front. They stood now with their hands in their pockets, staring at each other and then taking a good look around the room.

Two pairs of eyes landed on Andrea.

She shivered. The attention was direct, intense. Why the hell were they staring at her like that?

She was about to turn to Nina again, to turn away from the men, when one of them started shouting. He spread his arms and yelled something that was lost under the noise of the band. People in the crowd turned their way.

Both men suddenly had guns in their hands.

Andrea felt her heart start hammering. Nina was staring wide eyed at the men. Nobody in their vicinity could believe their eyes. People started backing away. The men lowered their guns and aimed at the band.

'Die,' Andrea heard one of them shout.

They opened fire. There was a terrible, animalistic scream that wrenched its way through the crowd. People were too crammed in to turn and run, but they had to try, anyway. The gunman's bullet caught the vocalist in the chest. Blood flew. The other man opened fire, shooting another band member, and then the men turned their attention to the crowd.

Or more specifically, to Andrea.

A moment ago, they'd both been staring at her.

Now, they were at it again, only this time they were training their weapons on her. Andrea couldn't move. Her mouth was dry. She felt like the proverbial deer trapped in the headlights. Why were they trained so specifically on her?

Nina jumped to her feet. 'Run!'

It was a great idea, but Andrea couldn't move. The gaze of the men was holding her in place, trapping her.

'I don't know if I can,' she said quietly.

The men fired again, this time into the crowd, but their eyes were still on Andrea. They started forward now as people screamed and tried to get away from them, crushing those behind.

Andrea stared up at approaching death.

The men fired point blank.

CHAPTER TWENTY NINE

It was the next morning. Alicia had spent a restless night and rose with the sun, headed to the shower. She left Drake snoring softly, then jumped on him when she reappeared. Drake was awake in a hurry, wide-eyed.

'Wanna fight me?' she asked playfully.

'Never,' he grunted. 'I prefer to win.'

'Well said.'

Drake showered and then they sat on the bed for a while before breakfast. 'It was a close call last night, love,' Drake said.

'Those men weren't trained properly,' Alicia replied. 'Hired thugs. Didn't stand a chance.'

Drake nodded. 'I guess having the higher ground didn't even help them.'

'It wasn't a bad idea, standing on top of those trucks. But they just didn't have the skills to pull it off.'

They talked and bantered for a while, then went down to breakfast to meet the others. Soon they were drinking coffee and tea and eating a buffet breakfast, and then the phone rang.

Hayden held up a hand. 'It's Karin.'

Alicia felt her heart sink. So far, Karin had only called them with bad news. Hopefully, though, today would be different.

'It's not good, I'm afraid,' Karin said immediately. 'Alicia, do you know a woman by the name of Andrea Agneson?'

Alicia blinked, frowned. She trawled her memory. There *had* been a woman by that name, somewhere in the distant past. It was a relatively striking name. It took her a few minutes to dig it up.

'When I joined the army,' she said. 'There were a few women. I'm sure Andrea Agneson was one of them.' Her heart was beating fast, her expectations brimming with misery.

'I'm sorry, but Andrea Agneson was shot dead yesterday as part of a gangland shooting in London. The gang targeted a bar owned by one of its rivals. Shot eight people. Andrea was one of them.'

Alicia bit her bottom lip. 'Bastards,' she whispered. 'Evil bastards.'

'Was she a friend of yours?' Karin asked.

Alicia took a deep breath and tried to pull herself together. The truth was, she hadn't thought about Andrea in years, hadn't even considered her an old friend. Once upon a time, they had gelled though, been there for each other, especially during those early army days.

'This is monstrous,' she said.

Inside, she wept for her one-time friend. To go all these years, to build an entire life and then have it taken away from you by one malevolent mastermind, by a faceless, vile, cowardly piece of...

'She can't keep this up forever,' Drake said. 'Soon, she's gonna start coming for us.'

'I wish she'd get on with it,' Kenzie said.

Alicia sat back, saying nothing. She was still reeling. A maelstrom of emotions beat at her. She didn't know what to think, what to do, how to act. The news had totally thrown her off.

'How many more?' she snapped. 'How many more old friends?'

Kinimaka was regarding her with sorrow in his eyes. They had recently got the news that Kono, his sister, had been targeted and had barely survived. There was now a larger guard on her, and she was isolated in a safe house. 'We have to end this,' he said.

'Isn't that what we're trying to do?' Dahl said simply. 'By tracking down the reaper.'

Alicia almost snapped at him then, at all of them, but she forced the emotion down, knowing it would do her no good. She looked at Drake and shook her head.

'My fault,' she said.

He leaned over towards her. 'Don't blame yourself for this, love. It's the action of a depraved killer, one of the worst. You can't put her sins on you.'

'I feel responsible.' She felt that, if she hadn't known Andrea, or rather *if she'd remembered* Andrea, then the woman wouldn't be dead.

'I had a chance to save her,' Alicia gritted. 'To protect her. I failed.'

'We can't remember everyone. It was nearly twenty years ago. The reaper's research is ridiculously good.'

'There's nothing good about it.' Alicia looked at him from under hooded eyes.

'Sorry, didn't mean it that way. We can't save everyone, Alicia. Never have been able to. But you're not to blame here. The reaper is.'

The table was quiet and subdued. Even Karin had sensed the atmosphere and had stopped talking.

'I have realised something through the night,' Hayden started in a soft voice, trying to steer the conversation away from Alicia's guilt. 'Because of Jarell, because he wouldn't give the reaper up, we now have no leads to her.'

Drake stared, trying to muddle that through his head along with a thousand other feelings. It was true. Jarell had been their last lead to the reaper.

'Bollocks,' he said.

It seemed none of the others had realised that. Alicia listened, her mood worsening. Did this mean they were back to square one?

'We might not have a lead on the reaper,' Mai said. 'But we *do* have a lead.'

Kinimaka nodded. 'The Tsugarai.'

'They're behind everything,' Mai said. 'They started all this. And don't forget, they know how to contact the reaper too.'

'You're saying that we should go after the Tsugarai?' Drake said. 'The entire gang?'

Mai shrugged. 'Why not? It makes sense. If we can cut the head off the snake, so much the better. I know it won't stop the reaper from coming after us, but it will get rid of a major threat.'

'Destroy the Tsugarai?' Alicia sat up, interested. 'That would help.'

'How big is this gang?' Drake stayed practical.

'Does it matter?' Mai said. 'We go to Tokyo, find them, root them out. Get a little payback of our own. And in the process, we hopefully dig up another lead on the reaper.'

Drake sat back. It was a good plan. He saw Karin was still listening. 'Can you organise us weapons in Tokyo?' he asked.

'I'll try my best. We have safe houses everywhere, especially in a city like that.'

'Then it looks like we're headed for Tokyo,' Drake said.

It was an odd feeling, Drake thought. Travelling through the day on an aeroplane, over thirty thousand feet in the air, when you knew the killer hunting you had a penchant for bringing down aeroplanes just to kill one or a minority of people. It was unsettling, and Drake, sitting in his seat, couldn't help but think about it and look at all the innocent people seated around him. The truth was, the reaper carried out this kind of attack whenever she wanted. Of course, they'd jumped on a plane pretty quickly, so she probably wouldn't have had the time to put something in place.

But still... it was worrying.

Drake spent the entire flight to Tokyo worrying about the plane's occupants, worried about the reaper, wondering if something was going to happen. He didn't sleep, didn't eat, just sipped a cup of water. To his left, Alicia also sat in silence, worried about different things. Her eyes were sad, and Drake thought she might be remembering the better times of her army days. In fact, the only member of their party totally switched on throughout the flight was Mai, who was working through what actions they might take when they arrived. Drake left her to it.

It was a long flight, hours in which to worry. Drake watched everything, everyone, his eyes constantly alert. He only managed a sigh of relief when the plane touched down.

They had arrived in Tokyo.

CHAPTER THIRTY

When they landed and rented a couple of cars, Mai immediately took them to the seedier side of Tokyo. It was dark here, approaching midnight and they were all dog tired, but they didn't stop, didn't seek the rest they craved. Mai had an old contact, and she wanted to use him.

First, they visited a safe house and tooled up. The weapons were nothing special, well used, even battered, but they made do. After that, they were trawling the streets, searching for Mai's old contact.

'You sure he'll still be there?' Kinimaka asked her. 'How long's it been?'

'He was my best asset. Ginko will never change. He'll work this network of streets until he dies. And I've checked with my Tokyo PD contacts. He's still around.'

Mai directed them to park on the street and then told them to wait. Soon, she exited the car and started walking along the benighted street. A stiff wind blew straight in from the bay, bringing with it the smell of sea salt. Mai listened and watched as she walked. There was the sound of rumbling traffic, of whispered voices coming from the shadows. The street was wide with cars parked on both sides and street lights blazing only intermittently. As she walked, she heard activity in the cars, saw some of them rocking from side to side. This was a busy street.

She walked to a corner, slowed, looked around. There were a couple of youths standing nearby. She asked for Ginko, gave them dead eyes, and waited for an answer. Eventually, it came. Ginko was famous around here.

'Dawn till midnight,' one youth said in Japanese. 'He never moves, old Ginko. Say hi from us.'

Mai continued her walk. Eventually, she came to a set of high black railings that formed an entrance to a park. On either side of the railings, a concrete niche had been set into the wall. Ginko sat on a plastic folding chair within one of those niches. As Mai approached, he looked up.

His eyes flew wide.

'It can't be.'

Mai stopped before him. Ginko was in his fifties with a long straggly beard and a full head of white hair. He looked seventy, but still moved with the fluid grace of a man far younger than his years. He unwound himself now, standing tall.

'Mai Kitano?'

Mai held out a hand. 'How've you been?'

'Oh, hey, I remember when you used to come around all the time. Those were the days, a favour for a favour, huh?' he winked.

'It wasn't so long ago,' Mai said with a smile. 'I knew you'd still be here.'

'Are you still... a cop?' He spoke the words with dread.

Mai shook her head. 'I'm not here in any official capacity. I'm here looking for the Tsugarai.'

Ginko chortled. 'What's left of them.'

'Exactly.'

Ginko eyed her. 'I don't know you anymore, Mai, and I have to live, sleep and earn off these streets. I'm no snitch.'

Mai knew he was. Ginko would do practically anything for a few dozen Yen. She put her hands on her hips. 'Come on, Ginko. I'm not asking for much. Just the location of their headquarters.'

'Information like that would get me killed. You don't want that, do you?'

'It's a simple answer to a simple question, Ginko. Where are the Tsugarai?'

But he wouldn't tell her. No matter how hard she tried, how well she cajoled, Ginko was clearly too scared to give up the gang. After a while he started becoming antsy too, asking her to move on before people took notice of her and started asking questions. Mai cursed inwardly and left Ginko to it, walked back to the car.

'Failure,' she said as she climbed in. 'He won't blab on them. Too scared.'

'So what next?' Drake asked of her.

'I have another move. Don't *want* to use it, but it's workable.'

She drew out her phone, checked the speed dial, and made a call. As she completed the action, she explained.

'You know Dai Hibiki. We've used him dozens of times before and he's married to my sister. If you remember, Dai is an ex-cop. He'll be able to find out where the Tsugarai's HQ is.'

'Shouldn't that have been option number one?' Hayden asked.

'Dai's in hiding, under protection, along with my sister. I didn't want to mess with that. Now we have no choice.'

She made the call, spoke to Hibiki. They hadn't caught up in a long time. But what should have been a pleasant call was purely business, as Mai asked for his help. Hibiki agreed and said he'd call her back with the information.

The team sat silently for a while in their respective cars.

'What do we do now?' Drake asked.

There was no answer. Instead of just sitting in their cars in the dark or just driving around, they found a respectable hotel and used it as a base. An hour later, Hibiki still hadn't called back. Mai said they might as well go to their rooms, and she'd place a group call the moment he rang with information. Mai entered her room and sprawled out on the bed, too wired to get any shut eye. Another hour passed. She raided the minibar, drank a couple of whiskies. It didn't take the edge off. She took a long hot shower, but that didn't help either. The night passed as slow as molasses.

It was just before sunrise when her phone rang.

'Dai?' she said.

'The very same. I spoke to a friend who works the gangs. You know the Tsugarai are pretty low key now.'

'Not low enough for my taste. They should have been ground into the gutter. Now, what do you have for me?'

Hibiki reeled off an address. 'It's a shithole, to be honest,' he said. 'A bit of a warren. Plenty of places to hide. Be careful, Mai.'

She assured him she would be and hung up. Next, she placed the group call and gathered all the others in her room.

'We finally have an address for the people who set the Devil's Reaper on us,' she told them.

'The Tsugarai?' Kinimaka wanted reassurance.

'What's left of them.'

'And the man to speak to?' Drake asked. 'Who's in charge?'

'A Man named Bushida,' Mai shrugged. 'I don't know him.'

'And the place we're going?'

'It will be easy enough to gain entrance. I'm told the Tsugarai now number around thirty in total. Some of those will be out doing their thing. Quite a few, actually. We shouldn't face any major problems.'

'When do we hit them?' Alicia asked.

'How about right now?'

CHAPTER THIRTY ONE

With the orange blaze of the sun rising steadily above the horizon, the team crowded into their two cars and headed in the direction of the Tsugarai's HQ. They were fed and caffeinated and totally unsure of what to expect. The traffic was steady but not too thick. Kinimaka drove the first car, Kenzie the second, and they had both tapped their destination into the sat nav.

When they arrived, they found a vast parking lot in which to turn around and park up. Across the street lay the Tsugarai HQ. It was a ratty but large secondhand car dealership with a garage, a rental area and a scrapyard attached. Drake saw many low buildings with cracked and dirty windows and doors with bars across them. He saw acres of cracked concrete and weeds and rusted vehicles. Even as they settled in to watch, they saw a bit of activity, a silver Nissan arriving and pushing through the front gates that were currently closed, driving up to one of the doors. A man wearing a hoodie got out and pushed inside.

They stayed in place and watched. About an hour after they arrived, Dai Hibiki sent them a photo of Bushida, the leader of the Tsugarai gang. The guy was tall and broad shouldered, with a face that looked like it had seen its fair share of fighting and hardship. His eyes were black, like his soul, and he had short cropped hair. Hibiki also sent a picture of Han, the second-in-command, a weasel-faced short man with a perpetual squint. From this distance, Drake doubted they could make anyone out too easily, but that was what the monoculars were for.

He used one now, fitting it to his right eye and taking a sweep of the property. First impressions were correct – the whole area was rotting away slowly. The few cars for sale were old and tatty. One of them had a pitted windscreen. The junkers in the back were stacked three high and not too carefully, almost toppling. As the morning wore on, the activity increased.

Alicia had the monocular to her eye when they first saw Bushida.

'Got him,' she said. 'Blue car.'

It had just arrived. They all sat forward. Bushida left the car parked at an odd angle, climbed out and didn't bother locking it. He stood for a moment, looking around as if surveying his kingdom. Then he disappeared into one of the buildings. More time passed, and they stayed on lookout, remembering all the comings and goings. There was a time between eight and ten when it seemed most of the thirty gang members were present, walking between buildings and generally receiving orders. Those who worked there went to their posts. After mid morning had passed, the gang seemed to go about their business proper, with most of them leaving. Drake and the others documented all of it in their heads.

'It's gonna be a long bloody day,' Dahl said with a sigh.

'I'm starving,' Alicia said.

Drake watched and took it all in. The Tsugarai seemed to run a tight ship, everyone knowing exactly what they were doing. The workers went straight to their posts, and the gang appeared to come in for a briefing and then depart. There were no more signs of Bushida.

The team stayed there all day.

When Bushida left for the evening, they followed. It had been a long day and, with food and drink unavailable, they were all feeling uncomfortable. They crawled through late evening traffic in slow pursuit of Bushida all the way to his home.

'Take a good look,' Hayden said through the comms. 'If we hit them, it either has to be at the workplace or at home.'

They followed Bushida up a tree-lined avenue, finally arriving at a gated three-storey dwelling that had a guard out front. So this was where the Tsugarai's money went. There was only one way in, one way out. High walls surrounded the property. As they watched Bushida park up, the guard came forward to open his door. The front door opened too, and another guard popped his head out. Both men were heavily armed.

Bushida ignored the guards as he walked up to his house and went inside for the night. The team watched until he'd disappeared.

'The Tsugarai have fallen so far,' Mai said. 'They live in the gutter. That place of business... it's a far cry from what they had.'

'A good thing,' Drake said.

Mai nodded her head. 'A great thing. Only, they haven't fallen far enough. Yet.'

'Did you see any guards at the workplace today?' Dahl asked.

'None that were obvious,' Hayden replied.

'I think we hit the workplace. Bushida has his home pretty tightly wrapped up. During the day, he only has a few men at the workplace. Most of the gang is out working. I think we can get to him there.'

'Lunchtime looked to be the quietest,' Kenzie said. 'If we sneak in then, we're golden.'

Drake thought it all sounded a little too easy. Essentially, they were right, though. They could only work with what they'd observed. He sat back as they drove back to the hotel and, most importantly, its restaurant.

They didn't dally. They ate, and they went straight up to their rooms, all knowing that, tomorrow, they would grab Bushida and teach the guy a lesson.

There was an unspoken question though – how far were they willing to go?

CHAPTER THIRTY TWO

The next day dawned with a dreary grey overcast, and they were soon back in place. They used the monoculars to find the best ingress and egress points, the exact positions of the workers and their routines, and probed the filthy windows to see if they could discern any movement inside. The morning passed quickly, and soon they were approaching midday, the time they'd decided to make their move.

The team climbed out of the car. The parking area was quite full; there was always someone coming and going, so their movements would be hidden until they reached the workplace gates. They checked their weapons, extra mags, and comms system. Everything was perfectly operating and in place.

They reached the road, waited incongruously to cross, and then approached the open gates. Drake could see only one member of the public inside, a guy getting his tyre changed. They took one last look at each other, then slipped in through the gates.

They split up, headed for various buildings until they were almost at the doors, then veered away and converged on Bushida's building. It wasn't pretty, and it wasn't covert, but they weren't going for covert. They were going for an all out attack.

As Drake reached the side of Bushida's building and flattened himself against it, the door opened. A sharp-nosed man stuck his head out, frowning, saw Drake, and instantly reacted. Some people, Drake knew, would take many seconds to react, but those tuned for violence would do so immediately. This man reached into his waistband for a gun and tried to tug it out.

Drake, also tuned for violence, was on him straight away. He didn't want to make any noise, so grabbed his gun arm and smacked him hard in the nose. The man's head whipped back, struck the door frame and his eyes closed. He would have slithered to the ground but for Drake's grip on him.

Drake eased his way through the door. The rest of his team either followed or found a different door. All doors would lead to Bushida, or so they hoped. There was no turning back now.

Drake stashed the man in a closet, then proceeded down a passageway. Ahead, another man popped his head out of a door and then frowned. His mouth opened. Drake flew forward, arms out, and grabbed him around the throat a split second before he shouted out. Drake gripped him hard, made the man choke, then forced him back against the wall. He smashed the man's head into the wall three times before his eyes closed and he, too, slithered to the floor in an untidy heap.

Along the corridor, Dahl took point. They crept along soundlessly. Soon, the Swede came to a row of windows that fronted an open office. He slowed, ducked his head. Drake was a step behind, Kinimaka a step behind him.

Drake turned to the Hawaiian. 'Nothing clumsy

now, hear? I don't want you falling over a mouse or anything.'

Kinimaka grimaced, obviously thinking the same thing. They all ducked and started creeping below the level of the window. If they could just-

It didn't happen. A man turned into the corridor ahead, saw them all. It was a shame, because Drake figured they were only two doors away from Bushida's office.

The man pointed and yelled. There was no grabbing him; he was a good twenty steps away. Luckily, though, he didn't have a gun.

Sounds came from the office to their right. Quickly, they ran in through a door – Drake, Dahl, Kinimaka, Alicia and Mai – and fanned out.

There were two men and three women, all seated at their desks with looks of shock on their faces. Computers faced them. Clearly, they were an admin team of sorts. Drake leapt across a desk, smashed the first man in the mouth. Dahl took the second. Alicia, Kinimaka and Mai hit the women hard, giving them no quarter. Drake whirled back to the corridor, seeing the first man still approaching. He froze when he saw Drake.

'Ay up,' the Yorkshireman said.

He ran at the man, who turned to flee. The guy didn't get far. Drake was pleased they hadn't come across any hardened gang members yet, but it stood to reason that they'd be all out doing their business.

He continued down the corridor, scanned the next room. It was a storage area, full of boxes and cans and piles of paper. Giving it a cursory glance, he continued on. Looked through the next door.

Saw Bushida.

The leader of the Tsugarai was standing behind his desk, gun in hand. The gun was trained on Drake with a steady hand. The tall man didn't look perturbed at all. Drake heard his colleagues approaching and made room.

'We know who you are,' Drake said. 'Put the gun down and talk to us.'

The barrel never wavered.

'*I* know who you are,' Bushida sneered.

Mai still hadn't shown her face yet. At this point, it didn't seem wise. She hovered behind the door frame, remaining silent.

'You are the team,' Bushida said, eyes still locked on Drake's. 'The team-'

'You sent the Devil's Reaper after,' Drake finished for him. 'That's why we're here.'

'Has she done a good job?' Bushida's face was severe. 'I asked her to make you suffer.'

'Call her off,' Drake said. 'Call this quits. And we'll let you live.'

'It doesn't work that way. Once you've given the reaper a job, she completes it. There's no calling it off. That's one of her stipulations.'

Both Dahl and Alicia had their guns trained on Bushida. Drake indicated them. 'Drop your weapon or you *will* die.'

Bushida looked left and right. Was he stalling? Obviously, Drake assumed he'd had time to call at least some of his gang before they reached his office. It was just a matter of time before they all arrived.

'Do it,' Drake said. 'Stop stalling.'

Dahl stepped forward into the room, gun still aimed. The movement intimidated Bushida, who stepped back. His gun wavered between all three of them.

'Is she here?' Bushida growled.

Drake was tempted to play it daft and say, "Who?" but there was only one person on Bushida's mind. The person who'd destroyed the Tsugarai in the first place.

'She's here. Put the gun down and I'll let you see her.'

'If she walks in with her head down, her hands in cuffs, I will consider talking to the bitch.'

Mai stepped into view, gun aimed directly at Bushida's head. 'I'd soon as kill you right here.'

Drake gave her a nervous look. Above all, they needed Bushida alive.

Bushida's finger tightened on the trigger, as did Mai's. There was utter silence for a long minute.

'You're hopelessly outnumbered,' Drake said finally. 'We could shoot you in the arm, the leg, the stomach. Give it up.'

Bushida was still staring at Mai with hatred. His eyes were glazed with it, open wide and fixed on her frame. Drake wondered if he'd even registered his voice.

But, with a slow motion, Bushida finally turned to him. He laid his gun on the table, held his hands in the air.

'There's nothing you can do to me,' he said.

'Oh, I wouldn't say that.' Mai walked into the room. 'You are the last leader of the Tsugarai. We can make your life hell.'

Bushida's eyes narrowed at the words "last leader." He glared at her with a hard determination. 'Your fate is sealed,' he said. 'Eventually, the reaper will come for you.'

'That's why we're here,' Drake said. 'How did you contact the reaper?' He hoped to God that it wasn't through Jarell.

'You want to *find* her? That is impossible.'

'Have you ever tried?' Drake didn't want to bandy words with the guy, but he needed to get him talking.

The minutes flew by.

Bushida cast another furtive glance at the window. Drake wondered how much time they really had before the bulk of the gang arrived.

Back in the corridor, the rest of the team were guarding all the approaches to the room. So far, they remained quiet.

'The reaper is a ghost, a deadly spectre. You will never see her coming for you. One moment you are living your life, the next you are dying hard. Just remember, she is the best of the best, and-'

'So are we,' Alicia said. 'The very best. Honestly, Bushida, you and your shit gang stand no chance against us.'

'We shall see,' Bushida said. 'They will be here soon.'

'But they won't save your life,' Drake said. 'Unless you tell me how to contact the reaper.'

'I could tell you. I have a very special way. But that would be cowardly of me, and I am no coward.'

Bushida was certainly setting his stall out. Drake took out his knife. 'Looks like it's the hard way then,' he said.

Bushida's expression changed from steely resolve to liquid nervousness in an instant. He backed away as Drake came around the table, looked once more at his gun and then out the window.

'Ah,' he said.

Drake followed his gaze. There were men pouring in through the open gates, at least a dozen of them. All had their guns out and were running at full pace.

'They're here,' Drake said. 'Grab him. We can't let him go.' Drake was hugely conscious that Bushida was their last connection to the reaper.

Alicia grabbed Bushida, holding him by the throat and the arm. She nudged his ribs with her knife, made him stand utterly still. She ran the point of her blade up and down his ribcage.

'Do as I say,' she said. 'Remember, I can cut and hurt you and still make you run.'

Bushida nodded. Drake caught his attention. 'Is there a back way out of here?'

'Out of the building, yes. Out of the site, no. You will have to go through the main gates.'

Drake had expected that. He was first through the door, checking the corridor both ways. Except for his own team, it was clear, but he could hear voices approaching from the front. His eyes switched to the back.

'Let's move,' he said.

They all ran out into the corridor, Alicia pushing Bushida before her. They formed a long line as they raced for the back door. Soon, Shaw, at the rear, yelled that she could see the approaching gang.

'Don't shoot,' she shouted. 'We have your boss!'

They probably knew that already, but it didn't hurt to remind them. Drake reached the back door and found it locked. He booted it open and ran outside, eyes flitting in all directions. His gun was ready, but he spied no one. So far, so good.

Then Shaw screamed.

CHAPTER THIRTY THREE

Shaw's voice rang out above all else.

'Engaging!'

There were no gunshots, so Drake assumed it was a knife or fist fight. Cam was back there with Shaw, and so were Kenzie and even Mai. He quickly scanned the area. What to do next?

Another two men were coming in through the front gate. They spied Drake and, probably not understanding what was going on, drew their weapons and aimed at him. Drake saw the way out cut off.

He ducked into cover. No gunshots came. Shaw and Cam were fighting at the back of the line. He had to give them some respite. The others were squeezing out of the back door, and now came Mai. Despite all that was happening, she couldn't help but give Bushida a look laced with hatred.

Drake, in cover, peered around a corner towards the front gate. The two men were inching their way forward, guns drawn, and were probably just twenty seconds away from Drake's position. A crunch was coming. Quickly, he decided what to do. He grabbed Bushida and shoved the man around the corner into view.

'Lower your weapons,' he shouted.

Took a look. Saw both men put their weapons on the floor and back away. Now, he motioned for Alicia to grab Bushida again and started making his way towards the front gates. The team followed. Now Cam and Shaw appeared, their arms and wrists bloody, still fending off men and women with knives. They fell out of the corridor into the open, spread out a bit. Their enemies streamed after them.

'We have your boss,' Dahl cried out. 'Back off!'

The attackers hesitated. There was clearly an unmistakable hierarchy here, a pecking order hanging over the gang members, for they saw Bushida in captivity and backed off. Drake watched the front gates. So far, they remained clear. He sensed that the stalemate was being stretched thin, at breaking point. All it would take was one wrong move.

Thick tension blanketed the scene. Alicia pushed Bushida along gently, still nibbling his ribs with the point of her knife. Drake led the way. The others followed in a long line. Drake also saw a couple of workers peering out of the garage, crouched so low they could be on their knees. Amid a thick soup of pressure and apprehension, he pressed forward.

Drake now counted at least twenty of the enemy. He saw guns and knives, could hear their tense breathing. Every time he moved, he was ready to duck and cover. Alicia kept her knife close to Bushida's ribs.

He neared the gates. Far away, across the road and the parking area, he could now see their parked cars, an uplifting sight. All they had to do was get there. The gates loomed invitingly. Drake reached them without incident. Maybe, just maybe, they would get out of this without incident after all.

Even as the thought flitted through his mind, he

noticed movement ahead. Two more gang members had just pulled up and were exiting their car. They saw Drake leaving the compound and didn't react at first. They started running, not looking at him. Then they saw the rest of the team and Bushida himself.

They stopped in their tracks, pulling up like sharply reined horses.

Drake watched them closely and saw their hands whipping swiftly towards their guns.

'We have your-' he began.

It was no use. The men weren't listening, just acting on instinct. Or maybe it was the language barrier. They saw their boss in trouble and they wanted to help. They pulled their guns out, aimed at Alicia and the others around Bushida, and opened fire.

Drake felt the taut stalemate break. Suddenly, everyone was going for their guns. The Ghost Squadron reacted instantly, diving for cover. Parked cars, oil drums, and two skips dotted the area. Drake ducked behind a car.

Gunshots rang out, dozens of them. Bullets riddled the air. Drake's team contented themselves by getting into cover. Alicia dragged Bushida with her, holding his head down. Lead smashed and clanged and deflected off metal, iron and steel.

Drake aimed his own gun, peered around the car, and fired off a shot. His bullet missed, but it was good to return fire. It gave their enemy something to worry about. Further away, Dahl and Kinimaka were crouched precariously behind an oil drum, trying to hide their bulks. Drake could see Kenzie and Shaw too, standing easily behind a large skip. The others were dotted around elsewhere.

Bushida's people yelled at each other and swore

and urged themselves on. They knew they had the numbers, but didn't want to hit their boss. No fire was directed at Alicia. Drake took another shot and hit his man in the chest, taking the enemy down. By now, the others were returning fire, too. The gang members hadn't thought to run to cover yet; they were still out in the open, and thus three took bullets to the chest in as many seconds. There was no leadership among their enemies, no direction; it was a basic free-for-all. Drake knew his own team would take advantage of that.

They did so now, ducking out and firing off shots, tagging the Tsugarai. Men and women with guns fell and twisted, crying out in pain. There were a lot of bodies on the floor. Alicia made Bushida watch it.

'Call them off.'

'You wouldn't understand.'

'They're your friends.'

'They work for me and, if they need to, they will die for me. They are not friends. That is not the Tsugarai way. As I said, you would not understand.'

'I understand one thing,' Alicia said. 'If you don't try to call them off, I'm gonna introduce your guts to the edge of my blade.'

'You can't kill me.'

'I think I'll do it, anyway.' Alicia steadied the knife in her right hand, preparing to thrust it forward.

'Whaaaat? *Wait!* You need me to give you the reaper.'

'But you won't even do that. You're of no use to us now. Might as well ditch the garbage.'

Bushida pulled away from her immediately, stuck his head out into the open. 'Stop!' he yelled. 'Stop firing!'

As if a curtain dropped over the Tsugarai, they did. There was a sudden lull. Drake had watched as Bushida stuck his head out, wincing. Now, he looked left and right at the long sprawl of their enemy. They were well spread out, and utterly untrustworthy. If they stepped out, Drake knew they'd be in the crosshairs of over a dozen people. But they couldn't just stay here.

Alicia looked over at him, spread her arms. Drake knew she was asking that they move, but didn't like it. There was no easy way out of here. He could see Hayden now too, and she just shrugged at him. The ceasefire stretched for another minute.

Bushida turned to Alicia. 'What are you going to do?' he spoke the words with a smirk on his face.

Alicia realised she might have messed up. Calling for the ceasefire hadn't really helped at all. She wondered what the hell they were supposed to do next.

It was an odd position to be in, Drake reflected. One option was to start the firefight again. Weirdly, that might be the safer alternative. The other was to trust that they could walk out of here with Bushida and not get fired on. Not only did they have to stay alive, but Bushida also had to.

Drake steeled himself and made the decision. They were walking out of here. Using the comms system, he conferred with Hayden, who agreed. As one, they readied themselves. Drake stepped out into the open.

'We're walking out of here,' he yelled, and heard his words being translated into Japanese by several people. 'With your boss. If you try to stop us, he dies.'

Drake glanced at Alicia and nodded. The whole team took that as a sign. As one, they all came out into the open, still holding their guns. The ceasefire held. Drake walked over to Alicia, stood close to Bushida as if emphasising his point, head always on a swivel.

They didn't group up too much, not wanting to present an easy target. They started carefully towards the gates. Every step of the way, an arsenal pointed at them, each barrel holding their lives in its small circumference. A blanket of silence hung over the scene, so quiet that Drake figured he could hear the faint squeak of a mouse.

They approached the gates, nearing freedom. Alicia had a tight hold of Bushida just in case he tried to run. Mai was within the group, wisely trying to stay incognito at this point. Just as Drake took another cautious step, one of the gang members rose and shouted out.

'Tsugarai! Attack!'

The enemy threw down their guns and burst into action. They flew at the Ghost Squadron, at least fifteen of them, their arms out, legs pumping. Drake wasn't phased and didn't lose a second. He aimed his gun at the runners.

'Stop!'

They didn't. He shot one man point blank in the chest, another in a thigh, a woman in the calf. By then, they were upon him, on the whole team, and a mass brawl broke out. Fists flew. Legs kicked out. Heads butted heads. People slammed into each other. Drake saw Dahl throw a man from left to right, saw him wrap an arm around another, and haul him off the ground. He saw Kinimaka pound on the head of a man as if trying to hammer him into the ground. Cam traded solid blows with a woman who knew martial arts and was giving him the runaround. Shaw was engaged with another woman who brandished a knife. Kenzie was struggling with two attackers, whipping from one to the other, barely able to fend them both off. Hayden and Alicia were battling three between them, darting left and right. Mai was up against two more, her skills showing as she made mincemeat of them.

Drake slammed his fist into a man's chest just as he saw Bushida try to make a break for it. The gang leader was in the clear, looking surprised, and trying to run back towards the main building. Drake threw himself at the guy with an outstretched leg, sent him face-planting the ground.

That would do for now.

Another man came at Drake, fists flying. He ducked left and right, struck out, missed. The guy punched him in the stomach and Drake folded straight into an upcoming knee. He saw stars. His nose started bleeding. The attacker sent another punch down on the back of his neck.

Drake staggered. This guy was fast and punched almost as hard as Cam. Drake decided on something new, fell purposely to his knees, and waited for the attacker to readjust. There were a few moments of stasis.

Enough for Drake to get his gun up. 'Run,' he said fairly. 'Or die.'

The attacker came at him. Drake had given him a fair chance. Now, he shot him squarely in the chest and wiped blood from his nose. He ducked another swing from another arm, tried to shrug off the pain and discomfort. The rest of his team were still engaged in the brawl.

They fought inside the Tsugarai's yard, a complicated mass of bodies throwing punches and kicks, and trying to grab and throw each other. Around Dahl and Kinimaka, the Tsugarai flew through the air, hitting each other and their colleagues, spinning off them and landing on spines or necks. Some of them didn't get up. Around Mai, they twisted and fell as she danced through them with her knife, rotating and whirling and striking, swift and true. She left a heap in her wake. Alicia and Kenzie struck hard, fast, taking out their opponents with barely a sweat. Hayden had her back to the wall, but Cam lunged in, fists pummelling like windmills, taking out her opponent in four devastating strikes.

Drake saw the Tsugarai herd thinning.

He took the opportunity to grab the prone Bushida by the neck, haul him to his feet. Now they would have the chance to...

Shots rang out. The last of the Tsugarai were getting desperate. Shaw yelled as a bullet zipped past her face. Hayden saw wood chips explode from the crate at her left shoulder. Drake ducked, but still felt an impact.

He blinked, shook himself. There was no pain. He was unhurt. What the hell? He had definitely felt... then it came to him. The impact he'd felt had passed through Bushida's body.

Drake cursed. Bushido slumped in his grip. Someone had shot their boss by mistake. The bullet had passed through the man's heart and ripped out the other side, travelling on. Bushida had died instantly.

Now we're fucked, Drake thought.

And he didn't mean right here and now. He meant in their hunt for the reaper. Bushida had been their last hope, and he had known what to do. They had come all this way for one man, one last hope, and now that man, that hope, had died.

The team sprang into action, taking out the shooters with extreme prejudice. Drake could see the new anger on all their faces.

He let Bushida slump to the ground, his nostrils filled with the stench of blood. One last Tsugarai remained standing, one whom Mai used her knife on, cutting in three different directions.

The team stood in the aftermath, stunned.

And they couldn't hang around here. They had to move. Not all the Tsugarai were dead. As they came to, they would only start causing more problems. Drake signalled his team should exit the place.

As one, they ran through the gates, leaving the carnage behind; the Tsugarai beaten.

Their last hope shot dead.

CHAPTER THIRTY FOUR

We've exhausted our lines of enquiry, Drake thought.

They weren't sure what to do, where to go, so they had returned to their hotel and, because it was only a little after three p.m., decided to drown their sorrows in the bar. Not a full on session, of course, just a few drinks to take the edge off.

First they had showered, cleansed their bodies of other people's blood, then, armed with a plethora of bruises and cuts, joined up at a corner table from which they could see anyone coming.

'We can't move before we have a plan,' Hayden said. 'That's a given.'

It made sense, Drake thought. Knowing their luck lately they'd fly from Tokyo to Miami, only to find they had to return to Tokyo again.

'The Tsugarai boss who put the contract out is now dead,' Kinimaka said. 'That's a different scenario.'

'But there's no way to stop the contract,' Mai said. 'Something we've been told several times.'

'Our focus now has to return to the Devil's Reaper,' Dahl said.

'That's where it's been for most of the time,' Drake said. 'Hasn't done us a bit of good so far.'

'It will,' Mai told him. 'Have faith.'

'Are you kidding, Sprite?' Alicia sighed, already on her second beer. 'It's got us nowhere from the beginning.'

They were all in a glum mood. Drake found he was far too despondent to lighten it. He swigged his own beer, wondering what state Alicia would end up in. To be fair, when it came to alcohol, she appeared to be a sponge.

'The contract will go on,' Mai said. 'Our only option is to go for the big one. We have to stop the Devil's Reaper herself.'

Drake was tempted to say *that's what we've been trying to do,* but knew it wasn't constructive. They would get nowhere with negativity. The fact remained that people had to work for the reaper; they had to stay in touch with her. People had to contact her in some way, even meet up with her. There simply had to be other avenues.

With no options, the team contacted Karin, wondering if anything new had turned up. Karin answered the phone on the third ring, sounding bleary. Drake hadn't realised it would be early morning in her part of the world.

'Sorry we woke you,' he said.

'It's no problem. I can barely sleep anyway. There are guards, you know, in my house. It's all I can do to keep them out of my bedroom.'

Drake felt the guilt twist in his stomach. 'Sorry about that.'

'Oh, I wasn't trying to guilt trip you, sorry. It was just an observation. Anyway, how can I help?'

Drake briefly explained the new predicament. They needed a way forward, something new to get their teeth into.

'There may be one chance,' Karin said after a while. 'But it's a long shot. A Hail Mary, really.'

'We're all ears,' Alicia said. 'All of us.'

'Right. Well, they recently captured the men who murdered Andrea Agneson. Remember, the woman who was shot in the bar? Three men were involved, apparently. They have them in a prison in Texas.'

'Texas?'

'After the murder in London, they were quickly on a plane to Texas. Captured on the tarmac. Cops used facial rec and all sorts of high-tech stuff.'

'Aren't they just worker ants?' Dahl asked dismally. 'Working for some boss who would really have the info we need.'

'Maybe, maybe not,' Karin said. 'The three men are part of a biker gang called the Draco Riders. They're big around Texas, well known. Into the usual shit. Probably a hundred strong, maybe more. A lot more. They're well respected among the other gangs out there.'

'And the three men?'

'Unknown where they stand in the hierarchy. Yes, they may be small fry, but they might also be players. This was a job for the reaper. Would you really send your small fry out to complete a job like that?'

Drake perked up. It was a good point. 'Do you think you can get us special dispensation to talk to them?'

'We're a federal agency... yeah, I think I can do that.'

Drake checked his watch. It was a little after five p.m. Karin was offering them a way forward, but it was extremely limited. He worried they were grabbing at straws, maybe playing into the reaper's hands. Was this what the monster wanted them to do?

'Talking to captured prisoners who happen to be part of a biker gang sounds pretty desperate,' Mai said.

'We took out all the Tsugarai,' Dahl said. 'Their leader's dead. Their organisation is in complete disarray if not destroyed. Where else can we go from this point?'

Mai inclined her head in agreement. Dahl raised a good argument, and it was one Drake had already contemplated.

'To Texas,' Kenzie said.

Hayden was already on her phone, looking for plane tickets. Drake felt a shudder, having that same feeling he'd felt coming to Tokyo. Did the reaper want them on that plane? *All* of them? It was all he could do not to voice his feelings aloud. He wouldn't feel safe until they landed.

'There's a flight early tomorrow,' Hayden said, looking up expectantly. 'Are we on it?'

Drake nodded his head. 'We're on it.'

CHAPTER THIRTY FIVE

The plane touched down safely near Austin, Texas. It was around eight thirty in the morning and the team was starving. Their appointment at the prison wasn't until 2 p.m. that afternoon and they had a little time to kill. They found a diner and ate and drank well and were then on their way to the prison. It was a long drive, but the vehicles they'd hired soon ate the miles up.

Drake noticed as soon as the prison came into sight. It was a modern affair, all right angles and high fences and thick tree-borders. They passed into the parking area and were soon seen into the lobby where they obtained day passes. They had dispensation to question all three members of the biker gang, but the governor had granted the permission to just Drake and Hayden. The others were forced to cool their heels in the lobby.

First, they walked through the prison and then found themselves directed to an interview room. They sat on one side of a bare white table, waiting for the first biker to be brought in. When the door opened, Drake saw a forty-something man with a haggard face and lank hair. The newcomer, a guy named Foster, licked his lips constantly as if his life depended on it.

The guy was seated, and then the guards withdrew. Hayden started the questioning. 'You killed several people in the U.K. You're waiting to be extradited. We were hoping you might answer a few simple questions.'

'Why should I?'

'Well, considering your position, how could it hurt?'

The guy spread his arms as far as his cuffs would allow. 'Good point.'

Hayden leaned forward to grab his attention. 'We know your target was Andrea Agneson,' she said.

Foster's eyes widened, and he licked his lips some more. He seemed at a loss for words. Hayden pressed her advantage.

'We also know who paid you to do the job.'

Foster closed his lips tightly apart from the flicking tongue.

'Will you talk to us? Tell us about the Devil's Reaper? How she contacts you. How you contact *her*.'

Following her every word, Foster fought hard to remain impassive. Hayden did her best to cajole him, to draw him out, and then Drake tried, asking with a little more venom. Foster swayed and looked scared but, ultimately, said nothing. The biker's faith, and his gang's culture, would not let him rat anyone out. Through the next half hour, they gained nothing.

The second biker was a man named Clement, and he turned out to be just as tight-lipped as Foster. This man had to be a world-class poker player, because his face betrayed nothing at all, not even when Drake mentioned the reaper's name. Of course, these bikers had nothing to lose, and Drake had nothing to offer them. They were dredging the last dregs of hope here.

The third biker was a man named Hamilton. He

was a long-haired, slim-shouldered rake of a man with a stoop. He sat and listened to them and smiled the whole time, giving them little but attitude. When Hayden mentioned the reaper's name, he laughed.

'She's a star, to be sure. All attitude mixed with sexiness and confidence. Really makes you wanna meet her, if you know what I mean. If I met her, I'd love to-'

'By all accounts, if you messed with her, she'd rip your balls off,' Hayden said.

Hamilton grinned. 'There's no other woman like her.'

'Oh, I know a few women like that,' Hayden also grinned.

Hamilton looked a little put out. 'I know how to contact her.'

Oh, how he played and he played them and kept leading them on. Dropping constant references to the reaper and how to contact her until Drake and Hayden decided he knew nothing. They had lucked out. It had been a long shot, anyway. Within minutes of making their decision, they had sent Hamilton back to his cell and were on their way out of the main prison with stooped shoulders. Along the way, they didn't even speak.

In the lobby, they shared gloomy glances with their colleagues. There were no words. It was obvious what had happened. The team sat for a while, making the area their own, and grabbed themselves coffees or water from the various machines. Still, they didn't speak, all lost in their own thoughts.

Nothing seemed to work. Nothing they did brought them closer to the reaper. Had the woman bested them, after all? Would she soon come for them? And what could they do about it?

Drake finally broke the silence. 'I don't often say this, but I'm all out of ideas. These murderers were really our last shot. How about we go searching on the Dark Web?'

'And look for what?' Hayden asked. 'She won't be an obvious contact. And Karin's already covered all that.'

'The Tsugarai might still know something,' Mai said. 'The survivors. I volunteer to go back and question all of them.'

'Bushida was our last shot,' Dahl said. 'Our best shot. And the bastard went and got himself killed. We know, by now, that the reaper only deals with the upper echelons of these crime syndicates, or whatever. It's one of her barricades.'

'Have any of the other murderers been caught?' Kenzie asked.

Hayden shook her head. 'Not that Karin has mentioned.'

'I'm surprised to be saying this,' Alicia said suddenly. 'But I think I may have an idea.'

Mai glared at her. 'Don't be stupid.'

'Well, I admit it's a long shot. But that's all we've got left, right? Do you remember when I was part of that biker gang?'

Drake frowned and cast his mind back. It had been a few years ago, but Alicia had run with a gang of bikers for quite some time. 'Lomas, right?' he asked.

'Yeah, I was with Lomas. Him and his entire gang. Well, they were an important group, famous even. They're kind of legendry in the biker world. And I got quite a reputation among them.'

Drake tried not to grin. He should have known that.

'So you were famous for shagging a biker,' Kenzie

said flatly. 'I'm guessing he was your boss. So what?'

'Funny,' Alicia gave her the finger, and then blinked. 'Actually, he was technically my boss. But... hey... what I'm saying is I'm famous among a legendary group of bikers. Maybe, just maybe, that might mean something to the hierarchy of the Draco Riders.'

Drake frowned. The biker family around the world was pretty tight-knit. Once you were in, though, you were in for life unless you betrayed them. Alicia had betrayed no one, just stepped away when Lomas died. In fact, her old biker gang was still very active, and could probably put in a good word for her.

'Would that be enough for the Draco Riders?' he wondered aloud.

'It's gotta be worth a try,' Alicia said.

The team decided it *was* worth a try. They left the prison facility in a hurry and listened to Alicia make calls as they sat waiting in the parking area. First, she contacted the old biker gang, identified herself, and shot the shit for half an hour. It was only when she'd verified who she was by passing a few old stories along that the man she was talking to, a man named Jaz, agreed to listen to her request. Alicia asked him if he could introduce her to the Draco Riders, pass along good words, and ask for their help. She wanted to meet them as an equal, as a preferred colleague, anything so long as they would listen seriously to her request. Jaz told her he'd make the call and signed off. They then made a few internet enquiries and found that the chapter of the Draco Riders they needed was based in L.A. Hayden found flights and they were off to the airport. Once there, they waited around for a while, cooling their heels. By the time they were at the gate and then on the flight, Jaz still hadn't called back. It was hours later, as they strode through LAX, that Alicia's phone started to ring.

'Jaz?' she answered quickly.

'Sure. I spoke to the Dracos. They know of us and our reputation. Our name is good with them. Got you an introduction with their big figurehead, the president. Man named Perdomo. He'll see you tomorrow.' Jaz reeled off an address. 'They know you're coming, Alicia. Only you. And I can only do so much over the phone. Be careful.'

Alicia thanked Jaz and looked up, met the eyes of her friends. 'I have a meet arranged with the Dracos,' she said. 'The president himself. If anyone has info that'll lead us to the reaper, it's him.'

'And you think a kind of biker's code will make him tell all?' Mai asked.

'It might,' Alicia said. 'The bikers hold that stuff pretty close, the ones that matter anyway. We can only hope the Dracos follow the code. And, to be fair, they have so far. They agreed to Jaz's request.'

Drake didn't like it, but they were all out of options. Alicia's idea was way out of leftfield, but it had merit. It just might work.

'Depends on the morals of a biker gang,' Kenzie whistled. 'Good luck.'

'They may be morally corrupt,' Alicia said. 'But I ran with them for months. There are some good men and women among them, people with big hearts and strict codes. If Perdomo is a strict biker advocate, he might put a biker's need, and creed, above the reaper.'

Drake looked at Alicia, saw the new danger she was

in, the peril that she bore on her shoulders without a word of complaint. She would do this for the team, for those who'd died, and to save future victims. And she wouldn't hold an inch of herself back.

Drake felt as close to her as he ever had done.

CHAPTER THIRTY SIX

With the sun beating down on her shoulders, Alicia Myles walked towards the black, wrought-iron gates that stood at the top of the driveway. She gave her name to the guy on the gate and was admitted through a side entrance. Then she had to walk all the way along the twisting driveway to the front doors of the house. It was a two storey extra-wide Mission Revival style with stucco walls, low-pitched red-clay covered tiled roofs, archways and parapets. Alicia slowed as she approached the high front door. So far, she had seen no sign of life other than the guard at the gate.

Then the door opened wide. A long-haired biker wearing a black leather jacket and sporting colourful arm tattoos emerged and nodded at her.

'Gotta search you,' he said. 'Don't hate me.'

She wondered if his words meant he knew of her reputation. She hoped so. She felt very alone right now. There was no backup, no cavalry. Alicia would live or die here today on her own skill-set. Drake and the others were sitting in a car somewhere about ten minutes away. Her comms had been disabled, and she carried no weapons.

The long-haired biker came forward and motioned that she should hold her hands out to the sides. The guy patted her down in a perfunctory manner, playing with fire. But, luckily for him, he wasn't too handsy, and Alicia had to play the game. She stood and waited until he was done, stepped away, and gave her a nod.

'You're good.'

'I know that.'

The guy nodded and let her in through the front door. She found herself in a wide, sparkling white lobby with a two-winged staircase ahead leading up to the first floor. The biker led her to the right and into a vast room where there were several bikers going about their business. One sat behind a desk, rifling through paperwork. Another looked to be sorting brown packages. Three more were standing over a table laden with weapons. Another biker had a sobbing man in his grasp and was threatening him with an iron bar. All wore leather jackets with the name "Draco Riders" on the back.

Alicia followed her guide. They left the room, went through another where men and women lounged and played card games and drank beer. There was a pool table in one corner, a row of video games in another. This must be the chill room then. Alicia didn't hold anyone's eyes, just let her gaze sweep through. So far, she'd counted fifteen bikers and, judging by the size of the house, there were dozens more.

Finally, they came to a closed door. Two large men stood outside, both with guns visible in their hands. They wore the generic leather jacket with nothing underneath, so their chests were bared. They shifted when the long-haired biker approached.

'She's here,' he said.

One of the men nodded, looked her over. 'I don't like the look of her. Have you searched the bitch?'

Alicia gritted her teeth but said nothing. Her hands curled into fists, but she forced them to loosen, kept her gaze neutral. She stared at a space between the two men as her guide vouched for her.

'Perdomo's waiting for you,' the guard told her. 'Be a good little bitch.'

That was it. Alicia felt herself unleashing, her fists and arms striking out, her body clenched for the fight. This guy was going to suffer more broken bones in a millisecond than he'd ever thought possible... .but somehow, some way, she managed to hold off, to hang on to her passivity. She didn't move a muscle, just let the scenario of violence run through her mind.

Long hair stared at her. 'Are you okay?'

She hadn't moved. The door was open. Now, she barged her way past the two guards and entered the room, stopping just beyond the door. She had to let her anger go. It would do her no good in here.

A man sat behind a wooden desk. He was bald, broad shouldered and tanned. His face was deeply lined, but in a regal way. He rose to his feet when she walked in, held out a hand. Alicia noticed he was well-muscled and moved with grace.

'Perdomo,' he said. 'Have they treated you well?'

Alicia covered her surprise at the question, at the man's soft voice. 'Fine,' she nodded. 'Nothing I can't handle.'

Perdomo waved her to a seat. 'Sit down. What can I do for you?'

Alicia glanced around the room as she sat. There was paperwork on a side desk, a computer, a pile of hardback books. It really wasn't the kind of office she'd been expecting. And in truth, Perdomo wasn't the kind of man she'd been expecting.

'You were one of us?' Perdomo suddenly asked.

Alicia nodded. 'A biker, yes. I guess Jaz filled you in. Lomas and I ran together for quite a while until he died.'

'Is that why you left the chapter?'

'They say I never left,' Alicia said with a smile. 'I could go back any time.'

Perdomo nodded, his bald head catching the artificial light in the room. 'Jaz said that too. You're very well respected, which is why I agreed to this meeting. Those who leave are normally outcast.'

'Special circumstances,' Alicia said. 'The team I'm with now saved many lives. We all did. Those were... hard times.'

Perdomo waved it off. He leaned back now, his leather chair squeaking. Alicia was glad to see he at least wore something under the ubiquitous leather jacket, even if it was only a white t-shirt.

'What can I do for you?' he asked again.

Alicia prepared to get into the nitty gritty. She had to remind herself that, despite Perdomo's pleasant appearance and manner, he ordered murders, dealt in drugs and ran guns across state lines. He was still a criminal.

'Recently, some of your people may have been involved in a murder,' she tried to stay on the diplomatic side of accusation. 'Of a woman named Andrea Agneson. Now, I mention those details only for clarity. I don't need denials or confirmations. What I'm looking for is the person who ordered that attack. I need to contact her, to find her.'

Perdomo narrowed his eyes. 'Her? So you know who we're dealing with?'

'The Devil's Reaper,' Alicia said. 'I... we... know her and have to reach her.'

'For what reason?'

Alicia bit her lip. This was where she lived or died. They had decided, because of her reputation in the biker community, to go with the truth. She took some time now to explain more of the reaper's history, who she was, what she did, who her mentor had been. She described several atrocities. And she ended up by explaining that she and her team – the same team that had helped Lomas' biker gang – were under direct threat and had had several of their old friends murdered. Alicia couldn't lay it out any clearer than that, and she hoped Perdomo respected her for it.

'That's quite a story,' he said after a while. He leaned back and stared up at the ceiling. 'And you say I murdered people to help the reaper?'

At least he wasn't denying her existence or his involvement. Alicia spread her hands. 'I'm not trying to hide anything here, and neither are you. We're both bikers, at the end of everything, bound by honour. I'm just asking for help.'

It didn't sit quite right with her though – asking for help from a gang who'd organised the murder of an old friend. She knew the Draco Riders hadn't killed anyone with prejudice against her; they were just following orders. The reaper's orders.

'You want the reaper,' Perdomo whistled softly. 'To contact her and then, I assume, to somehow engineer a face to face?'

'Something like that,' Alicia said. 'The reaper won't stop coming after us, so we have to go after her.'

'On the attack,' Perdomo mused. 'I like it.'

Alicia inclined her head, waiting with bated breath.

'If anyone else came in here asking this question, do you know what I would do to them?'

Alicia now saw the shark smile beneath the placid face, the visage of a man who knew how to kill. 'I know.' She said.

'I respect the creed,' Perdomo said. 'Some chapters these days, they run alone. They respect no one. Nothing. Some have no honour. Some even see other chapters as rivals. That is not the way with the Draco Riders. We have honour and we expect to receive it in return.'

'You have spoken with Jaz,' Alicia said, reminding him of her credentials.

'Of course. But what you are asking – it is huge.'

'You can't be scared of the reaper.'

'Scared? No, that is a stupid word. But do I fear what she could do? Do if fear what would happen if you fail and she finds out it was I who gave her away? Yes, I fear that.'

'She won't find out,' Alicia said.

Perdomo just smiled. 'They always find out.'

'You're our last hope.' Alicia let it slip out. She didn't want to sound so desperate, but they were living on the edge here, all out of moves.

'Are you going to kill her?'

Alicia hesitated. Just to hear it spoken that way – it was cold, harsh, callous. It made her take a step back and reevaluate. Finally, she said, 'We have no choice. We have to take her out before she kills anyone else we care about, and then us, of course. We're slated to be the last course in her deadly banquet.'

'Do you want to draw her out?' Perdomo's face took on an even more shark-like grin.

'You can do that?'

'We're high on the food chain. We have a way.'

'You can get her to a certain place at a certain time?'

Perdomo nodded. 'Yes.'

'I couldn't ask for more.'

'I could,' Perdomo said.

Alicia narrowed her eyes, wondering what was coming. Perdomo had them over a barrel. He could literally ask for anything. 'What do you want?' she asked.

'The hardest thing to give me.'

Alicia didn't say anything, just looked him in the eye.

Perdomo got to his feet, walked over to the window and looked out. Alicia watched him. After a long moment, he looked back at her.

'I want you to kill the reaper.'

Alicia felt surprised. 'Why?'

'Because I am honour bound to give you what you need, and by doing that, I am opening myself up to her wrath. My only way out of this is for you to kill her.'

'She will recognise you by the method you use to draw her out,' Alicia said. 'I understand.'

'When you meet her,' Perdomo said. 'Do not miss.'

Alicia looked him dead in the eye. 'We never do,' she said.

CHAPTER THIRTY SEVEN

When Alicia walked out unscathed, Drake drew a huge sigh of relief. She gave them a brief call, asked to be picked up, and soon they were driving through the manic Los Angeles traffic to a discreet hotel where they could camp out in the lobby. They knew Alicia had something juicy for them, but didn't want to ask until they were all together, in a safe and relaxed place.

It was an hour before they found somewhere suitable.

Drake sat on a leather couch opposite her, noting she looked unmarked. He had been worried they would hurt her in some way. She had, in effect, walked alone into a lion's den. It hadn't been easy for any of them. But now she was here, and she was fine.

'Did you get anything?' Hayden asked first.

Alicia couldn't keep the smile off her face. 'I got it all,' she said.

'A way to take down the reaper?' Kinimaka asked.

'Everything,' Alicia said. 'Now, listen up. The president of the Draco Riders believes in the biker's creed. He's honour bound to help us. But in doing so, he's exposing himself and his gang. The reaper will know it's him who set her up. She... has to die.'

'Wasn't that the idea, anyway?' Mai said.

'We always try capture first,' Hayden said.

'Not this time,' Alicia said. 'The reaper is the worst kind of evil. You all know what she's capable of, even before she turned her attention to us. We'll be doing the world a favour by getting rid of her.'

Drake nodded. 'I agree. She's the worst kind of scum.'

'So what did Perdomo tell you?' Dahl asked.

Alicia sat forward. 'There's a way to draw the reaper out. To actually get her to meet you face to face. Nobody ever uses it, of course, because they don't want or need that kind of heat. Plus, she always completes her job. But... if needs be... there's a way.'

'And that is?' Masi prompted.

Alicia took a breath. 'You put out a news story that archaeologists have found what they're calling a stairway to hell in Arizona. There's a guy who's been paid off who will run that for us. Just run it in a particular paper. I'm guessing the reaper has people who monitor that paper and will pass the message on to her.'

The team were all staring at her as if wanting more. Finally, Drake said, 'Is that it?'

'What else do you want to hear? It's an answer to our problems. This is our chance for a face to face with the bloody reaper.'

'But where's the face to face?' Kenzie asked.

'Highway one,' Alicia said. 'A diner called Morrigan's at high noon, three days after the news article runs.'

'High noon?' Drake repeated. 'Shit.'

'And the reaper just turns up there?' Mai asked.

Alicia shrugged. 'Nobody's done it before, so no one knows. But that's how Perdomo sees it.'

'She'll be expecting a trap,' Dahl said.

'Not necessarily,' Alicia shrugged. 'Yeah, she'll be wary, but you'd expect that. She won't be expecting the Ghost Squadron to come crashing down on her.'

'You have the details,' Hayden said. 'You're sure he's being honest?'

'As I can be.'

'Then let's run the damn story. Draw her out and end this. Before anyone else gets hurt.'

'I agree,' Alicia said and pulled out her phone. 'Perdomo gave me the reporter's contact details.'

CHAPTER THIRTY EIGHT

Three days later, Matt Drake was lying in wait.

It was only ten o'clock, and they were early. Purposely so. The newspaper article had run without issue, no questions asked. They had to assume the reaper would get the message.

They were positioned all around the diner. They were in it, behind it on the low bluffs, in the parking area across the road. Everyone had splendid views.

The diner sat off Highway One in Los Angeles, with low hills ranging behind it and the blacktop highway running in front of it. Beyond the highway lay the beach and then the ocean. People just pulled straight into diner's car park off the highway, parked up, and wandered in through the glass front doors. The diner was long and low, with rectangular windows and a red sign that read *Morrigan's*, and a pitched roof. It had steps leading up to the front door, a dozen signs for the best beer in the west, and a big A-board with specials standing outside. It was a busy old place. Drake and the others had come here three times in as many days, and they felt they knew the layout as well as anyone.

Drake was inside with Alicia. The two shared a small square table. Around them, dozens of patrons filled the place, causing a loud hubbub. Waiters and waitresses dressed in yellow with red pinafores threaded through the tables, loaded down with plates and drinks. The bar area was full, truckers and single folk sipping drinks and eating plates of pancakes and donuts. Drake kept his eyes on the door, well aware that they were extremely early.

Across the highway, he could see the distant figures of Dahl, Kinimaka and Hayden, stood waiting, surveilling the area. Slightly above and behind them, and with an easy path down, he knew Mai, Kenzie, Cam and Shaw were lying prone with monoculars, looking down over the diner and giving a running commentary on who was driving up and who was about to come through the door. Would the reaper send a recce team first? Would she fill the place with her guards? Would she turn up in an SUV, a car, a truck? There were a ton of questions, and their survival depended on them being at least able to answer a proportion of them.

Drake toyed with his food. It was cold by now, anyway. He drank the coffee, getting refill after refill, and then getting a little jittery because he was high on caffeine. They all carried their weapons, fully loaded Glocks with lots of spare mags. They all carried knives, too.

Karin had initially been wary of the showdown. A high noon showdown wasn't the best scenario, and the diner was frequented by thousands of civilians. But they had argued that this was not just their best chance to catch the reaper, it was their *only* chance. And soon, very soon, the reaper would be coming for them.

This turned the tables. It put them on the attack.

And they had prepped as well as they possibly could. They were just waiting now.

Waiting for high noon.

Time passed incredibly slowly. Drake ate a little bacon, drank more coffee, ignored the bill that the waitress had placed prominently on the table. He was worried.

'There are too many people in here,' he said, both to Alicia and through the comms system they had in their ears. 'When the reaper arrives, we must get her outside.'

He looked through the window to the front of the diner, saw a wide collection of vehicles parked there, from cars to trucks and vans, all baking under the morning sun. It was a beautiful day, and Drake could see the top of the ocean sparkling in the distance as it rolled and swayed. He checked his watch.

10.30.

They waited. They checked their weapons, watches, spare mags time and time again, watched out for anything untoward. As far as they could tell, the reaper hadn't sent anyone ahead, hadn't surveyed the area, the diner. Drake wondered just how many guards she would turn up with.

It didn't matter. They had to take her down.

'How are we gonna recognise her?' Cam asked from his place above on the bluffs.

'I don't think that'll be a problem,' Mai said. 'She'll come with an honour guard.'

'However many she brings, it won't be enough,' Alicia said.

Drake nodded. 'She's murdered our old friends, fucked up our lives. This time, she'll find out what revenge is all about.'

'And don't forget that protégé of hers,' Hayden said. 'Vicius. Don't know what he looks like, but he's going down too.'

'Don't worry,' Alicia said. 'He'll stand out like a massive-'

'Wait,' Shaw said. 'I think I see something.'

Alicia looked aggrieved at being interrupted. Drake checked the time. It was 11.45. 'What do you see?'

'In the distance for now, approaching along Highway One. Three limos, all driving close to each other. If that's the reaper, she travels in style.'

'You ruined my dick joke for that,' Alicia moaned. 'You need to get a better sense of timing, Shawnasee.'

They fell silent. They waited. Those on the bluffs reported the approach of the limos. Those near the beach came a few steps closer. Drake and Alicia got to their feet to stretch, then sat back down, ready.

'Limos approaching and slowing,' Shaw reported. 'It has to be her.'

'Don't jump to any conclusions,' Hayden said. 'Can you report what's happening in real time?'

'Sure,' Shaw said. 'All three limos are pulling into the parking area, looking for a place to stop. They're heading for the far side, where there's space, now parking so they're facing the road. They've all stopped and are waiting. Maybe getting last-minute orders. We're just waiting now.'

Long moments passed, loaded with tension. Despite the cold as ice forced air system, Drake felt a trickle of sweat slide down his spine. He held Alicia's eyes, neither of them speaking, both in the zone and ready to act. Seconds felt like hours as they waited for something to happen. All the noise in the diner fell away – the sights, the sounds, the smells. There was nothing except the space to the door, the door itself, and what might be just beyond it. Drake slowly licked his lips.

Shaw's voice came through the comms. 'Doors opening everywhere. I'm seeing guys and girls in dark suits, all climbing out at the same time. I see six, eight, ten. Still counting. One of them is opening the back door of the first limo. All are standing in place and looking around, studying the terrain as if looking for trouble. Okay, the back door is open, and a man is climbing out. Young-ish, maybe late twenties. Tall and thin, wiry. His hair is all over the place. Looks fit, mean, agile. The guards are showing him reverence. I think that could be Vicius. Wait... the guards are now headed towards the back door of the third limo. If this is a woman...'

Shaw trailed off. Drake rose and walked to a place where he could see what was happening. His gaze was obstructed, but he saw several guards in their well-cut suits, standing around the limos and surveying the immediate area. He saw the man who might be Vicius, but not much more than that. Slowly, he turned on his heel and went back to Alicia.

'It has to be her,' he said. 'She's bang on time.'

'Good,' Alicia grunted. 'Because I'm ready to do some damage.'

Shaw once again interrupted them. 'Okay, so the back door is open. There's a guard holding it, looking around, and now he's speaking to someone. Yeah, there's a figure getting out. Wait... wait for it...' Shaw trailed off.

Drake sat forward, unconsciously. Alicia cursed and told Shaw to get on with it. Across the road, Dahl, Hayden and Kinimaka were already looking for a way across.

'Oh, yeah,' Shaw said then. 'A woman is getting out. She's over six feet tall. A brunette. Hair looks styled, expensively so. Lips are bold, bright red. She's wearing black leather pants and trainers, standing tall. She's well muscled too. Looks like she can take care of herself. Striking. Eyes everywhere. Guys... that has to be her.'

Even though he'd already come to the same conclusion, Drake felt an arrow of anticipation shoot through him. Adrenalin spiked, making him ready to act.

'Doors are closed,' Shaw went on. 'The woman just made a gesture. She's headed for the diner. They all are. Total count: twelve guards, Vicius, and the reaper. I see the occasional glimpse of a Glock under their suits. We're coming down now, but I can still see them. Let me see... they're twenty seconds away... fifteen... ten... approaching the door.'

'They're here,' Alicia said softly.

CHAPTER THIRTY NINE

Drake saw the door open, saw the guards in their suits filing in. He stayed seated, hiding his face with a menu. Hayden reported that she, Dahl and Kinimaka had crossed their road and were in the parking lot. Mai reported her group was three quarters of the way down the bluff and approaching. Drake and Alicia waited in place.

The guards entered with Vicius at their centre. They headed for the counter. Finally, the reaper herself pushed through the doors and stood in place, just beyond the entrance, looking around.

Tension stretched through the diner like an unbreakable sliver of taut steel, resonating hard.

There was only one way to play this. Drake rose to his feet, pulled out his gun, and aimed it directly at the reaper.

'Outside,' he said. 'We're not doing this in here.'

The reaper turned her flawless face towards him, locking eyes. She suddenly looked put out. 'Matt Drake,' she said softly. He couldn't hear her, but could see her lips moving. 'How cool.'

Alicia now stood up too, also covering the reaper.

'And Alicia Myles,' the reaper said. 'Where's the rest of the crew?'

Drake motioned to the door with his gun. The guards could all see that he was covering the reaper. For now, they couldn't act.

All around, people were starting to see the man with the drawn gun. A woman screamed. A man went to cover his kids. This was starting to unravel.

And suddenly Vicius exploded into action. He grabbed hold of the coffee pot and launched it at Drake. The heavy glass object flew through the air, spilling coffee as it went. Drake dodged it easily, but the distraction allowed the guards to spring into action. They ran towards Drake, cutting through the tables.

They flowed through the gaps. Drake met the first with a smash on the nose, breaking it. Blood flew across the nearest table. People shrieked and tried to scramble out of the way. The next guard approached. Drake holstered his gun for now and went forward, grabbing the guard under the arms and hoisting him in the air and on top of a table, smashing him down on its surface so that it shattered. Food, plates, and crockery flew everywhere.

Alicia ran forward, also choosing not to discharge her weapon in the busy diner. She led with an elbow to a guard's throat, sent him choking to his knees. Then she span and kicked out, catching another guard in the sternum, her foot gliding over the top of the table and impacting hard with his chest. The man stopped in his tracks and went down face first, the top of his head glancing off the edge of the table.

At the door, guards surrounded the reaper, at least five of them, but they didn't reckon on enemies coming up from behind. Hayden and Dahl and Kinimaka crashed through the door, sweeping through them. The reaper herself staggered away as her guards went down under the onslaught. More guards, still standing near the bar, now rushed forward.

Dahl flung men left and right, smashing them into a bench and the front windows. Kinimaka smashed two across the tops of their heads, felling them like trees. Hayden was more subtle, but no less effective, taking out another two. Together, they made sure their moment of surprise was highly effective.

As he fought, Drake kept his eye on the reaper.

She grabbed hold of the edge of a table, steadying herself. And then she faced Hayden. Drake's friend could end it all here, a bullet to the heart, but she wouldn't fire inside a diner full of people. Not even to rid the world of one of its greatest evils.

Hayden struck at the reaper. The brunette dodged the blow and hit out; her own attack vicious and perfect. The blows staggered Hayden, made her think twice. The reaper pressed her advantage, not shying away from the fight. Hayden had to defend herself against the other woman's competent attack.

The doors flew open again, and then the rest of the Ghost Squadron was in the diner. They pinpointed guards, started fighting them. Drake and Alicia had already felled three between them, left them in groaning heaps. Now, though, the diner's patrons were getting in the way. There was a lot of screaming and crying out and shuffling away, and now some of them were getting to their feet, milling around, running between Drake and his opponents. It was a total melee, and Drake's view was blocked by rushing civilians. A man shouted in his face. A woman hauled her boyfriend out of the way. Some guy was protecting his plate of chicken and chips. Drake tried to push his way through to the fight.

The noise inside the diner was tremendous. A guard flew over the counter, clearing it by several feet, propelled by Kinimaka's arms. Dahl lifted a table, slammed it against a guard's face, sending him into dark oblivion. Cam pressed forward with a flurry of punches, taking on two men. Mai fought to find space in which she could do her thing. The diner was packed.

The reaper stared Hayden in the face, pulled out a gun and started firing high in the air, at the tops of the windows. There was a nightmare sound of glass shattering and people screaming. All the broken shards fell down like a deadly waterfall, spraying across the floor.

Hayden wrestled with the gun. Now though, other guns were being produced, the guards seeing the reaper's action as a sign. Drake's team fought to neutralise guns everywhere.

Drake reached the bar, vaulted over it just in time to grab a guard who was lining up Dahl's head in his sights. He broke the guy's wrist, kneed him in the face. He span. Another guard, on the other side of the bar, was also pulling out a weapon. Drake grabbed a steak knife and sunk it between his shoulder blades, giving him something else to think about.

The fight now fell out into the parking lot. People ran here and there, escaping to their cars. Drake's team hadn't fired a shot in the diner and didn't intend to. Hayden staggered down the steps, a guard raining blows on her. Dahl lifted another table and used it as a battering ram, forcing two guards back into a door frame so that they smashed against each other. By now, most of the guards had been injured, but not permanently taken out of the fight.

Drake ran around from behind the bar. Alicia was to his right, elbowing a guy in the knackers. Drake began to wonder if it was her trademark move. Then, abruptly, he came face to face with the reaper.

'Well played,' she said.

Drake raised his fists, then paused. 'Care to surrender?'

'You'd like me in that position, wouldn't you?'

Drake ignored the provocative way she spoke. 'Last chance to live,' he said, and somehow, despite all he'd said previously, actually meant it.

'You're going to have to take me, I'm afraid.'

Drake didn't mind that at all. He struck out at her, saw his blows deflected, tried again. She was good, dancing from side to side, meeting his attacks with grace. She assaulted him, catching him a solid blow to the ribs. He saw guards they'd felled earlier starting to get back up.

The reaper darted away from him straight for the open, shattered windows. She was a dark shape leaping through into the bright day. He glanced around, wondering if he should go after her or keep helping Alicia.

'I'm good,' the Englishwoman said, fighting two. 'Go after the bitch.'

Drake ran. On the way, he smashed a guy in the head, but the guards were starting to make their way after their boss. Drake saw one guard down and out for the count. He saw two more destroyed by Dahl and Kinimaka's joint unstoppable attack. Another man lay crumpled in the doorway, not moving. That left eight guards and Vicius still operating with the reaper.

All of them were racing for the limos.

Drake saw his team suddenly at a loss, having been

fighting opponent's hand to hand and then just forced to watch them run away.

'Get after them!' he yelled.

But the guards were already at the cars and the reaper was hurling herself inside.

CHAPTER FORTY

Drake started running after the guards, but two of the limos were already moving. Their doors were wide open. Guards leapt in on the run, legs kicking as they landed across the seats and pulled themselves inside. Drake and his team closed in on them.

The cars put on a spurt of speed. Dust and gravel flew from underneath the tyres, sending up clouds of dust. Drake ran in front of one and found himself on the bonnet, sliding off the far end and rolling away from the tyres. The cars headed for the exit to the diner's parking lot.

The Ghost Squadron surrounded the moving vehicles. They reached inside, tried to pull guards out but were harshly rejected. Doors were closed. The reaper could no longer be seen behind the smoked glass.

They were escaping.

Desperate, Drake tried all he could. He ran at the nearest car, grabbed the door handle and yanked it open. Shock coursed through his system as he was faced with the barrel of a gun. Without thinking, he threw himself to the right just as a shot rang out. The bullet missed his head by inches.

He was left kneeling in the gravel.

The cars were going to get away. Drake cursed. The reaper had left with most of her entourage intact, engineering a surprise escape. He stared after the cars now, consternation across his face.

The team was still attacking the cars, being driven back. Gunshots rang out. There was no getting close to the vehicles without risking a bullet. Both limos were now approaching the exit and soon, would be on Highway One.

And in the clear.

Drake cursed. They had come so close. The reaper would redouble her efforts now. This had actually turned out to be a disaster.

And then lady luck intervened. As the limos reached the exit of the diner, a big truck pulled across, blocking it off completely. It was open-sided, carrying several crates, and it pulled abruptly to a halt with a squeal of air brakes. The driver leaned out of his window to yell and curse but then saw the severe visages of the people who were suddenly leaping out of the limos.

Eight guards, Vicius and the reaper threw open their doors. Drake rose to his feet. The guards swarmed all over the truck, yanking open the cab doors and pulling the driver out, leaping onto the back and taking cover behind the crates. The reaper jumped into the back; Vicius took the front cab. The Ghost Squadron was racing for the truck as one.

Someone was already behind the wheel, goosing the gas pedal. The truck gave a lurch. It didn't set off right away, though. It gave a groan, its engine roared. It pitched and rocked again. The guards settled in the back.

The Ghost squadron arrived.

Without slowing, together, they leapt at the sides and doors of the truck. They were a fast-flowing stream of bodies, an unbroken flow. Dahl and Kinimaka landed a split second before the others, taking the back of the truck and hiding behind crates. Mai and Kenzie reached up for the cab door, throwing it open, followed by Cam. Drake and the rest all leapt for the truck's rear.

They landed as one, scattered. Guards were peering from behind the wooden crates, pulling out guns.

The truck roared once more and then set off. It jerked and pulled out into the traffic flow, gaining speed. Drake balanced as best he could on the balls of his feet as the air rushed past his face. Now he could take out his gun.

The truck raced through traffic, swerving from lane to lane. Drake crouched next to Alicia in the back, hidden behind a crate, taking potshots at the enemy. There were five guards back here with the reaper and three in the cab, along with Vicius. It was a bullet-laced free-for-all. Lead flew around the back of the speeding truck, slamming into the wooden crates and smashing off wood chips. Some of them whined high in the air, over the tops of the cars and heading for the ocean of the higher bluffs to the right.

In the cab, it was crowded. Mai was on her knees, lashing out at a guard, with Kenzie crammed right up against her, Cam just inches behind, still trying to pull closed the door. The driver was spinning the wheel and yelling. Vicius was seated next to him.

Vicius pulled out a gun. Mai hurled herself across her opponent's lap, batted the gun from Vicius' hand so that it rattled down into the footwell. She felt a blow to her spine, pulled herself back up and sent stiffened fingers into her opponent's throat. He rocked back. She grabbed him around the head and yanked him forward, smashing his forehead into the dash with force. She didn't let up, did it twice more. The man slumped in her arms.

Vicius was trying to climb over him to get to Mai.

Kenzie pulled her gun on the driver.

'Pull over.'

'Fuck off. At this speed, if you shoot me, we'll all die.'

It was a mad, desperate bluff, but Kenzie hesitated. The truck was flying along at speed, swerving between lanes as it overtook slower vehicles. And it wasn't just their own lives, she knew. If the truck lost control, it would plough into other cars. In the cab, as long as the driver stayed at high speed, they were at a stalemate.

Drake ducked and ran from crate to crate. His teammates did the same, closing in on the guards and the reaper. They covered each other with volleys of bullets as they crept closer and closer. Soon, Drake was on the other side of the crate to a guard. He climbed on top; the wind whipping through his hair, and looked down the other side.

Saw the guard; fell on top of him.

He fought for the man's weapon. Drake grabbed it and threw it away. He threw out several punches, then shot the guard in the stomach. Another down. Dahl, Kinimaka and Hayden streamed past his hiding place, followed by Alicia and Shaw. Together, they fell on the remaining guards.

Atop the speeding, slewing truck, they fought. Dahl smashed his opponent against the side of a crate, holding him by the neck. Kinimaka disarmed his man, twisted him sideways and hooked an arm around his throat. Alicia came up against a capable woman, both of them standing toe to toe and trading blows. Drake left his fallen opponent and raced to help his friends.

They felled guard after guard. More shots rang out. A bullet grazed Drake's shoulder, ripping his jacket. He dived to the side, rolled, fired back. His own bullet took chunks out of a crate right next to the reaper's head.

The truck bounced over the uneven road. Drake held on tight but still went sprawling. He slid towards the open back end, saw a guard bounce right off, and winced. The guy disappeared down the asphalt, rolling unstoppably.

In the cab, Mai jumped onto her unconscious opponent's lap so that she could easily reach Vicius. The reaper's protégé hit out immediately, turning towards her and fighting in the uncomfortable confines of the cab. His own left shoulder was right up against the driver's right and every movement made the driver grunt and wince. His eyes were wide with concentration and fear.

But Mai concentrated on Vicius. She jabbed at his eyes and throat and didn't let up. She led with palm and edge of hand strikes and finger daggers. Vicius covered up and deflected, but he was no match for her. Soon, his face was bloody, his eyes bruised. He abandoned his battle with her to reach down and try to grab the gun from the footwell.

Unimpeded, Mai broke several ribs, but still he scrabbled in the footwell.

Her last blow made him slump. The problem was, he slumped hard to his left, falling into the driver, knocking one of the man's hands off the wheel. The truck veered hard, lurching to the left, just missing the front of a slowing car. Its engine roared. Its front left tyre struck a kerb and bounced up and then hit an obstruction. The truck slowed, it heaved and wobbled. Its front end yawed and then the back came around in a wide arc.

Drake held on desperately as the back end flew past the front. He had hold of one of the ropes tying the wooden crates down and held on with everything he had. Gravity wrenched at him. The rope abraded his flesh. Even now, from a safer position, the reaper fired at him, and he couldn't return the favour. As he watched, a guard flew over the side of the truck, bouncing down into the roadway, his gun left behind and clattering across the ridges of metal that formed the floor.

The truck came to a shuddering stop. Everyone flew forward, slamming into metal and wood. Drake couldn't hold on any longer; he rolled into the front bulkhead, bruising his shoulder. He lost this gun.

Looked up.

The reaper loomed over him.

But she had also lost her gun. The truck was still shaking. The reaper looked down at him, kicked out. Drake rolled away. Three guards were at her back. Dahl was on his knees alongside Kinimaka. Hayden was splayed out, trying to sit up, and Alicia was half-dazed after slamming into a crate. Shaw looked almost unconscious.

Drake fought to stand, couldn't quite make it. The reaper turned away and ran with her three guards to the side of the truck, jumped down.

Drake wondered how they were all fine, and his team was struggling. The answer was obvious. They'd had had good, safe positions behind the crates and had been able to hold on to the guide ropes. Drake's team had been running, crawling. They hadn't had that luxury.

Now, the reaper was escaping with what remained of her guards.

Drake yelled at his team, forcing them to their feet.

In the cab, Mai kicked Vicius into a final oblivion and then turned to the driver. She didn't need to. During the crash, his head had come into contact with the window and he was out for the count. Mai turned to Kenzie and Cam.

'Out now. The reaper's escaping.'

Together, they scrambled out into the white hot day.

CHAPTER FORTY ONE

The Devil's Reaper ran across the thick white sand, down the beach towards the rolling, boiling surf.

Three guards were around her, all but one unarmed. Drake and his team pelted in pursuit, their boots slamming in the soft sand, the blazing sun glaring down from above. Behind them, the wreck of the truck still ticked over.

The guard with the gun turned and fired off several shots. Each bullet slammed the air above Drake's diving head. He rolled in the sand, sat up, saw the reaper halt and spin towards the guard, demanding the gun.

The man hesitated, but then gave it to her. She ordered him, judging by her hand gestures, to stand and fight. To gain her more space.

Drake was up and running in no time, closing the guards down. His team was spread out to left and right, all racing through the sand. They said nothing, just tried to close down their target. It was a fast, tense, silent sprint, and they were all concentrated on their ultimate prey.

The three guards were waiting for them, but they stood no chance.

Dahl didn't even slow down. He was running at top

speed, turned to the side, lowered a shoulder, and barged into his man without mercy. There was the sound of breaking bones, of rushing air. The guy couldn't even whimper. He was launched several feet off the ground, in flight, and then landed on the top of his head as he came down. There was a crunch. The guy didn't move again.

Cam went for the second guard, striking out with both fists. The blows were so hard they debilitated the guard almost immediately, making him grunt and fold over. Cam didn't let up. He punched the guy until he collapsed, holding his ribcage. As he fell, Cam smashed him across the temple for good measure, knocking him cold.

The third guard had the misfortune of coming up against Kenzie, who didn't waste a second. She hammered him under the chin, ducked his own blow and sidestepped a knee he threw out. She grabbed his left arm, twisted and broke it, and then stepped behind him, still holding it. He was putty in her hands. She put a knee in the small of his back, pressed hard, and sent him to his knees. Then she rained down blows at his neck and temples until he fell face first in the sand, unmoving.

Drake and the others had bypassed the guards and were racing in pursuit of the reaper.

She looked back, saw them catching up to her. She angled into the surf. The waves crashed up her legs. Alicia was the first to arrive, striking out. The reaper blocked, moved away and threw punches, driving Alicia back. Drake slowed, not wanting to get in Alicia's way. The reaper led with an elbow, and then a spinning kick, the water catching her trainers and flying off them in white sheets. The kick caught Alicia in the solar plexus, made her grunt and fold just a little. The reaper kicked again, but Alicia danced aside, splashing through the surf. A large wave tugged at their knees, making them stumble. Alicia threw her arms up to ward off several strikes, then staggered backwards. The reaper was matching her blow for blow. The woman pushed forward, wading through the running waters.

Drake and the others were ready to act. The reaper had to see how ineffectual her efforts really were, but she didn't let up. She fought on until the very end, coming at Alicia with a flurry of big hits, knocking the blonde's head from side to side. Alicia ended up dropping to her knees and delivering a punishing thump to her attacker's stomach, one that sucked all her breath out and doubled her up. It stopped her in her tracks. Alicia, on her knees in the surf, rose like an avenging angel, shedding water, and brought both hands, clasped together, down on the reaper's neck, driving her even further into the waters.

Then she kicked out, smashing the woman's head to the side. The reaper drooped. She held up a hand. Alicia hesitated, watching it closely. Everyone's attention fixed on the upraised hand.

Which is why they didn't see the other hand. *It* came up holding a Glock 45; the barrel aimed at Alicia's face.

Two feet parted them. No way could Alicia reach the woman before she pulled the trigger.

'So here we are,' the reaper panted.

Alicia glared at her, giving nothing. 'You're finished,' she said.

Drake stared at the reaper, soaked and defiant as she was. This was the woman he had vowed to kill and, even here, even after all this, she still held his heart in her hands – the choice to end or spare Alicia's life.

The reaper's aim didn't waver. 'I had plans for all of you. A shame it's come to this.'

'Put the gun down,' Dahl said. 'You can't kill all of us.'

'I don't need to. Killing just one will devastate the group beyond repair. Don't you think I know that?'

Drake remained silent and started edging forward. Maybe he could push Alicia out of the way, take the bullet himself.

The reaper just smiled. 'I get one shot. I'll give you a choice. Who wants it?'

Ice trickled down Drake's spine. She was right. One if them was going to die. At least one. There was no way around it. The reaper was competent and deadly and utterly evil. She would take great pleasure in killing one of them whilst the others watched, so that they would never forget what happened. And there was nothing they could do about it.

'Which one?' the reaper asked again.

'You choose,' Alicia snarled at her.

'All right then,' and she kept the gun pointed at Alicia. 'I choose you. I'm gonna blow your fucking face off.'

Drake tensed. If he saw that finger tighten on the trigger, he would act. He would throw himself across Alicia, try to...

All around the others inched closer. They should rightly fan apart, create a harder shot for the reaper to pull off, but their collective concern for Alicia overrode everything, and here they were... crowding in.

'How touching,' the reaper said. 'You all want to save her.'

'I killed Vicius,' Mai said.

'I took half your guards apart,' Dahl said.

'I think that was me,' Kinimaka said.

'If you kill her, you will lose all your advantage,' Hayden told her.

The reaper didn't look phased. 'Maybe that's what I want. You've caught me. What's left for me now?'

'Prison is too good for you,' Drake snarled.

'I agree,' and with that the reaper suddenly stepped back and turned the gun on herself. She stared at all of them. 'There's no way I'm going to prison,' she said.

And, point blank, she pulled the trigger. Drake winced. The reaper's head took the full force of the blast and she fell back into the surf, very dead. Alicia checked the gun, and noted that it had been the last bullet. She heaved a sigh of relief and turned to the others.

'Thanks,' she said simply. 'I thought that was the end there for a while.'

'We had your back,' Mai told her.

Alicia nodded. The surf turned red around their ankles. Drake and the others stepped away, headed once more for the beach. They rendered the guards unconscious once more and started on the long slog back towards their vehicles. If the cops had arrived by the time they got there, they could easily pretend to be victims. Drake, especially, felt like a victim. And so would the others. Most of them had lost good friends or old acquaintances to the reaper.

'I'm glad it ended that way,' Hayden said. 'If she'd lived, we'd be fighting her forever.'

'Good riddance to bad rubbish,' Alicia said. 'As they say.'

They looked up towards the sun. It was turning into a bright and beautiful day

CHAPTER FORTY TWO

A few days later, they were back on the beach, seated at an enormous table at an outdoor café. The table cloth was orange, the crockery chequered and the knives and forks edged in gold. The seats were comfy, plush, leather covered. All of them had glasses and cups full of drinks, sodas and beers and teas and coffees, and had just placed their food orders. It was midday, the sun at its zenith and dazzling, a warm breeze playing off the white tops of the rolling waves. They could all hear the undulating surf as it crept and crawled and whispered across the beach.

Drake shielded his eyes as he gazed across the ocean. He ached and was bruised far more than he cared to let on. 'A few grazes,' he said. 'Could be worse.'

'I'm a slab of black and blue meat,' Alicia groaned. 'Naked, I look fantastic.'

Mai choked on her drink. 'Please, please, do not put that image in my head.'

'Oh, come on, you know the thought appeals to you.'

'Not if you were the last person on earth.'

'I'm hurt,' Alicia pouted. 'I always thought we'd eventually get it together.'

'Well, they do say the more you fight, the more attracted you are,' Cam pointed out.

'Do you want a slap?' Mai asked him.

'Not from you. Not today.'

One by one, they recounted their aches and pains. It had been a long, hard battle against the reaper, and none of them were unscathed.

'But she's gone now,' Kinimaka said. 'Along with her entire operation. We even got her protégé, so there's nobody to carry on her vile business. Of that, we can be glad.'

'Unless she has another protégé,' Mai put in. 'Which we can't be sure about.'

'Let's not think that way,' Drake said. 'Let's call it a big win for both us and the world.'

They didn't cheer, didn't even smile. As a team, they were in mourning. Many people had died during the reaper's campaign, some of them so far removed from the team that they hadn't thought about them since the day they last saw them. But, because their relationships were a matter of record, the innocent had suffered. No matter how hard the sun shined, how perfectly the surf rolled, it wasn't a good day. Drake would see the faces of the dead in the night. They would haunt his dreams.

But they would move on. A step at a time. Since they became team SPEAR, they had never stood still. Every day was a new adventure, every step one in the right direction. But now, they needed to give themselves time to grieve.

The meals arrived, and they tucked in. There wasn't a great deal of conversation for a long time. A server broke Drake out of a deep reverie by asking if they wanted desserts and, for once, he said yes. He smiled briefly at his colleagues, his team, his friends.

'We look to the future,' he said. 'And hope that the next adventure is not as sorrowful as this one.'

'We all survived,' Alicia pointed out. 'There were moments when I didn't think that was gonna happen.'

Drake nodded. 'Yes, we're all in one piece. I think we've found something we can drink to.'

He raised his cup of steaming coffee. The others raised their own cups and glasses, brought them clinking together. Around them, the sun blazed and the Pacific Ocean rolled and Los Angeles turned minute by minute, second by second, a vast half-asleep giant.

Matt Drake was surrounded by his friends. There wasn't anywhere else preferred to be.

THE END

Hope you enjoyed the latest Matt Drake and are already looking forward to see what happens to the team next! I'm not sure what the next release will be yet, but look for it in January 2024.

If you enjoyed this book, please leave a review or a rating.

Other Books by David Leadbeater:

The Matt Drake Series
A constantly evolving, action-packed romp based in the escapist action-adventure genre:

The Bones of Odin (Matt Drake #1)
The Blood King Conspiracy (Matt Drake #2)
The Gates of Hell (Matt Drake 3)
The Tomb of the Gods (Matt Drake #4)
Brothers in Arms (Matt Drake #5)
The Swords of Babylon (Matt Drake #6)
Blood Vengeance (Matt Drake #7)
Last Man Standing (Matt Drake #8)
The Plagues of Pandora (Matt Drake #9)
The Lost Kingdom (Matt Drake #10)
The Ghost Ships of Arizona (Matt Drake #11)
The Last Bazaar (Matt Drake #12)
The Edge of Armageddon (Matt Drake #13)
The Treasures of Saint Germain (Matt Drake #14)
Inca Kings (Matt Drake #15)
The Four Corners of the Earth (Matt Drake #16)
The Seven Seals of Egypt (Matt Drake #17)
Weapons of the Gods (Matt Drake #18)
The Blood King Legacy (Matt Drake #19)
Devil's Island (Matt Drake #20)
The Fabergé Heist (Matt Drake #21)
Four Sacred Treasures (Matt Drake #22)
The Sea Rats (Matt Drake #23)

Blood King Takedown (Matt Drake #24)
Devil's Junction (Matt Drake #25)
Voodoo soldiers (Matt Drake #26)
The Carnival of Curiosities (Matt Drake #27)
Theatre of War (Matt Drake #28)
Shattered Spear (Matt Drake #29)
Ghost Squadron (Matt Drake #30)
A Cold Day in Hell (Matt Drake #31)
The Winged Dagger (Matt Drake #32)
Two Minutes to Midnight (Matt Drake #33)

The Alicia Myles Series

Aztec Gold (Alicia Myles #1)
Crusader's Gold (Alicia Myles #2)
Caribbean Gold (Alicia Myles #3)
Chasing Gold (Alicia Myles #4)
Galleon's Gold (Alicia Myles #5)
Hawaiian Gold (Alicia Myles #6)

The Torsten Dahl Thriller Series

Stand Your Ground (Dahl Thriller #1)

The Relic Hunters Series

The Relic Hunters (Relic Hunters #1)
The Atlantis Cipher (Relic Hunters #2)
The Amber Secret (Relic Hunters #3)
The Hostage Diamond (Relic Hunters #4)

The Rocks of Albion (Relic Hunters #5)
The Illuminati Sanctum (Relic Hunters #6)
The Illuminati Endgame (Relic Hunters #7)
The Atlantis Heist (Relic Hunters #8)
The City of a Thousand Ghosts (Relic Hunters #9)
Hierarchy of Madness (Relic Hunters #10)

The Joe Mason Series

The Vatican Secret (Joe Mason #1)
The Demon Code (Joe Mason #2)
The Midnight Conspiracy (Joe Mason #3)
The Babylon Plot (Joe Mason #4)

The Rogue Series

Rogue (Book One)

The Disavowed Series:

The Razor's Edge (Disavowed #1)
In Harm's Way (Disavowed #2)
Threat Level: Red (Disavowed #3)

The Chosen Few Series

Chosen (The Chosen Trilogy #1)
Guardians (The Chosen Trilogy #2)
Heroes (The Chosen Trilogy #3)

Short Stories

Walking with Ghosts (A short story)
A Whispering of Ghosts (A short story)

All genuine comments are very welcome at:

davidleadbeater2011@hotmail.co.uk

Twitter: @dleadbeater2011

Visit David's website for the latest news and information:
davidleadbeater.com

Printed in Great Britain
by Amazon